# I'm *not* going to speed date!

"I don't need some guy complicating my life," I muttered as I rushed down the sidewalk. "It's complicated enough. I—"

"Did you say something, Ophelia?" a voice to my left called.

I stopped short and whipped around. Edna Walters stood beside her parked car staring at me. Her arthritic hands clutched her walker tightly while she watched me with a puzzled look.

Peachy. Edna, the biggest gossip in town, second only to Darci's friend, Georgia. By this afternoon, the whole town would hear how I'd finally lost it and had started talking to myself. There were already enough people in the community thinking I was a bit odd. My habit of stumbling into the middle of murder investigations tended to give people that conclusion. That was just one reason I was determined to turn over a new leaf—another was the danger! Nope, no more murder and mayhem for me. I didn't care how much Aunt Dot thought my lifestyle sounded like "fun." I was putting all that behind me. Starting now.

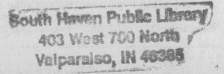

*Books by*
**Shirley Damsgaard**

THE SEVENTH WITCH
THE WITCH'S GRAVE
THE WITCH IS DEAD
WITCH HUNT
THE TROUBLE WITH WITCHES
CHARMED TO DEATH
WITCH WAY TO MURDER

# SHIRLEY
# DAMSGAARD

# THE
# WITCH IS DEAD

## AN OPHELIA AND ABBY MYSTERY

**A V O N**
*An Imprint of HarperCollinsPublishers*

This is a work of fiction. Names, characters, places, and incidents are products of the author's imagination or are used fictitiously and are not to be construed as real. Any resemblance to actual events, locales, organizations, or persons, living or dead, is entirely coincidental.

AVON BOOKS
*An Imprint of* HarperCollins*Publishers*
10 East 53rd Street
New York, New York 10022-5299

Copyright © 2007 by Shirley Damsgaard
ISBN: 978-0-06-114723-4
ISBN-10: 0-06-114723-0
**www.avonmystery.com**

First Avon Books paperback printing: September 2007

Avon Trademark Reg. U.S. Pat. Off. and in Other Countries,
Marca Registrada, Hecho en U.S.A.
HarperCollins® is a registered trademark of HarperCollins Publishers.

Printed in the U.S.A.

10  9  8  7  6  5  4

**To Sheba.**
**May your spirit run with the wolves,**
**my old friend.**

# THE
# WITCH IS DEAD

# *Prologue*

A hot, summer wind tossed the clouds across the night sky and tugged at the girl's nightgown as she walked down the path. Above her, leaves whispered, calling her deeper and deeper into the woods. From a distance came the hoot of a solitary owl.

The girl lifted her head, sniffing the humid air. The smell of damp vegetation tickled her nose. She paused. Another scent rode the night breeze, swirling around her like a fog. She took a deep breath and her stomach twisted. Rotten meat. Did a carcass of a dead animal lie spoiling past the trees on her right? Violet eyes searched the darkness but saw nothing.

A trickle of dread shot up her spine. Should she turn and run, back to the safety of the Victorian cottage she shared with Ophelia, her guardian? But something pulled her forward. She took another step, and the smell intensified. Again her stomach threatened to revolt. She struggled to swallow the rising bile. Her breath hitched in her throat, and her dread changed to fear.

What waited in the woods?

She turned and swiftly retraced her steps along the path.

Sanctuary waited for her beyond the trees that lay ahead. A soft bed with cool sheets, her room with her familiar things, her pets.

Her steps quickened.

Suddenly she froze. Behind her she heard the low moan of someone in pain. Lowering her head, she felt a current of panic travel through her nerve endings like electricity. She willed her feet to move, but they wouldn't. The moan, closer now, was more like a hiss.

Slowly, she turned.

Chalky gray faces with dark hollow eyes peered at her from the shadows, moving in noiseless unison from behind the trees. As if a silent signal had been given, they gathered in a group at the end of the path. Their clothes hung in tatters from their decaying bodies. Bony hands stretched out in supplication, while their bloated lips moved in wordless pleas.

She recoiled in horror.

The corpses moved toward her, and their pain washed over her in waves. Her throat tightened. A scream rose from deep inside her. She wanted to run but couldn't. Helpless, she watched the horrible sight drift closer and closer.

She tried to jerk her body free, but seemed glued to the pathway. What was wrong with her legs? Why couldn't she flee?

*Ophelia,* she cried in her mind, *Ophelia, help me! Help me, please!*

They were nearly upon her, and she felt their foul breath surround her.

Her mind cried out again for rescue, but silence was the only reply.

Resigned to her fate, she clenched her eyes shut and

waited for the skeletal hands to grab her. Any second now the horror would touch her.

The seconds stretched into minutes. She sniffed the air. The stench that had enveloped her was gone. Slowly, she peeked from scrunched up lids. Nothing. Cautiously she opened her eyes wide.

The vision was gone.

The woods were gone.

The ghouls were gone.

She was safe in her own bed, in her own room. Relief flooded her. Her body began to relax.

Abruptly, the relief she felt fled. She knew what the dream meant.

With heavy hands she threw off the sheet covering her and rose stiffly. Silently, she walked out of her room, down the hall, and into the next bedroom. Approaching the bed, she reached out and shook the sleeping figure.

"What?" Ophelia bolted up and scanned the room, disoriented. Spotting Tink standing over her, she lay back against her pillows with a sigh. "Tink."

"I'm scared, Ophelia," the girl whispered.

"Here," Ophelia said, patting the mattress and scooting over.

Without a word, Tink sank down next to her.

"Did you have a bad dream?" Ophelia asked, softly stroking Tink's blond hair.

Silently, Tink shook her head.

Alarmed, Ophelia sat upright. "What's wrong, Tink?"

Tink wrapped her thin arms around herself. "Ophelia, the shadows are back."

# One

Tink stood with her nose pressed to the large plate-glass window, then whirled around, her thin face a picture of excitement. "Look," she said. "Do you think that's Aunt Dot's plane?"

From where I sat next to Abby, I searched Tink's face to see any lingering signs of last night's vision. Her eyes seemed clear, not shadowed as they had been. Her smile seemed real, not forced. Relieved, I smiled back. "It should be landing soon." I glanced at my watch, then up at the large monitor showing the arrival times of flights. "It's three-thirty now, and the flight from Raleigh is supposed to arrive at 4:05."

Tink turned away and went back to her vigil. Out of the corner of my eye, I saw Abby studying me, her face mirroring the consternation my face had worn when watching Tink.

"What?" I said defensively.

My grandmother lifted an eyebrow. "Are you going to tell me what's going on?" Her voice carried the soft lilt of the mountains in Appalachia where she was born.

Scrunching my eyes shut and rubbing my forehead, I thought about how to answer her.

*Do I tell her about Tink's nightmare?* I didn't want to upset her. Abby hadn't seen her mother's sister, Dot, since her visit three years ago to her girlhood home. My grandmother had anticipated Aunt Dot's visit to Iowa for months. I didn't want anything to mar it.

Opening my eyes, I slid a look at Abby sitting there, the picture of calm. Her silver hair was done in a neat twist at the back of her head. She wore a floral skirt and ivory shell with a matching scarf. An understated amethyst broach, one that my grandfather had given her many years ago, held the scarf in place on her shoulder. She was elegant and charming.

Unfortunately, it's hard to hide things from your grandmother when she's a psychic witch. Even if you're one yourself.

I blew out a breath. "Okay," I replied reluctantly. "Tink had a dream last night—"

"A dream or a *dream?*" Abby asked, breaking in.

"A vision. Rotten corpses walking toward her in the woods."

"How awful for Tink." Abby's lips tightened. "What did they want?"

"I don't know. Tink said they definitely wanted something. They were approaching her with their hands outstretched, as if they were pleading, but they never spoke."

Abby tapped her chin. "Hmm, whether we like it or not, evidently some sort of connection with Tink has been made." Her eyes wandered over to where Tink stood at the window. "That girl is a strong medium. Her energy must be a beacon to restless souls."

"Any way we can tamp that energy down?"

Abby shook her head. "No, she and I have tried. She's gaining more control over her talent, but as she grows older, the talent is growing stronger." She paused. "Did you say 'corpses,' not 'corpse'?"

"Yeah. Why?"

"So it's more than one spirit trying to reach her?"

"I guess. Is that important?"

She gave me a knowing look. "Ophelia, as a psychic, by now you should know every little detail can have meaning."

I glanced back at Tink. "It's significant that there was more than one?"

"Yes." Abby's face lightened. "She hasn't been by a cemetery recently, has she?"

"I don't think so. She doesn't like them, you know. She says there are too many voices to overcome. A few always manage to break through her guard."

"Well, another explanation might be a mass death somewhere."

"You mean like a plane crash, or train wreck?"

She nodded again. "Yes. The combined energy of the spirits is breaking through her resistance."

"I haven't heard of any recent tragedies, have you?"

"No, but Tink's vision doesn't have to be about something that happened recently. It could be out of the past."

"How 'past'?" I asked with a frown.

Abby lifted a shoulder in a shrug. "I don't know. Maybe once Aunt Dot arrives, she can shed some light on what's happening to Tink. After all, she's lived all these years with Aunt Mary, and Mary's the most powerful medium that I've ever known."

I shuddered at the mention of Great-Aunt Mary's name. I'd met her as a child when Abby took me to the mountains. Great-Aunt Mary had struck fear in my adolescent heart. Towering over me, she had a way of drilling me with her green eyes that made me want to confess every childhood misdemeanor I'd ever committed.

Abby picked up on my reaction and patted my knee. "Don't worry, dear. Aunt Dot is nothing like Mary."

"I know. She's the exact opposite, if I remember correctly."

She smiled. "Yes, she is. She's still as wide as she is tall. Whenever I think of her, I see her standing in the kitchen, in her cotton dress and orthopedic shoes, with both hands in some bowl, mixing away. And she always smelled like cinnamon."

Abby's memories of Aunt Dot matched mine. I grinned as I let my gaze fall on the book Tink had brought to read. Picking it up, I thumbed through it.

"That kid!" I exclaimed.

"What is it, dear?"

Holding out the book, I showed it to Abby. "Tink marks her place by turning down the corner of the page. I don't know how many times I've told her not to do it."

"Isn't that one of the paperbacks she bought last week at the bookstore in Aiken?" Abby asked.

"Yes."

"So it's her book. She can do what she wants," she said with a lift of her shoulder.

"But it's disrespectful."

She gave me a playful nudge with her elbow. "Quit being such a *librarian,* Ophelia."

"I suppose," I responded reluctantly, and put the book back on the seat next to me.

To kill time, my eyes traveled around the room, looking at the others who were waiting.

My gaze halted as I noticed someone sitting on the other side of the room who seemed familiar.

His eyes, behind horn-rimmed glasses, were downcast as he studied the papers he held in his hand. He wore black pants and a pale pink oxford shirt open at the throat. His expensive loafers were polished until they gleamed, and his dark blond hair was streaked and artfully tousled. A successful businessman waiting for his flight.

But something about the way he held himself struck a chord in my memory. He lifted his head. To my chagrin, he caught me staring at him.

Sleet-gray eyes dared me to respond.

It was Cobra! The biker I'd threatened not only with my Louisville Slugger, but also with a hex.

At the time, I wanted nothing more than to see him thrown in jail. That's what he and the rest of his biker gang deserved for trying to take over our town of Summerset.

That is, until I found out he was an undercover DEA agent.

I cringed, recalling my behavior, and felt my face grow warm. The hex and the bat weren't my most shining moments. But it wasn't all my fault—I really had thought he was one of the bad guys. And he'd played along.

Here was my chance to redeem myself.

He looked away, engrossing himself again in his papers.

How had he signed that note he'd passed to me? The one I was given as he loaded the last of the bikers into the police van? Oh yeah. "Ethan." That was it.

Mumbling a quick "Pardon me" to Abby, I crossed the room.

"Hi, Cobra," I said, taking the seat next to him.

"Excuse me?"

"Or should I say 'Ethan'?" I asked, trying to sound confident.

He acted confused. "Ethan?"

Crap, had I made a mistake? I decided to brazen it out. "Yeah, Ethan. That's your real name, isn't it? It's how you signed the note you gave me. You know, the one that said, 'Until we meet again, keep your head down, and don't fall off your broom.'"

"Broom?" He shifted in his seat and gave me a wary look. "Some guy thinks you're a witch?"

"Ah, well . . . " I studied his face more intently. Nope, he was Cobra—I'd know those gray eyes anywhere. I nudged him in the arm. "Come on, Co—er, Ethan, you know I'm the librarian in Summerset." I wiped my suddenly sweaty palms on my denim skirt. "And about this witch thing . . . I'd like to apologize for my remarks. You see—"

"You're a librarian who's a *witch*?" His voice carried a note of alarm as he shrank farther away from me.

I felt the heat creep up my neck and into my face. "You're not Ethan?" I asked with a squeak in my voice.

"No," he replied, shuffling the papers in his hand. "You've obviously mistaken me for someone else."

Peachy. I'd just convinced a complete stranger that I was a psycho. *Good one, Jensen.*

Dropping my head, I stared at my hands clutched tightly in my lap and tried to think of some witty response.

Finally I peeked over at him. "Sorry," I muttered through clenched teeth.

With a rapid shuffle of his papers, he shoved them into his briefcase and stood.

Sensing him staring down at me, I raised my head and watched as he hooked his glasses in his front pocket. Again I was struck by his gray eyes.

Only now they weren't cold.

Instead, they sparkled with humor.

He hoisted his carryon to his shoulder and grinned. "Give my regards to Sheriff Wilson, Ophelia," he said with a wink. He spoke so quietly only I could hear him.

Before I could close my gaping mouth and utter a scathing reply, he turned on his heel and walked swiftly to the escalators. He gave me one last look over his shoulder, accompanied by a salute, before he disappeared up the escalator.

Dang, Cobra had tricked me again.

* * *

Twenty minutes later we were standing near the metal detectors watching the passengers disembark the plane from Raleigh. Tink shifted from one foot to the next as she craned her neck, trying to be the first one to spot Aunt Dot.

I smiled. Tink could strain her neck all she wanted and she still wouldn't be able to spot short, squat Aunt Dot over the heads of the crowd.

Suddenly, one of the passengers jumped as if someone had goosed him. On another side, someone stepped forward quickly. Before we knew it, the whole group had parted and Aunt Dot came barreling up the center. From behind her, a balding man in his late fifties struggled to keep up. With her head down, she reminded me of a quarterback making for the goal line. For a ninety-one-year-old woman she sure could move.

The cotton dress I was accustomed to seeing Aunt Dot wear was gone. Instead, she wore a sensible dark purple polyester pantsuit. In her right hand she held a knotted cane, its wood polished to a fine sheen by years of use. And her hair? Wow—tight curls frizzed around her head in a decidedly blue halo.

Lifting her head, she paused for a moment as her aged eyes scanned the people waiting. Sighting us, a wide grin lit her face and she resumed her march toward us, the balding man still following her.

Abby closed the distance between them and gathered Aunt Dot's plump, little body in a tight hug. Next to me, I heard Tink utter a small gasp. Glancing over at her, I noticed her face had lost what little color it had and her eyes were focused on the man standing with Aunt Dot and Abby.

Reaching out, I laid my hand on her arm. "What is it?"

"Nothing," she said with a slight shake of her head. "I'll tell you later."

The man with Aunt Dot smiled, shook Abby's hand, and handed her a heavy cloth bag before turning and joining a young man who seemed to be waiting for him.

The young man's pale blue eyes glanced my way, and I saw a spark of curiosity light his face. The man's son? Maybe. The guy who'd helped Aunt Dot off the plane clapped him on the shoulder in greeting before they turned and joined the other passengers making their way to the baggage claim.

I turned my attention back to Abby and Aunt Dot.

With a smile, Abby guided Aunt Dot over to where Tink and I waited.

Aunt Dot looked first at me, then at Tink, her face bright with expectation.

"Aunt Dot, you remember Ophelia, don't you?" Abby asked in a loud voice.

"No need to shout, girl. I'm not deaf yet," she said with a glance at Abby. Her voice sounded a lot like Abby's, but with the cadence of Appalachia more pronounced. "Of course I remember her." Aunt Dot stepped forward and clasped me around the middle in a quick hug.

Only five-four myself, I still had to lean down to give her a squeeze. And it felt like I was embracing a down-filled pillow. Abby was right. The scent of cinnamon seemed to cling to her.

"Hi, Aunt Dot," I said, smiling over the top of her kinky curls.

"You've grown, Ophelia," she said, stepping back and studying my face. "But then again, maybe I've just shrunk," she ended with a cackle.

Releasing me, she turned to Tink. "And this must be the girl that I've heard so much about."

Suddenly shy, Tink nodded, sending her long ponytail bobbing.

Without a word, Aunt Dot crossed to Tink and took her face in her weathered hands. Her eyes roamed over Tink, taking in the violet eyes and the smooth skin. It was almost as if she was trying to see into Tink's mind.

Tink squirmed under her scrutiny.

Aunt Dot dropped her hands to Tink's shoulders. "This one's special," she said in a satisfied voice. "Welcome to the family, Titania."

Surprise flitted across Tink's face. "You know my real name?"

"Yes, Abby wrote me. The name fits you, child. Titania—Queen of the Fairies. But we'll speak more of that later," she said, throwing an arm around Tink's shoulders.

I shot Abby a questioning look, but her only response was an innocent smile and a careless shrug. Hmm, as a child, I hadn't spent much time with Aunt Dot, or Aunt Mary, but I *had* with my grandmother. Along with the various psychic abilities that ran through the women of our family, there was also a certain amount of caginess. And I didn't need to use my sixth sense to know something was up. I also knew I wouldn't pry what it was out of Abby until she was ready to tell me.

"Come on, Aunt Dot," Abby said, taking her arm. "Let's find your luggage and get you home. You must be tired after your long flight."

She steered Aunt Dot in the direction of the escalators, with Tink and I bringing up the rear.

"Careful, child," Aunt Dot called over her shoulder after stepping carefully on the descending stairs. "I've heard of people getting their foot caught in these contraptions. Took their leg right off."

From behind her, Tink did a slow eye roll, but stepped gingerly on the first step. With a smile, I followed.

After retrieving Aunt Dot's battered blue suitcase, we were all finally loaded in Abby's SUV and headed back to Summerset. The interstate miles flew by, and soon we were pulling into Abby's winding driveway.

As we approached her house, Abby pointed out her plots of vegetables and flowers growing in the rich Iowa soil to Aunt Dot. During this time of year—midsummer—Abby's greenhouse shifted from selling bedding plants to fresh vegetables. And Tink found working for Abby was a great way to supplement her allowance.

Abby slowed the SUV to a stop in front of her large farmhouse. The windows, framed by dark green shutters, gleamed as the sun sank lower on the horizon. As we exited the vehicle, I heard the hum of Abby's bees flitting from flower to flower in the beds that grew along the wide front porch. Nasturtium, snapdragons, Shasta daisies, and foxglove bloomed with abandon, and I watched Aunt Dot and Tink pause on their way up the steps to look at them. Aunt Dot leaned forward, pointing at the blossoms, and said something to Tink in a low voice. I couldn't make out all her words as I hoisted her heavy suitcase out of the back, but I thought I heard the word "fairy."

"Hey," I whispered to Abby. "What's the deal with Aunt Dot and fairies? She just said something about them again to Tink."

"Ah, well," Abby stuttered, shouldering Aunt Dot's cloth bag and slamming the passenger side door. "She likes them?"

"You're asking me?" I set the suitcase on the gravel drive.

"Umm, maybe it's a little more than that." She turned and started up the sidewalk to the house.

"What do you mean 'a little more'?" I called after her.

"Shh," she said, laying a finger to her lips. "Aunt Dot will hear you."

I waved her concern away. "They're already inside. Are you going to tell me what's going on?"

Abby sighed. "Oh, all right, I didn't want to tell you this right away. I know how skeptical you can be. I wanted you to get more acquainted with Aunt Dot first. You haven't seen her since you were a child, and I didn't want you thinking she was a doddering old woman—"

"Abby," I said, cutting her off. "Get to the point."

"Okay," she hissed. "Aunt Dot's particular talent is that she sees fairies. There. Happy now?"

"What?" I fisted my hand on my hip. "There's no such thing as fairies."

"Humph," Abby snorted over her shoulder. "Tell that to Aunt Dot."

I closed the back door of the SUV with a bang and, after picking up the suitcase, made my own way up the path to the house.

I had a feeling this was going to be *some* visit.

# Two

Before I reached the front steps, the screen door slammed and Tink came out onto the porch.

"Do you need help?" she asked, grasping one of the large pillars and leaning to the side, swinging back and forth.

"No," I replied with a smile as I mounted the steps, "but thanks." Setting the suitcase down, I took her other hand in mine. "What happened at the airport? I heard you gasp when you looked at the man who'd helped Aunt Dot off the plane."

Tink's face took on a worried expression. "I don't know—it was weird. It felt as if something was poking at me, mentally, trying to get my attention."

"A spirit?"

She lifted a thin shoulder. "I guess. I've noticed it before, when there's been a recent death in someone's family. It's kinda like the spirit is still hovering around the family member and zeros in on me."

"Maybe this man was flying home from attending a funeral." I paused for a moment. "Do you ever drop your guard long enough to let them contact you?"

"No." Her ponytail whipped back and forth as she shook

her head emphatically. "I'm afraid once I let them contact me, they'll keep bugging me until they're ready to leave."

I squeezed her hand. "Don't worry kiddo. As you get older, you'll gain more control. When I was your age, I had a hard time shutting out the thoughts of others. I felt constantly bombarded by their feelings, but now I don't sense things unless I want to."

A grin drifted across her face. "That's what Abby says, too."

"There you go." I picked up the suitcase and gave Tink's hand a tug. "Come on, we'd better get inside."

In the house, we were greeted by the sound of sharp toenails skittering across Abby's hardwood floors. Lady, and Tink's rambunctious terrier puppy, T.P., came careening around the corner of the living room. Part wolf, part German shepherd, Lady's white tail wagged in greeting, while T.P. ran straight to Tink and jumped on her. Lady, polite as always, sat at my feet and watched me with a long suffering look that said, "Kids! What are you going to do with them?"

Laughing, I bent and scratched her ears. "Had problems keeping the youngster out of trouble, did you?" I glanced over my shoulder at Tink. "You'd better go check Abby's bathrooms."

With a groan, Tink headed down the hallway, with T.P. in hot pursuit.

Unable to think of an appropriate name for the puppy, Tink had started calling him "T.P.," standing for "The Puppy," until we could come up with a better name. Unfortunately, now the name also described his fondness for eating toilet paper. And he was absolutely psychic when it came to sensing a bathroom door left carelessly open. I hoped Abby had extra toilet paper.

Setting the suitcase in the hallway, I joined Abby and

Aunt Dot in Abby's old-fashioned kitchen. Although the house was "modernized," Abby preferred to keep her kitchen as her mother had in the mountains of Appalachia. A gleaming wood-burning cook stove sat along one wall, looking incongruous next to the electric refrigerator. A large kerosene lamp sat in the center of the table waiting to cast its warm glow throughout the room when darkness fell. A ceiling fan whirred softly overhead, sending the scent of Abby's drying herbs drifting through the house. As always, stepping into the kitchen gave me a feeling of taking a step into the past.

Abby bustled around the room, laying out homemade bread, pickles, and meat for sandwiches. "Aunt Dot, it's been a long day for you. After we eat, I'll show you to the guest room so you can rest."

"Ach, nonsense." Aunt Dot waved a gnarled hand in Abby's direction. "I'm not tired." Glancing at the old-fashioned clock, she pointed to her canvas bag resting against a table leg. "Drag my bag to where I can reach it, Ophelia."

Grabbing the bag by its handles, I scooted the bag over to Aunt Dot. She bent and began to pull out bottles filled with dark ruby liquid, placing each one carefully in front of her on the table. From across the kitchen I heard Abby's soft moan.

"You really should get some rest, Aunt Dot," she said in a firm voice.

"Fiddle." Aunt Dot unscrewed the cap from one of the bottles, and the smell of fermented juice mingled with the aroma of herbs. "I haven't been off that mountain and away from Sister for fifteen years." She was referring to Abby's aunt, and my great-aunt, Mary. "I intend to enjoy myself, so I don't have time to be tired." She reached up and patted her frizzy curls. "Why, I even went to the beauty parlor and had my hair done while Sister was at the general store getting supplies."

Well, that explains the blue halo, I thought.

"Fetch me some glasses, will you Abby?"

Without a word, Abby placed three small glasses in front of Aunt Dot, who filled each one to the top and handed a glass to each of us. Holding her glass high, she looked first at Abby, then at me. "*Salinte*," she said, and took a deep drink.

I took a cautious sip of the deep red liquid. The rich, sweet taste slid smoothly down my throat. Yum. I fought the desire to smack my lips.

"This is really good, Aunt Dot. What is it?" I asked, taking a larger swallow.

"Homemade elderberry wine." She drained her glass and poured another one. "Sister and I make it every summer for our Saturday night wine time. The recipe's a secret."

I finished my glass and poured another, ignoring Abby's raised eyebrows. It was only homemade wine, bottled by two little old ladies—how potent could it be?

Aunt Dot topped off her glass and settled back in her chair. Looking over her shoulder, she spied Tink standing in the doorway. She grabbed the chair next to her. "Here, child, come sit next to me." Taking a quick peek at Abby, busy making sandwiches, she said, "Put the food away for now, dear, and join us. Sister and I never eat until wine time is over."

Silently, Abby did as Aunt Dot requested and joined us at the old oak table.

"Now," Aunt Dot said, turning to Tink. "Has Abby told you about the women in our family? About your legacy?"

"A little," Tink replied, "but I'm not related to you by blood."

"It doesn't matter." Aunt Dot fixed her bright blue eyes on Tink's face. "You share our spirit, and fate made you a member of this family. You'll carry on our heritage. A heritage that goes back over one hundred years."

With a timid smile, Tink lowered her head. "Margaret Mary, Ophelia's mom, didn't inherit the gift, did she?"

"No," I piped in. "Mother's talents lie in other areas."

Like being able to control all she surveys, I thought, but didn't voice my opinion out loud.

Tink looked up and cocked her head. "So what are some of the different talents?"

"Ahh," Aunt Dot said, pouring another glass of wine and passing me the bottle.

I filled my glass, too.

Aunt Dot continued. "Sister is a medium, like you. And you know Ophelia and Abby are both psychics, but their talents are a little different. Abby is good at sensing the future, and Ophelia seems to have a knack for finding things."

"Things?" I said. If the past two years were any indication, those "things" usually turned out to be dead people.

Aunt Dot motioned in Abby's direction. "Abby's mother, my sister, Annie, was a healer. By laying hands on a sick neighbor, she could see the disease in her mind. If the illness was one she could help, she'd treat it using herbs and crystals."

"Weren't there any doctors?" Tink asked.

"Back then there weren't many. And it took days to reach one. Some of our neighbors had no choice but to seek one out. Their illness was beyond Annie's skills." Aunt Dot stared off into space as if images from the past flickered through her mind. "Annie was also a midwife, and many women of the mountain had an easier time giving birth, thanks to her talent for easing the pain." Aunt Dot's eyes traveled to me. "Annie also used runes, like Ophelia here."

"But I'm not as good as Annie was," I said.

"Don't fret about it. You haven't had anyone to help you. Our grandfather, Jens, taught Annie."

"I thought Annie was taught by your mother?"

"Mette Marie? No, our mother's talents laying in sensing the weather, as did my grandmother's, Flora Chisholm Swensen. At times, Mother could even call the rain."

"Really?" I asked, surprise ringing in my voice. "I'd always assumed the runes came from Mette Marie."

"No, from Jens. He was Danish, a descendant of the Vikings, and he had his own kind of magick." Aunt Dot chortled. "It was fun as a child to visit my grandparents—a Scottish weather witch and a Vitki."

"That's a Viking shaman, right?" I broke in.

"Yes. We never knew what to expect."

All this family history was confusing me. "But I thought your heritage was strictly Scottish."

"No, my mother was half Danish, and the maternal side was Scottish—the Clan Chisholm—so Mother's background was fine with my father, Walter Cameron. The Chisholms had fought on the right side with the Clan Cameron at the Battle of Culloden."

"When was your father born?" I asked, even more confused.

"Hmm, let's see . . . 1896, I believe."

I was shocked. The Battle of Culloden had occurred in the mid-1700s.

"But that battle happened over a century before Walter was even born!" I exclaimed. "Why would what side your ancestors fought on matter?"

Aunt Dot shook her head. "People in the mountains have long memories. Especially when it comes to the clans. It was one of the reasons my father was so against Annie marrying—"

"I really think we should eat now," Abby said, popping out of her chair.

"Oh, sit back down." Aunt Dot flapped her hand at Abby as she refilled her glass of wine—and mine. "After Annie laid eyes on Robert Campbell, she'd have no other, much to my father's disgust."

"I don't mean to sound stupid, Aunt Dot, but what's wrong with the Campbells?"

"They were on the wrong side. They fought with 'Butcher' Cumberland—"

"'Butcher' Cumberland?"

"The Duke of Cumberland—he led the British forces at Culloden, and even after the battle, continued to slaughter the clans, and the Campbells were with him." Aunt Dot shook her head sadly and downed the rest of her wine. "My father always said 'never could trust a Campbell.' He—"

"Tink, dear, aren't you hungry?" Abby said, cutting off Aunt Dot and smiling brightly at Tink.

"Gosh, I guess."

"See, we need—"

I held up my hand, stopping her. "Wait a second."

Aunt Dot's little family history lesson was just getting interesting, and I wasn't going to let anything, like food, interfere until I ferreted out all the dirt Abby was trying to hide.

"More wine, Aunt Dot?" I asked sweetly, and ignored the evil look Abby cast my way.

"Oh, I shouldn't," she said, holding out her glass for more.

"So," I said after filling her glass, "Walter didn't want Annie to marry Robert?"

"No," she replied vehemently. "Father was dead set against it, and nothing Annie or my mother could say would move him. Finally, Robert and Annie took matters into their own hands—"

I scooted forward in my chair. "They eloped?"

Aunt Dot gave Abby a wary look. "No—they had a lovely spring wedding in 1932. I think Father would've rather given Robert a horsewhipping than his daughter's hand in marriage, but they didn't leave him much choice."

I did some fast mental arithmetic. Spring of 1932, huh? Abby was born in the fall of the same year. What a juicy family secret—Abby was conceived out of wedlock. I caught her shifting uncomfortably in her chair as a red stain spread across her cheeks.

Trying to put Abby at ease, I gave her a big grin. "I think that's really romantic."

"Humph, that's not how most people looked at it back in the thirties," she said as she firmly grasped the remaining wine bottles and removed them from the table—a safe distance from Aunt Dot and me. "Tink, would you set the table, please."

Guess wine time was over.

# *Three*

Oh, Lord, even my eyelids hurt, I thought, as I cautiously peeked at the bright sunshine spilling through the windows in one of Abby's spare bedrooms. I had the mother of all hangovers, thanks to Aunt Dot's lethal elderberry wine. Not even the wonderful sandwiches, homemade pickles, and potato salad that Abby served us last night had soaked up the alcohol contained in that wine. At the images of food, my stomach threatened to revolt, so I shoved them out of my head.

*Coffee. I need coffee.*

I grabbed one of my old robes from the closet and made my way down the stairs to the kitchen. Each step seemed to jar the headache pounding right behind both eyes.

*Aspirin. Add aspirin to the coffee.*

*Wow, if I feel this bad, I can't imagine how Aunt Dot must feel. I had a good sixty years on her. She's probably still in bed.*

I rounded the corner of the kitchen, and there she was. She was dressed in an old flannel robe that had seen better days, and was hustling around the kitchen without a care in the world. And to my bloodshot orbs, her hair looked even bluer than it did last night.

"Aunt Dot, what are you doing up? Are you feeling okay?" I stumbled over to the freshly made coffee and poured a generous cup.

"Ach, of course I am," she replied, dismissing my concern. "It would take a lot more than one little bottle of our wine to get me snookered." Aunt Dot gave me the once-over. "But I must say, Ophelia, you don't look so good."

A sound suspiciously like that of a sob came out of my mouth. *I'd been drunk under the table by a ninety-one-year-old woman.* Digging around in Abby's cupboards, I searched desperately to find something to take away the throbbing.

"I think you need agrimony, centaury, and wormwood tea, Ophelia."

I turned to see Abby in the doorway, her hand resting on her hip.

Taking pity on me, and tsk-tsking all the way, she crossed to the sink and filled the teakettle with cold water. She removed packets of herbs from the cupboard and set about making the tea. While the leaves steeped in the boiling water, she removed a bottle from the refrigerator, and after sprinkling a bit of liquid on a square of muslin, handed the cloth to me.

"While you're waiting for your tea, hold this on your forehead. It's tincture of witch hazel."

I did as Abby told me, and instantly the throbbing in my head lessened.

"Ohhh, thanks."

"Humph. I could've told you about the elderberry wine. It may taste like juice, but it's got a kick like a mule."

"Yeah, I found that out," I said without opening my eyes. "And it feels like he kicked my head. Man, that's potent wine."

"It's the 'shine," Aunt Dot said casually.

I opened one eye. "'Shine?"

"Umm-hmm. Moonshine. It's part of the secret recipe. We add a little bit to each bottle." Aunt Dot laid a finger to her lips. "Don't tell Sister I told you."

Wincing, I rubbed the cool cloth against my forehead. No wonder I got tanked. If Aunt Dot had shared her secret with me last night, I might not have gulped down as many glasses.

"Sit down, and I'll get you that tea," she said. "That will help, too."

Peering out of one eye, I walked to the table and sat, placing my elbows on the tabletop and holding the cold cloth to my head. The smell of frying bacon now filled the kitchen, and miraculously, my stomach rumbled in response.

"I've read all of Abby's letters about the wonderful ways you've used your talents, Ophelia." Aunt Dot set the steaming cup of tea in front of me. "Annie would be proud of you."

Taking the cup in both hands, I let its warmth seep into my fingers before taking a sip. "I have her journals, and when I don't understand what the runes are saying, it helps to read the notes she made."

Aunt Dot gave my arm an affectionate pat. "The more you use the runes, the more you'll hear their song." She hesitated. "I got so wrapped up in telling you family stories last night that—"

From across the kitchen I heard Abby snicker.

Ignoring Abby, Aunt Dot continued. "We didn't talk about you and your life. I'd like to know more about your adventures."

I guess you could call getting shot, shut in a box, hexed until you were ill, throttled, and threatened with jail several times "adventures." I didn't. I called it "being scared spitless." And after my involvement with the latest murder investigation a scant couple of months ago, and almost taking another bullet in the process, I'd hung up my snooping for good.

"Oh gee, Aunt Dot, I, ah . . . " My voice trailed away.

"You don't want to hear those stories, Aunt Dot," Abby said, rescuing me. "Let's make plans for your visit. We have a wonderful art center in Des Moines . . . I thought we'd drive in, have lunch, then—"

"I don't want to go to an art center." Aunt Dot folded her arms over her ample chest and gave Abby a mutinous look. "I told you, I'm planning on having a good time—I want an adventure of my own."

I choked on my tea.

"That nice man on the plane, you know, Mr. Buchanan, the funeral director?" Aunt Dot settled back in her chair. "We talked a great deal about you and Ophelia."

Funeral director? Well, that explained Tink's reaction to him. The man dealt with death as his occupation, and Tink picked up on it. In much the same way as when she passed a cemetery.

"You told him about us?"

Aunt Dot uncrossed her arms. "Yes, and he was very interested, particularly when I told him about my fairies."

I set my cup on the table. "You told him you see fairies?"

"Yes. So?"

My eyes met Abby's. We needed to fill Aunt Dot in on the ground rules around here. We *did not* talk about our talents to strangers.

"Ah, Aunt Dot, this isn't the mountains. People around here are kind of funny when it comes to witches."

She cocked her head as if the idea was totally foreign to her. "How so?"

"Umm, well . . . " I struggled to think of a way to explain it. "They see witches as evil—"

"We're not," she said, interrupting me.

"I know, but there are a lot of stereotypes—old crones in league with the devil—you know, that kind of stuff. It's just easier if we don't broadcast what we do."

Aunt Dot looked puzzled. "That's a shame you have to hide your talents. How do you explain what you can do?"

How did we explain?

We didn't.

I suspected Sheriff Wilson wrote off my talent for stumbling over bodies as just his bad luck and a product of my overactive and unhealthy curiosity. And Abby? She'd always been careful not to give away too much information whenever someone came to her with a problem. She'd mask her psychic intuition as good old-fashioned common sense. And the neighbors never wondered what lay behind Abby's amazing wisdom. My assistant and friend Darci had been the only one who ever questioned whether there was more to Abby than met the eye.

Aunt Dot's bottom lip stuck out in a pout. "You're not expecting anything to happen while I'm here?"

"No, sorry to disappoint you, Aunt Dot. Summerset is really pretty quiet. It's not a hotbed of crime, and I don't expect any bodies to be popping up in the near future."

"Shoot." Aunt Dot frowned. "I really wanted to help you solve a murder. Life is so boring on that danged mountain."

Boring. Right. Two little old ladies, living in the boonies, one was a medium who talked to spirits while the other believed that she communed with fairies. Oh, and what about their wine's secret ingredient? Illegal booze. Did they run their own still, or just know people who had one? It didn't sound boring to me, but now she wanted in on a murder case? The thought made me shudder.

"Nope, no bodies, Aunt Dot," I reiterated, and as I did, I sent a silent plea that I'd be right.

Monday morning, as I returned the stack of books that had filled the library's night drop over the weekend to the shelves, Darci came bounding in the front door. Dressed in her usual skin-hugging blue jeans, today she had her blond hair piled high on the top of her head. Her mules with their three-inch heels slapped her feet as she strode toward me.

"Ophelia, I need to talk to you," she said in a breathless voice and grabbed my arm, pulling me toward the counter.

"Okay," I replied, gently extricating my arm and following her. "You're late, by the way."

She fluttered a red-tipped hand in my general direction. "Yeah, yeah, I know, but I couldn't find this." She plopped a magazine down on the counter and pointed at it proudly. "Look."

"What?" I asked. "The latest copy of *In Style?* Or is it *People* this week?"

She gave me a quick nudge with her hip. "Silly. It's a catalog for Des Moines Area Community College." She grasped my shoulders with both hands and gave me a slight shake. "I'm going to college!"

I was stunned.

Even though several people in the community liked to think of Darci as the poster child for the phrase "dumb blonde," I knew better. The "silly, little me—I don't get it" attitude was nothing more than a big act. She was shrewd, sharp, savvy, and could cut right through the bs when she wanted to. But going back to school?

"I thought you didn't want to try college because of your dyslexia?"

"I've thought it over, and I'm not the same person I was in high school. I know how to deal with the dyslexia now. Before, I was so afraid of failing that I didn't want to try." She faltered and I saw tears suddenly spring into her big blue eyes. "You don't think I'll fail, do you?"

I threw my arms around her and gave her a big hug. "Of course not. You're one of the smartest people I know. In fact, you're so smart that sometimes it's almost like you're psychic."

She stepped out of the hug and sniffed. "Good. I really, really need you to support me in this, Ophelia."

"I will—that's what friends are for, isn't it?"

"Will you help me study?"

"Sure, no problem. I might be a little rusty. It's been a few years, you know."

Darci snorted. "You always talk like you're sooo old. You're only thirty—"

"Hey," I said, stopping her. "Let's not talk about age." Turning my attention to the catalog, I flipped it open and scanned the classes. "So what are you taking?"

"Just the general education classes for now, but I want to go on and major in psychology."

"That's terrific. Are you going into counseling?"

"Um-hum." Darci's eyes wandered over to the bookshelves. "Ever since last spring, I've thought about that waitress out at The Viper's Nest." She turned and looked at me. "You remember her, don't you?"

"Sure, Janet? Wasn't that her name? She lived in a crappy trailer and was trying to support two little kids on her tips as a waitress."

"Right. I want to help women like her, help them make better lives for themselves and their kids." Darci glanced over her shoulder nervously and then back at me. "And if you promise not to say a word to anyone, I'll tell you what I really want to do."

I made an X over my chest. "Cross my heart."

"I want to open a women's shelter here in Summerset for women down on their luck. Give them a place to live until they can get back on their feet."

"Darci!"

"Shh," she said, giving my arm a shake.

"That's very admirable. Why don't you want people to know?"

"They'll laugh."

"Ah, let 'em laugh," I said with a wave of my hand. "You're going to be making a difference in someone's life."

"You don't think it's too high a goal?"

I shook my head. "Are you kidding? If anyone can do it, you can. You're a master at getting people to do what you want." I laughed. "I can just see you at fund-raisers—you'll have the men turning out their pockets before they know what hit them."

"Yeah," she said thoughtfully, "I would be good at raising money, wouldn't I?"

"Yes, you would," I said with a big smile, but as a thought struck me, I sobered. "What about the library? Are you going to quit?"

I felt like a rat, a selfish rat at that, asking the question, but I couldn't imagine the library without Darci.

"No, silly. I've already talked to Claire, and she said it would be fine if I went to half time, and that you could hire another part-time assistant."

A soft groan slipped out before I could stop it. "I'll have to train someone new."

"No, you won't. I'll train them. And who knows? Maybe

you'll find someone who actually understands the Dewey Decimal System."

"Humph." I still didn't like the idea of a new assistant, but I wasn't going to let my feelings stand in the way of Darci pursuing her dream. "Life's full of changes, I guess," I said reluctantly.

Darci's face immediately took on a shrewd expression. "Funny you should say that—"

"What do you mean?"

Why did I feel that I'd just walked into one of Darci's traps?

"Here," she said, pulling out a piece of paper from between the pages of the catalog and handing it to me.

"Is this one of your latest plans to drag me off to some day spa?"

"No, but a facial certainly wouldn't hurt you." She looked me up and down. "Though, I must say the blond highlights in your hair look nice." She lifted a strand of my long brown hair. "But you need a touch-up. And I like how Nyla has cut your hair this time. It frames your face, accentuates your high cheekbones." She crossed her arms and studied me as if I were some science experiment. "You could wear more makeup. You have such expressive brown eyes—a little more mascara and taupe eye shadow would really make them pop. And your clothes—"

"Okay, okay," I said, tugging on my beige linen jacket and smoothing the matching linen slacks. "I get it. I need to put more care into my appearance."

"It would help, but you have come a long way over the past couple of years."

I arched an eyebrow. "Why, thank you very much, Ms. Make-over Queen," I replied sarcastically. Looking down at the paper in my hand, I said, "Now, what's this?"

"It's next Friday night at the Marriott. We're going and we're going to have a great time."

As I skimmed the words printed on the flyer, a feeling of apprehension marched down my back, making me shiver with distaste. Dropping the flyer, I grabbed a pile of books from the counter and stomped over to the shelves.

Darci followed on my heels.

"Not going to do it," I muttered. "No way, no how. So you can forget about trying to talk me into it, Darci West."

"Oh, come on, we'll have fun," she wheedled.

"No."

She took a book from my hand and shoved it onto the shelf. "You're going to let me go by myself? That's not being a very good friend."

I wheeled on her, my eyes wide with horror at what she had planned for us. "Darci, I'm *not* going to speed date!"

# *Four*

A quick look at my watch told me that I was late. I'd agreed to meet Tink, Aunt Dot, and Abby for lunch at Stumpy's Bar and Billiards, owned by Abby's eighty-year-old boyfriend Arthur. And thanks to Darci's little bombshell about the plan to drag me to a speed dating event, I was running behind.

As I scurried past the turn-of-the century storefronts that made up the downtown section of Summerset, I thought about Darci's latest plot to set me up with a guy. I don't know why she couldn't get it through her head that I was happy without one. When did it become her life's mission to find my soul mate? Ha! Like that would happen anytime soon. I'd already been engaged once, and it had been disastrous. When my former fiancé found out about my "gift," our relationship ended. He explained he had a real problem with the idea of marrying a witch. Well, I had a problem with marrying a jerk, so we were even.

"I don't need some guy complicating my life," I muttered as I rushed down the sidewalk. "It's complicated enough. I—"

"Did you say something, Ophelia?" .

I stopped short and whipped around. Edna Walters stood

beside her parked car staring at me. Her arthritic hands clutched her walker tightly while she watched me with a puzzled look.

Peachy. Edna, the biggest gossip in town, second only to Darci's friend Georgia. By this afternoon the whole town would hear how I'd finally lost it and started talking to myself. There were already enough people in the community who thought I was a bit odd. My habit of stumbling into the middle of murder investigations tended to give people that conclusion. That was just one reason I was determined to turn over a new leaf. Another was the danger! Nope, no more murder and mayhem for me. I didn't care how much Aunt Dot thought my lifestyle sounded like "fun." I was putting all that behind me. Starting now.

"Oh, hi, Edna. Didn't see you standing there."

Her forehead wrinkled in a frown. "But—"

"Sorry, can't chat now," I cut her off, and tapped on my watch. "I was supposed to meet Abby for lunch fifteen minutes ago. Got to fly," I said, wiggling my fingers in her direction. "Oh, stop by the library . . . we just got a new shipment of books." I spun on my heel and hurried on my way.

Flinging open the door at Stumpy's, I scanned the room, looking for Abby. I spotted Agnes McPhearson, talking earnestly to Ned, my friend and editor of *The Courier,* while he tried to eat his lunch. As usual, her dark slacks were covered with cat hair. I grinned. Agnes was a compulsive photographer, and no doubt trying to convince Ned to run some of her pictures in the next edition of the paper. If I had the time, I'd try and rescue him from Agnes's clutches, but I didn't want to keep Abby waiting.

Spotting our little group at a table near the back, I joined them.

"Sorry I'm late." I slid onto a chair and grabbed a menu.

"We already ordered for you." Abby's voice was tight with irritation.

Setting the menu down, I tried to get a read on her mood. She didn't seem happy, but I didn't know if her attitude was a result of my tardiness or something else. I cocked my head questioningly.

She shook hers slightly, as if to say, *I'll tell you later.*

"What have you ladies been up to this morning?" I asked with what I hoped was a sunny smile. "I see you're still in your work clothes, Abby. Been out in the greenhouse?"

Abby's lips tightened. "Yes, since five a.m.," she answered in a low voice. "Aunt Dot got me out of bed so we could try and find the fairies that she's sure are camping out in my flower beds."

Next to me, Tink gave a soft chuckle.

I nudged her with my foot.

Aunt Dot's eyes glowed as she leaned closer to the table and said in a stage whisper, "I caught a glimpse of one last night, hiding in the foxglove. They do love foxglove." She glanced at Abby before returning her attention to me. "Abigail should put some pots in with her flowers. Set them on their side. Fairies need a place to get out of the rain, you know," she said a little louder.

I peered quickly over my shoulder to see if anyone at the next table might have overheard Aunt Dot. The last thing we needed was everyone speculating about her and her fairies. Nope, they weren't paying any attention to us. *Whew.* But maybe now would be a good time to change the subject.

"Aunt Dot—" I began.

"What about in the winter, Aunt Dot?" Tink piped in. "Do fairies migrate like hummingbirds?"

"Oh no, child. They live in underground tunnels and caves. On a warm winter's day, they like to sun themselves." She turned to Abby again. "That's another thing Abigail needs in her garden—some nice flat rocks. The fairies—"

"Oh, gee," I said, rudely interrupting her. "I didn't see Arthur. Is he here today, Abby? Did he—"

I stopped abruptly, sensing a presence to my right. My eyes traveled up to see Sheriff Bill Wilson, bald head gleaming, standing at the corner of our table.

Great. I wondered if *he* heard our discussion.

"Hi, Bill," I said in a cheery voice. "Whatever it is, I didn't do it."

Instinctively, he made a motion to rub his bald head. Halfway there, however, his hand stopped, and I smiled. Bill liked to joke around and say he hadn't started losing his hair until I started bungling his investigations. It was a lie—Bill had been bald ever since I'd known him. However, he hadn't been kidding a couple of months ago when he threatened me with jail time if I didn't stop my snooping.

"Afternoon, ladies," he said with a nod.

After Abby had made introductions, Bill eyed me with speculation.

"You haven't been to Aiken recently, have you, Ophelia?" he asked, wiping his head.

His question caught me off guard, and I stuttered, "N-N-No."

"Not planning on going there any time soon, are you?" He rubbed his head again.

"No." Perplexed, I frowned. "Why?"

"No reason," he replied, and turned his attention to Abby and Aunt Dot.

Aunt Dot sat forward in her chair practically vibrating with excitement. She fixed bright eyes on Bill. "You're the sheriff?"

"Yes, ma'am, I am." Bill smiled down benevolently at her.

Ha, I thought. I bet he wouldn't be smiling if he knew about Aunt Dot's dreams of adventure.

"And you arrest bad men?" she asked.

Bill shifted his weight to one foot. "Yes, if I find any."

"Have you found any lately?" Aunt Dot asked, tilting her head and gazing up at him.

Bill gave me a nervous glance before answering Aunt Dot. "Why no, ma'am, I haven't."

"Do you *need* any help finding some?"

I was right—Bill quit smiling as tiny beads of sweat speckled his forehead. He quickly broke eye contact with Aunt Dot. The arrival of our lunch saved him from answering her question.

He said a hasty good-bye, and as he walked away, scrubbing his head, I heard him mutter, *"Must run in the family."*

I'd been so interested in the exchange between Bill and Aunt Dot that I hadn't noticed Tink fall silent. I observed her pale face.

Concerned, I touched her arm gently. "Aren't you feeling well?"

"I'm just not hungry," she replied in a small voice.

"Not hungry?" Abby asked in disbelief. "Eating one of Arthur's hamburgers was all you talked about this morning at the greenhouse."

"I know." Tink pushed her plate away. "I changed my mind."

"Would you like something else?"

Tink shook her head and, shoving her chair back, stood. "I'm going to the restroom."

Before any of us could respond, she left the table and headed toward the back.

I followed.

I found her standing at the sink, applying a wet paper towel to the back of her neck.

"What is it, Tink?" I asked, placing a hand on her shoulder.

"I don't know. I got an icky feeling when Sheriff Wilson was talking to Aunt Dot."

"What kind of an 'icky' feeling?"

Tink took a deep breath. "Like the one I had when I saw that man at the airport with her."

"Mr. Buchanan, the funeral director?"

She nodded. "Only this time the feeling was worse. My skin felt all prickly."

Resting a hip against the porcelain sink, I pondered what she'd said. "Well, Mr. Buchanan, as a funeral director, deals with death. As a sheriff, Bill does, too. I hate to say this, but maybe Bill had to handle an accident this morning. He did mention Aiken, something might have happened over there."

"You don't think it has anything to do with me?"

"No," I replied with more confidence than I felt. "Aiken is fifteen miles from Summerset. We don't know anyone there, so what could happen in Aiken that would affect us?"

Later, I'd regret asking that question.

After work that afternoon, I hurried home. I'd promised Tink that we would take the dogs for a run out at Roseman State Park. After whipping into the drive of my Victorian cottage, I ran to the curb and opened my mailbox. I pulled out the mail and thumbed through it.

Gas bill, electric bill, a new credit card offer, Tink's subscription to *Seventeen*. Nothing too interesting here. Then a letter with a Minnesota postmark caught my eye. It was from an attorney's office in St. Paul.

Jason Finch, Tink's uncle and former guardian, lived in Minnesota.

Her former guardian who still had legal custody.

# *Five*

I noticed my hands were shaking, and I felt icy fingers of fear squeeze my heart.

What if this letter was to notify us that Juliet, Tink's aunt, had been released from the mental hospital? But a moment later I realized that wasn't possible. A year ago Juliet had killed a man and been declared legally insane. I couldn't see the legal system letting her out anytime soon. Then I wondered if Jason's attorney was writing us to renege on our agreement that I raise Tink. The thought left a sick feeling in the pit of my stomach. Tink was such an important part of my life that I couldn't imagine it without her. And it would kill Abby if we lost her.

*Stop it, Jensen,* said a little voice inside my head. *Open the letter and read it.*

Taking a deep breath, I tore open the envelope with trembling fingers. Quickly, I read the letter and let out a whoop of joy. The attorney proposed, on the request of his client, that Jason permanently surrender custody of Tink, clearing the way for me to start adoption proceedings. He also stated that a trust, containing the funds Tink had inherited from her deceased mother, would be set up. Our friend from Minnesota, Rick Delaney, and I would be named as the trustees.

The relief I felt was so strong, I almost dropped to my knees in the middle of the driveway. Clutching the letter, I tore into the house, searching for Tink. I found her in the kitchen making a peanut butter and jelly sandwich while Lady, T.P., and my cat Queenie watched with rapt attention, just waiting for something edible to drop on the floor.

I grabbed her in a fierce hug, causing the knife in her hand to clatter to the floor.

"Ophelia!" she squealed. "What's gotten into you?"

Releasing her, I quickly explained the contents of the letter. Her reaction disappointed me. She didn't seem to share my elation.

"This is great news, Tink! Aren't you happy?"

"Yeah," she said, bending to pick up the fallen knife, which by then had been licked clean by T.P. Tossing it in the sink, she turned and faced me. "It's a lot to absorb."

"I know, but now we can make this arrangement permanent." Uncertainty hit me. "That's what you want, isn't it?"

"Sure." Her voice sounded noncommittal. "I thought we were going to Roseman State Park?" she said, changing the subject.

"Umm, yes, we were." My eyes darted to the clock. "Give me five minutes to change, okay?"

In my room, I quickly changed out of my linen slacks and blazer and into a pair of shorts and a T-shirt. As I tied my tennis shoes, I thought about Tink's reaction. Obviously she didn't want to tell me her feelings right now. Maybe after we reached the park, I could get to the bottom of what was bothering her.

We drove to Roseman without talking. Lady and T.P. sat in the back. I'd opened the windows a crack, and they both had their noses pressed to the opening, sniffing the air excitedly as the fields of corn, hay, and soybeans went flying by.

At least someone was excited, I thought.

Once we arrived at Roseman, I drove down the quiet lane to the back side of the park, away from the campgrounds. I stopped the car and we let the dogs out. They immediately took off down the path and into the woods. Tink and I followed.

A light summer breeze ruffled the leaves overhead and helped keep the bugs at bay. I took a deep breath and smelled the scent of newly mown hay as we walked.

"Ahh," I sighed. "I love that smell."

"What smell?" Tink asked, breaking her silence.

"Hay," I replied, taking another deep breath. "It reminds me of when I was a kid and spent the summers with Grandpa and Abby."

"You spent a lot of time with them, didn't you?"

"Yup, a few weeks every summer until I was eighteen. I think Mother thought it was a good way to keep me out of trouble. It let Abby put me to work in the greenhouse."

"And you enjoyed it?" Tink stopped to pick up a broken twig and began to strip off the leaves as we continued walking.

"Sure did. I don't have Abby's knack with plants, so after I killed several, she thought it wise to keep me busy watering and weeding." I looked at her. "You like working with Abby, too, don't you?"

Tink threw the stick into the bush. "Yeah . . . " Her voice trailed away and she kept her eyes focused ahead. "Ophelia, I'm scared."

I put my arm around her shoulders and pulled her close, our steps matching. "Why, Tink?"

She scuffed at the leaves on the path. "What if the judge decides to put me in a foster home instead?"

I dropped my arm and stopped in the path. "How did you come up with that idea?"

"Nell. We talked about it the last time I stayed the night at her house." She kicked a rock. "A judge took Roger Jones away from his family."

"Tink," I said in an exasperated voice. "Roger Jones's parents were mistreating him. I may not be the best mom in the world—I don't bake you cookies, and home-cooked meals are in short supply—but I don't think a court would call that mistreatment."

A small smile played at the corner of her mouth. "I guess you're right." She sobered. "But what if the judge says no for some other reason?"

"I won't let that happen," I said with determination.

"Could you stop it?"

She had a point. Whatever ruling the court made, I'd be forced to follow it.

"Look, why would a judge say no? Jason is willing to let me adopt you; I *want* to adopt you; you want to be adopted . . . " A sudden thought brought back my fear. "You really do want to stay here, don't you?"

Tink rolled her eyes and snorted. "Duh!" Her shoulders suddenly drooped. "This is my home now."

T.P. came running over to Tink with a stick in his mouth.

She bent to take it away from him, but not before I saw her eyes fill with tears. She straightened and threw the stick.

The happy puppy scrambled after it.

I put my arm around her shoulder again and gave her a squeeze. "You have to have faith it will all work out—"

"But . . . " she said, pulling away.

"But what?" I asked when she didn't continue.

"The past three days have been weird," she said, rushing her words. "First, I had that dream about the shadows in the woods. Mr. Buchanan at the airport. Sheriff Wilson at lunch. I—I—"

"Hey, slow down. You think all of this means something?"

"Yeah." She looked at me with worry written all over her face. "What if they're some kind of premonition? It's left me feeling bad every time it happened. Isn't that what premonitions do to you?"

"Tink, first of all—you're not a psychic, you're a medium—"

"But what if a spirit is trying to warn me of impending doom?" she asked, cutting me off.

If she hadn't been so concerned, I would have laughed. "Impending doom" sounded just like Abby.

"Sweetie, if something tragic were about to happen, don't you think Abby or I would've sensed it?" I asked her calmly.

"Yeah."

"Have you had any more dreams?"

"No," she mumbled.

"See? It was probably just a random dream," I said, and squeezed her again. "Everything's going to be okay."

I felt Tink's mood brighten.

"A judge would really let you adopt me?"

"Sure, I'm a fine upstanding citizen," I said as I tugged on my T-shirt and stood tall. "Aren't I?"

A cheeky grin washed over her face. "Yeah, but I don't think I'd ask Aunt Dot to be a character witness. She might start telling the judge about her fairies. Wouldn't look good for our family. He might think we're all crazy."

Now my eyes suddenly filled with tears. That was the first time Tink had ever said "our family."

Wiping my eyes, I laughed and looked up at the sky.

"It's going to be dark soon." I whistled for the dogs. "We'd better get back to the car." The dogs had just scampered back in response to my whistle when I turned and jumped, startled.

A man stood in the path, blocking our exit from the woods.

I grabbed Tink and shoved her behind me. As T.P. ducked behind Tink's leg, Lady took a position in front of me. A low growl rumbled in her throat as the hair along her spine stood straight up. An insane thought popped into my head: *Where was my Louisville Slugger when I needed it?*

The man took one look at Lady and held his hands out in front of him. "Sorry, I didn't mean to scare you," he said, his voice apologetic.

He appeared to be around forty, and from the way he was dressed, I would've guessed he was a farmer. His denim overalls, stained with rust, were worn over an old plaid shirt. Bits and pieces of twine hung out of his side pockets, and the center pocket of his bibs appeared stuffed full. He wore an old slouched hat on his head that shadowed the upper part of his face, and it was hard to see his eyes. His stance was relaxed and nonthreatening.

Deciding he was harmless, my heart slowed to its normal rhythm.

"I own the property over yonder," he said, pointing to the trees behind Tink and me. "I was out checking my fence lines and on my way home." He dropped his eyes, then suddenly bent down and picked up an object from the path. "Look, a quarter," he said, holding the shiny coin high in the air. "Not yours, is it?"

I shook my head.

"Just never know what you're going to find in the woods," he said as he tucked it in his already full pocket. I'm Silas Green, by the way."

Silas Green? The name wasn't familiar to me, but I didn't know everyone in the area. Darci did. I'd ask her about him tomorrow.

"Nice dog," he commented, eyeing Lady. Returning his attention to me, he smiled to reveal a set of very crooked front teeth with long incisors. Immediately, he didn't look so harmless.

Lady now stood glued to my leg. Never taking my eyes off Mr. Green, I reached down and patted her head. "Yes, she is." Taking Tink's hand, I started down the path. "Excuse us, we need to get home before dark."

"That's wise, miss. The woods aren't a good place to be come nightfall."

I paused and gave him a puzzled look.

"The mosquitoes. Once the breeze goes down at night, they come out. They'll eat you alive if you don't watch it." With a tip of his hat, he turned and walked off in the other direction.

I watched in the growing dusk until he was out of sight. Dragging Tink behind me, I hurried us to my parked car.

We made it in record time.

# Six

Since Darci's classes started in two weeks, I struggled to come up with a schedule for the library that worked around her. But it was Claire Canyon, our library board president, who saved the situation. While talking causally with a woman who'd recently moved to Summerset, she learned the newcomer needed a part-time job. Claire had been impressed enough with to offer her an interview.

"This is pointless," I said to Darci as I stared at the blank piece of paper lying on the counter.

Darci paused while checking in books. "What's pointless?"

"Trying to come up with questions for the interview this afternoon." I tapped the counter with my pen. "Claire's vote of confidence is good enough for me."

"But you have to at least go through the motions." Darci flipped the book shut.

"I suppose. Hmm, how about 'What are your favorite authors?'" I said, scribbling it on the blank sheet.

*Are you familiar with the best-seller lists?* came next. "Hey, I'm on a roll here," I said as I started to write the next question. A nudge from Darci interrupted me.

I turned my head to see Abby escorting Aunt Dot through the door. As soon as Aunt Dot cleared the doorway, she shook off Abby's hand and proceeded across the room like a steamroller, her head whipping from side to side as she took in the library.

"She's so sweet," Darci murmured next to me.

"Yeah? Well, just don't mention murder or fairies, okay?"

"Huh?"

"Trust me on this one, Darce." I plastered a smile on my face. "Hi, Aunt Dot," I said loud enough for her to hear me.

"This is where you work, eh?" Aunt Dot trooped up to the counter, her walking stick thudding with each step.

"Yup. What do you think?"

"You have a lot of books," she replied in a matter-of-fact voice.

My eyes traveled around the room. She was right—we had thousands of books in our circa 1920 library. Its heating and cooling system might leave something to be desired, and the blinds covering the arched windows were ancient, but I loved the old place. Our library had character. Crown molding ran around the high ceilings, and light from the antique light fixtures reflected off the soft gold walls, warming the room even on the darkest day. The floors had recently been redone. Wonderful pegged planks had been discovered underneath the worn carpet and restored to their original beauty. The whole building smelled of old leather and lemon oil polish.

My gaze settled on Abby, standing directly behind Aunt Dot.

The skin around her eyes looked pinched, and I noticed a faint twitch in one eyelid. Her normally immaculate braid had tendrils of silver escaping this way and that. And the aura of calm that usually floated around her was missing.

But before I could open my mouth to say anything, Darci stepped from around the counter to greet Aunt Dot.

"Hi, I'm Darci, Ophelia's assistant," she said, holding out her hand.

Aunt Dot took her hand in both of hers and studied Darci closely. "My, she's a smart one, isn't she?" she said over her shoulder to Abby.

Darci's eyes widened in surprise at Aunt Dot's remark.

Boy, I would have to explain that one later, I thought. Oh well, by now, Darci was well-acquainted with our family's talents.

Abby smiled. "Yes, she is," she replied with affection. "Ophelia told me you're starting college in a couple of weeks,"

Darci gave a hesitant nod. "Um-hum. I'm a little nervous."

Abby stepped forward and gave Darci's arm a squeeze. "You'll do fine," she said, her voice reassuring. "I'll miss seeing you around the library."

"Oh, I'll still be here on the weekends." She shot me a look. "Someone has to keep Ophelia out of trouble."

Ha! Since Darci had done more than her share to *get* me in trouble, I thought her remark very inappropriate.

"Aunt Dot," Darci said, her eyes returning to my diminutive aunt. "Would you like me to give you a tour of the library?"

Uh-oh. I didn't like that idea at all. Darci had her own fascination with our "adventures," and I didn't think it wise for her to spend unsupervised time with Aunt Dot. I shuddered to think of what kind of trouble two excitement junkies like Aunt Dot and Darci could get into.

I stepped quickly around the counter. "I'll take her."

"No." Darci's eyes sparked with wry humor. "I'd be happy to show her around. You have to finish the questions for the interview." She extended her arm to Aunt Dot. "Would you like to see the children's section and Ophelia's office?" She took a worried glance at the stairs leading to the basement. "But maybe the stairs might be a problem."

"Ack, these old legs still work," Aunt Dot said, setting off at her usual pace, pulling Darci with her.

I couldn't help but grin. "She's something else, isn't she?"

My grin fell away when I saw the expression on Abby's face. The pinched features warned me of problems brewing.

"You have no idea." Abby's voice rose on an exasperated note. "She's only been here four days and she's wearing me out!" She blew a stray strand out of her face. "If she isn't up until all hours trying to make contact with the fairies she's convinced live in my flower garden, she's messing with the plants in my greenhouse. She quizzes every customer that comes in. And—and . . . " Abby was on a roll, "she's decided, since she's on vacation, it's okay to have wine time every night. I'm going to be glad when that damn wine's gone," she muttered. "I swear—I've never known such a meddler."

I had to drop my head to hide my smile. Abby was a fine one to talk about meddling; in my opinion, she was the expert. Maybe it ran in the family, along with our psychic gifts. But if that were the case, it meant that I—

I didn't get to pursue that line of thinking. Abby's next statement broke into my thoughts.

"Have you had a chance to speak to an attorney about the letter from Minnesota?"

"Yes, I talked to Warren." I scrunched my face, thinking back over the last couple of days. "Today's Wednesday, so yeah, Tuesday. I met with him over my lunch hour. He said it might be a little more complicated since Jason is in Minnesota, but Tink lives in Iowa, so the proceedings will be in this county."

"Will Jason have to appear?"

"Gosh, I hope not. I don't think it would be good for Tink to see him again. We'll have to deal with it as it comes up. Right now, Warren is drafting a response to Jason's attorney."

"Don't worry, dear, you have to have faith it will all work out."

I exhaled. "That's exactly what I told Tink. Do you think she's doing okay?"

"She seems fine. I think it was a good idea to let her spend the night at Nell's. They were going to the beach at Saylorville today with Nell's parents. And there's the campout this weekend."

I slapped my forehead. "That's right—we're supposed to join Nell and her family out at Rosemen State Park on Saturday night." I grimaced. "Spending the night in a tent isn't exactly my idea of fun."

Abby chuckled. "You'll have a good time, and it will be a nice distraction for Tink—" She stopped abruptly. "She hasn't had any more nightmares, has she?"

"No, or any 'icky' feelings."

Abby nodded wisely. "That's good. It wouldn't do for her to wake the whole campground because of a bad dream."

I shivered at the thought. "No."

"Have you done a rune reading? One might shed some light on what's going on with her."

"No, but I will, if it happens again." I shook my head. "I'm not sensing anything, so I just don't—"

I broke off when Georgia, owner of the local bed and breakfast—and Darci's source of all gossip concerning the citizens of Summerset—came striding in the door.

Her red ponytail bounced as she hurried over to the counter where Abby and I stood. She plunked down the stack of books in her arms and turned to me. "Where's Darci?" she asked in an agitated voice.

"Down in the basement, giving Aunt Dot a tour? Why?"

"Haven't you heard—" Georgia stopped at the sound of Aunt Dot and Darci coming up the stairs. She waited, fidgeting back and forth, until they reached us.

"What's up, Georgia?" Darci asked, reading her excitement.

"Did you guys hear about what happened over in Aiken?"

Bill had mentioned Aiken at lunch on Monday. I felt my stomach clench with apprehension.

"No," Darci replied, her eyes widening with curiosity.

From where she stood next to Darci, I noticed Aunt Dot go on alert, too.

"A man was embalmed alive!"

Everyone's jaws dropped as the gruesome image lodged in our minds. No one spoke.

Abby was the first one to break the silence. "Georgia, that has to be a rumor. A body isn't embalmed until a doctor has examined it to make sure the person has passed. It's impossible for someone to still be a—"

Georgia didn't let Abby finish. "Not if it was murder."

"Murder?" Aunt Dot quivered with anticipation.

I stifled the groan rising in my throat as Georgia continued.

"Alan said the victim was hooked up to the embalming machine via an IV." She held out her right arm and pointed to a vein. "Then another IV was placed in the other arm," she said, holding out her left arm. "As the fluid was pumped in on one side, the blood was forced out on the other side, and—"

I held up a hand, stopping her. "That's enough. We get the picture."

"Wait a second," Darci said. "You just can't grab some-body, break into the nearest funeral home, and embalm them."

"The victim was already in the funeral home. No one had to snatch him," Georgia explained breathlessly. "His name was Bu—"

I finished for her. "Buchanan."

Georgia pivoted in surprise. "How did you know?"

Aunt Dot gasped. "I know him. I met him on my plane ride from North Carolina. I sat right next to him!" Her eyes glowing with fervor darted first to me, then to Abby. "It's a sign. We're destined to solve his murder!"

Claire's candidate was late for her interview. Not a good way to impress the interviewer. But it was just as well. Her delay would give me some time to recoup from Georgia's news. And deal with the headache nagging behind my left eye. One not caused this time by Aunt Dot's wine. No, the cause of this headache was the tension in the back of my neck. What was causing it? Simple: How did I explain Mr. Buchanan's murder to Tink?

Tink had already voiced a concern that her "icky" feel-ing at meeting Mr. Buchanan had been a warning. Once she learned that he'd been murdered, I knew she would feel guilty. She would think that she had somehow failed to avert a tragedy.

And boy, oh boy, did I know all about that feeling—when my best friend, Brian, had been murdered several years ago, and my vision had failed to stop his death. The event sent me into a tailspin that took me years to recover from. I'd shut myself off from everyone except Abby, fearful of getting close to anyone again, turning my back on my gift and my heritage. It wasn't until I was pulled kicking and screaming into a murder investigation that the walls I'd built around my life began to crumble. My involvement made me realize that I couldn't hide from who and what I was.

I couldn't let the same thing to happen to Tink.

Rubbing my forehead, I wished the headache away.

It didn't work.

Frustrated, I began to pace my small office. From the shelves, pictures of Abby, Tink, my parents, stared down at me. As in my office at home, several crystals lay scattered about my desk. Pausing, I picked up a disk made of moonstone. Moonstone—calmness and awareness—did I need that. I rubbed the milky white disk between my fingers and tried to let its energy seep into my mind while I resumed my trip around the room.

Why hadn't either Abby or I picked up on Mr. Buchanan's approaching death? We both were psychics.

I felt the blood drain from my face.

If Bill had known about Buchanan's death on Monday, and we met him on Saturday, the murder had to have happened either Saturday night or Sunday. Had Buchanan's killer been waiting for him when he returned to the funeral home? The idea made the tension in my neck squeeze harder.

How could we *not* have sensed the tragedy waiting to happen? Especially Abby. I'd been standing with Tink, away from Aunt Dot and Abby. Maybe I was too far away to get a read on him, but Abby? She'd stood next to him, even shook his hand when Aunt Dot made the introductions. And Abby was very, *very* good at reading people she touched.

I grasped the moonstone tighter.

These thoughts and pacing around weren't getting me anywhere. The only way to find answers would be to discuss the situation with Abby, preferably without Aunt Dot around.

I sighed deeply. Abby was going to have her hands full with Aunt Dot. She'd hustled Dot out of the library right after Georgia's announcement, but it was too late. Even as they left, I overheard Aunt Dot asking how we were going to help the sheriff solve Buchanan's murder. I didn't envy Abby the job of keeping her out of this. Long ago, I decided another trait the women in our family shared was persistence. And I had a feeling Aunt Dot possessed that quality in spades.

But Abby would have to handle it on her own. I had Tink to worry about.

A sharp knock on my door interrupted my musings.

"Come in," I called out as I placed the moonstone back on my desk.

The door swung open to reveal Darci standing there. "Your interview is here." She stepped aside and allowed a woman to cross the threshold.

With a deep breath, I looked at the person who might replace Darci.

# Seven

"Ophelia," Darci said, "this is Gertrude Duncan."

The woman Darci ushered in was tiny. Dressed completely and immaculately in black, she wore understated pearl studs in her ears and a carved silver pendant. Her age was hard to judge—she could've been anywhere from her late forties to mid-fifties. Her demeanor was both refined and assured. She could have looked dowdy, but she'd added a little "funk" to her appearance by wearing her dark red hair in short spikes. From behind burgundy framed glasses, brown eyes studied me expectantly.

"It's wonderful meeting you, Ms. Jensen," she said, extending her hand. "Claire speaks very highly of you."

Her voice was low and well-modulated. Her words carried a faint southern drawl, but different from Aunt Dot's.

"Have a seat, and please call me Ophelia," I said, motioning to a chair at the corner of my desk. Turning to the door, I caught Darci's questioning look and gave my head a slight shake. Smiling, she wiggled her eyebrows and mouthed *Good luck* as she quietly shut the door.

"From your accent, Ms. Duncan, I take it you're not from the Midwest?" I said as I seated myself behind my desk.

She chuckled. "It's obvious, isn't it? All I have to do is open my mouth. And call me Gert." She inched back in her chair, demurely crossed her legs at the ankles and folded her hands in her lap. Her posture was impeccable.

Wow, I thought, this woman could almost outlady Abby.

"I was born in St. Tammany Parish in New Orleans," she replied softly, "but Mama grew up here in Iowa. We moved back to help with my grandma. Even though Grandma's passed, Mama wants to stay. We were living in the city, but Mama didn't like it." She lowered her eyes. "Mama's not well—her nerves. She still mourns Grandma, you know, and all the noise in the city bothered her something terrible. Now we're renting a sweet little farmhouse south of town. The old Blunt place."

"I know that place. I didn't realize the Blunts were renting it out," I commented, leaning back in my chair. "Your mother won't mind being alone while you're at the library?"

"Oh no, Mama loves to cook. She keeps herself busy in the kitchen all day long. I'm the one who has the problem." Gert lifted her chin. "And if I may be forthright, though I love my mama to death, being out in the country day in and day out is driving me a mite stir crazy." She smiled broadly as she rubbed her pendant. "That's why I rushed right in and applied for this job. It would suit me to a T. I could still spend time with Mama but get out once in a while, too."

"I see. As Claire told you, we only need help two or three afternoons a week."

"Like I said, Ms. Jen—er, Ophelia, this would be perfect for my situation." Gert removed an envelope from her purse and handed it to me. "Here's my job résumé. I'm afraid my most recent employer is no longer in business. I would have to call friends in New Orleans to obtain his current phone number. I'd be happy to do so, but I was in a bit of a hurry to meet with you today."

I had a strong feeling Gert knew how to conduct an interview better than I did. *Jeez, Jensen, you should be writing stuff down. At least look like you know what you're doing!*

Placing the envelope to one side, I picked up a pen.

"Ahh . . . do you enjoy reading, Gert?"

Her face beamed "'Course I do. I adore mysteries—*Rebecca* is my favorite."

I made a note. "What about the current best-sellers?"

"Oh yes," she exclaimed, and rattled off a list of titles and authors, some of whom I'd never even heard of.

"Romance? Do you read any romance?"

A faint tinge of pink bloomed on her fair cheeks. "Yes, but Mama thinks they're unseemly."

"Ah, don't worry about it," I said with a flip of my hand. "We have several closet-romance readers as patrons. The steamier, the better. If you know what's popular, you'll be able to help them find the newest releases."

"I also love true crime," she said in a hushed voice, as if Mama might be able to hear her confession from her little house clear out in the country.

"Ann Rule?"

"Oh my," she said, clasping a hand to her chest. "The way she gets into the mind of those killers, it's amazing." She scooted forward to the edge of her chair. "You can learn from reading Ann Rule, too. Her books show how the authorities go about catching those bad people."

Gert seemed sweet and kind of naive. She also seemed to be under Mama's controlling thumb. I could see where working at the library would be a release for her.

I tapped my pen on my desk. "How would you rate your people skills?"

"I don't like to brag, but I have a knack for handling difficult people."

*Hmm, like Mama?* But I didn't voice my question.

"I'm also proficient at the computer and I type eighty-five words a minute."

Thoughts of the never-ending project of entering our entire inventory into the computer sprang to mind. I'd been working on that sucker for over a year and had about given up on ever finishing. A fast typist would be an asset.

I asked her a few more inconsequential questions, but as far as I was concerned she had the job.

Finally, I put my pen down. "Do you have any questions for me, Gert?"

"No," she replied as she stood to leave. "I do thank you for taking the time to speak with me, and I'll look forward to hearing from you."

She extended her hand, and I gave it a firm shake. "Claire and the board do the actual hiring, but I'll pass along my recommendation. Their next meeting is tomorrow evening." I glanced down at the envelope. "Is a number where you can be reached included on your résumé?"

"It surely is." A look of concern crossed her face. "Please, if Mama answers the phone, don't be alarmed. She can be a little gruff at times."

"I understand," I replied, walking around the corner of my desk. "Thanks for coming in, Gert."

"My pleasure." Her gaze fell to my desk, and before I could stop her, she picked up the moonstone. "What a lovely crystal," she said, turning it over in her palm.

Terrific. Crystals are programmed to each individual owner and imprinted with their personal energy. Now, thanks to Gert handling my stone, I'd have to cleanse and rededicate it.

She replaced the moonstone and picked up my hematite. "What's this little black rock?" she asked as she rubbed it.

"Hematite," I answered, trying not to wince at the sight of her handling yet another of my crystals.

"And this?"

She made a move toward my jade, but I grabbed her hand before she could touch it. Pumping her arm, I smiled.

"Thanks again for coming in, Gert." With a hand firmly in the middle of her back, I steered her away from my desk and my crystals.

With reluctance, Gert allowed me to direct her toward the door. "It was delightful, Ophelia. As I said, I've heard so much about you."

With a nod of her spiky head, she walked confidently through the children's section and toward the stairs.

When I arrived home late that afternoon, I let the dogs in, checked the bathroom doors to make sure they were shut, and called Abby. I didn't have much time. Tink would be home soon.

Abby picked up on the second ring.

"Is Aunt Dot with you?"

"No."

"Good. Why didn't we pick up on Mr. Buchanan's murder?"

Abby let out a long breath into the receiver. "I've thought about that question all day, and I don't know the answer." She sighed again. "The only reason I can come up with is we don't always sense everyone's death."

"But this wasn't a simple case of someone meeting their natural end. This man was brutally murdered."

"I know," she murmured.

"Do you think Tink knew what would happen if she let

down her guard? Were the spirits trying to give her a warn-ing? Spirits do warn the living, don't they?"

"I think so," she replied softly.

"Okay," I said, my voice rising, "so how do I explain to a fourteen-year-old that she might have known in advance that someone was going to die? That she might have been able to stop a murder? That she failed because she didn't listen? You know what kind of guilt she'll feel, and you know what that can do to a person."

"I also know just because you're a psychic, or a medium, you can't stop every tragedy. It—"

"That sucks!" I broke in with a shout, causing T.P. to yelp in bewilderment.

"Yes, dear." Abby's voice was calm. "You've always made your feelings on that subject quite clear."

Shouting at Abby would serve no purpose, so I took a deep breath to get control of myself. "How do I help Tink?" I asked in a more reasonable tone. "I'm not sure I'll be able to answer her questions."

"Would you like me to come over?"

"With Aunt Dot in tow? I don't think so," I replied with sarcasm. "The less we say around her, the better."

"I agree."

I heard the front door slam. "Tink's home. Got to go." I ended the call before Abby could answer.

Tink blew into the kitchen and went directly to the re-frigerator. "I'm starving," she said, flinging the door open. "What do we have to eat?"

To my tired eyes, Tink's hair looked even blonder after her day in the sun. A slight tan had kissed her fair skin. She looked so young, so happy, and I'd have given anything to shield her from what I was about to tell her. A deep sense of sadness settled in my heart, making it ache. How was I ever going to teach this child in one night the lesson that had taken me over thirty years to learn? But unless I wanted Tink to pay the same emotional price I had, I needed to try.

"Tink," I said in a quiet voice. "I'd like to talk to you. Let's go in my office."

Alarmed, Tink turned and stared at me. "What's wrong? Has something happened to Abby—"

"No, no," I said, cutting her off.

"Jason's changed his mind?"

"No. I'll explain in my office."

Taking her hand in mine, I led her to the room I used for my magick. The weight of my responsibility slowed my steps. I had to make her understand. I couldn't let guilt crush her as it had me for so many years.

I settled Tink in the chair beside my desk and picked up a blue lace agate for wisdom and communication, hoping it would help me find the right words.

Tink watched me with confusion and fear written on her face. Her violet eyes begged me to get to the point.

"Mr. Buchanan was murdered," I said quietly.

"But—but—" she stuttered.

"Georgia stopped by the library today and told us." I ignored the shocked look on Tink's face.

"Message . . . they were trying to give me a message." With a sob, Tink raced out of the room.

I ran after her and finally found her outside, underneath one of the trees ringing our backyard. T.P. lay cuddled on her lap. Lady and Queenie sat protectively on each side, like guardians. Picking up Queenie, I slid down next to Tink, our shoulders touching, and for a moment neither one of us spoke.

"It's not your fault," I said at last.

"You don't know that," she said with a sniff.

T.P., hearing the sad note in her voice, licked her hand as if to comfort her.

"Okay, Tink, let's suppose you were receiving a message." I glanced at her. "I'm not saying you were," I stressed. "But we'll go with the idea that's the case. What would you have done?"

"Walked up to him and told him."

"You would've walked up to a complete stranger and told him he was about to die a terrible death?"

"Yes," she said in a small voice while her hand scratched the puppy's ears.

"And if you had, what would his reaction have been?"

"He would've thought I was crazy."

"Right . . ." My voice trailed away. "And as a result, he wouldn't have heeded your warning." I picked up a twig and rolled it around in my hand. "How many tragedies do you think Abby's seen but been unable to stop, for whatever reason, in her seventy-plus years?"

Tink cuddled T.P. to her chest and rubbed her chin on his head. "A lot."

"Right again." I broke the twig in two and cast it on the ground. "If there's one thing I've learned—there are some things we can't change, no matter how much we want to."

Tink stared off at the woods in the distance. "We should be able to use our gift. We should be able to change the outcome. It's not right when we can't."

"I agree, but you have to accept the reality of it. Or you can let it destroy you."

"You learned this because of what happened to Brian?"

"Yes," I said in an even tone.

A tear slid down her cheek. "How can you shrug off failure?"

"You can't, and I wouldn't want you to. A person would

have to have a cold, hard heart to do that. And we both know that's not you."

"So what do I do?"

Reaching over, I took her chin and turned her face until she faced me. "You mourn, and then you let it go. You have faith that next time, you *will* make a difference." I tucked a strand behind her ear. "If you don't, sweetie, your talent will drive you insane."

Tink dropped her gaze. "I don't want to wind up crazy like Juliet."

I gathered her in a tight hug, squeezing the poor puppy between us.

He yelped and scampered off Tink's lap.

"Oh sweetie, you could never be like Juliet. She was bad to begin with, and the evil inside her drove her over the edge." I leaned back so I could see her face. "You do have to believe that what happened to Mr. Buchanan was for a reason." I caressed her cheek. "Abby and I share in this, too. Neither one of us sensed anything wrong."

Her brow gathered in a frown. "I wonder why?"

"I don't know." I gave her a determined smile. "But I intend to find out."

# *Eight*

The light on the base of the cordless phone glowed bright as I poured my third cup of coffee that evening. And its glow gave me a strange sense of peace. It meant Tink was at least talking to her best friend, Nell.

Dinner had been silent. Tink pushed her corn around on her plate with her fork and only took a bite when she caught me watching. I tried to keep up some form of conversation, but soon even my food lost its appeal. Any appetite I'd had was crushed by the weight of silence that hung around us. I gave up, asked Tink if she was done, and filled up the dog bowls with our scraps.

Taking my coffee back to my office, I ran my fingers idly over my pictures, my crystals, and my books lined up neatly on the shelves. If only I could find the answer to my dilemma between their pages. Worry picked at the corner of my brain, no matter how hard I tried to ignore it.

I could deny it, I could run from it, but the cause of the worry was inescapable. We had a problem. And it started Friday night with Tink's dream of rotting corpses pleading for help. Abby liked to say that there was no such thing as a coincidence, and Tink coming in contact with a man whose occupation was death was no coincidence. Then to have the man die on his own embalming table. I didn't need a map to know something was up. The question was, what? And how did I protect Tink, and for once keep my family out of a murder investigation?

I glanced at the phone. Light still on. Good, I thought, taking a sip of coffee. I hoped Tink would share her troubles with Nell.

I wondered how much Nell knew about our gifts. She'd been a front row witness to Tink's misadventure with a Ouija board in May. The troubled spirit of Summerset's last murder victim had tried to choke a participant when Tink inadvertently summoned him by way of the board. The five girls at that session had all learned that messing with the Ouija board was *not* a harmless game.

I frowned. Maybe Tink had taken her lesson too much to heart and now was afraid to let her guard down at any time.

The shrill ringing of my cell phone filled the room. I leaned across the desk and flipped the phone open.

"I can't get through on your land line," came Abby's voice from the receiver.

"I know," I said, sitting in the chair behind my desk and placing my bare feet on the edge. "Tink's talking to Nell."

"How did she take the news about Mr. Buchanan's death?"

I pulled one hand through my hair. "You can talk now? Aunt Dot isn't around?"

A slight sniff sounded in my ear. "No, she's out in the yard looking for fairies. Seems she does better seeing them after a couple of glasses of wine."

A sudden thought occurred to me. "Abby, what if all these years, Aunt Dot's fairies have been a result of her tippling?"

"Who knows?" Abby gave a long sigh. "Right now, I don't have time to worry about fairies. I'm concerned about Tink. What happened?"

Quickly, I repeated my conversation with Tink and her reaction to Mr. Buchanan's murder.

"What are you going to do now?" Abby asked when I'd finished.

"A rune reading. I want us to stay out of whatever's going on, Abby," I said in a firm voice. "The only reason I'm doing the reading is to find a way to protect Tink."

Two hours later, I'd made my preparations and my office was ready. A circle of salt ringed the polished oak floor in the center of the room. A thick purple candle sat in heart of the circle, waiting to be lit. My runes, along with a square of linen, lay next to the candle. I had one last thing to do before I did my reading.

After climbing the stairs, I walked quietly down the hall and slowly opened the door to Tink's room. Moonlight filtered through the lace curtains on the windows, creating a shifting pattern on the rag rug. From the bottom of Tink's bed, T.P. lifted his head, and two bright eyes stared at me in the darkness. He sighed and settled his head back on his paws. A sleeping form sprawled in the center of the bed, her pale blond hair fanned across her pillow.

I tiptoed over to the bed and gazed down at her. Instinctively, my hand moved to stroke the soft strands of hair away from her face, but I stopped halfway for fear of waking her. As I watched her sleep, a jumble of emotions ran through me. Pride at what Tink was becoming, fear of losing her, panic at the thought that her talent might destroy her as mine had almost destroyed me, and most of all, the fierce need to protect this child at any cost. I clenched my hands.

I *would* keep this child from harm, I *would* learn where these events were leading us, and I *would* stop it.

Taking a deep breath, I turned and left the room.

In my office, I crumbled dried leaves of sage into my abalone shell and lit them. The aroma of burning sage soon filled the room. Closing my eyes, I inhaled the pungent smoke. Instantly, I felt a sense of peace and purpose blanket me. Placing the shell on the desktop, I grabbed two crystals from my desk—amethyst and ulexite. The energy of the amethyst would increase my psychic talent, and the ulexite would help clarify what I saw with my sixth sense. I moved to my circle and stepped over the line of salt, careful not to disturb it.

After seating myself in the center, I lit the candle. The wick caught, making the flame dance. Holding the amethyst in my left hand, I placed the ulexite against the center of my forehead. My eyelids drifted shut and I concentrated on feeling the energy from deep within the Earth. Slowly, I let the force surround me as I imagined sitting in a circle of light. I framed my question carefully.

"How can I protect Tink?"

Placing the two crystals on either side of the candle, I picked up the worn leather pouch containing Annie's runes. I opened the bag, slipped my right hand inside and let my fingers play over the round stones. When one felt warm, I removed it and set it gently on the linen square in front of me. Soon three runes lay gleaming on the white cloth.

The Norns—the Three Sisters. Past, Present, and Future.

I ignored my trembling fingers as I flipped over the first rune.

Berkano. *"Bear-kawn-oh,"* I whispered. It was reversed—the rune that resembled a B was facing left instead of to the right. Not good. Berkano was the rune for birth, family, children—that which the heart holds dear. Reversed indicated problems in those areas. Strife and stress. A permanent split.

Okay, that made sense. In the past, while living with Juliet and Jason, her aunt and uncle, Tink's life had been a mess. Juliet had been bent on using the child's gift for her own evil purpose. We had thwarted her efforts, and as a result, Tink came to live with me. Juliet was no longer a part of Tink's life.

I turned over the next rune—the Present.

Kenaz. *"Kane-awze."* Again I said the name aloud.

Dang. The sideways V faced the left, too. Another rune reversed. Kenaz represented the warm fire of the hearth and new beginnings. Facing in the opposite direction, it indicated an ending fraught with anxiety. Did it mean an ending to Tink's connection with the Finches?

Maybe the last rune would shed light on what Berkano and Kenaz meant.

The rune indicating the Future stared up at me, and I felt my heart thud.

Isa. *"Ee-saw."* I choked on the word. That rune was a simple straight line and had no reverse. But just because the rune had no opposite meaning, it wasn't a positive sign. It stood for "ice." A freeze on all activities. No movement forward or backward. Whatever the heart held dear would be locked away in a block of ice until the Wheel of Fortune decided to turn.

I tugged on my bottom lip as I stared at the runes before me. How in the hell did these three glyphs answer my question? They were all negative. All indicated some kind of separation relating to home and family. A loss that would be full of frustrations.

Did Kenaz mean Tink would be lost to the Finches because I adopted her? Given the way the legal system worked, an adoption was bound to be full of delays, as indicated by Isa. And I would experience anxiety, another element shown by Kenaz, until the whole process was finished. Frustration? Well, if Juliet were sane enough to realize what was going on, losing Tink would certainly vex her. All in all, bad news for the Finches—good news for me.

My apprehension lightened.

Wait a second—my question hadn't been about the adoption. It had been: How can I protect her?

I felt dread come crashing down as the answer stared up at me.

Strife, stress, and loss relating to the family. And in the end, any efforts to prevent them would be frozen. I wouldn't be able to protect Tink. Whatever the Fates had planned, the course was set, and I was powerless to change it.

The next morning, I stood staring out the window over the kitchen sink as I finished my bowl of cereal. I'd tossed and turned all night while my brain searched for another interpretation of the runes. I didn't like what they told me. There had to be a way to keep Tink safe, and I wouldn't quit searching until I'd found it. I had no intention of letting a little thing like Fate stop me.

I turned as Tink walked into the kitchen. She was dressed in shorts and a T-shirt, as if she were ready to spend the day working at the greenhouse, but her eyes were shadowed.

"Feeling okay?" I tried to keep my tone light.

She lifted a shoulder. "Yeah. I guess," she replied after getting a bowl out of the cupboard and pouring cereal. She picked up one of the puffed balls and popped it in her mouth.

"Don't you want milk on that?" I asked, opening the door to the fridge and handing her the jug.

"Whatever."

"Wait a second." I took her arm and pulled her toward me. Laying a hand on her forehead, I studied her face. "Are you sick?"

She shrugged me off and walked over to the table. "I dreamed about Walks Quietly last night."

We'd met Walks Quietly, a Native American shaman, at the same time we'd had our run-in with the Finches. He'd been Tink's protector and friend. I never did quite figure out exactly what kind of gift he possessed, but whatever it was, it was powerful. Dang, why hadn't I thought of calling him for advice? It would be difficult to reach him—he didn't have a phone in his cabin. But I could call the sheriff and ask him to contact Walks Quietly for me. I filed the idea away in my memory banks.

"Really?" I said, following her. "You haven't dreamed about him for a long time, have you?"

Sitting at the table, she poured the milk over her cereal. "No." She took a spoonful and chewed it thoughtfully. "In the dream, we were in the woods. Walks Quietly was ahead of me, and I was running after him." Staring off into space, she took another spoonful. "I never reached him," she mumbled with her mouth full. "He disappeared into the woods. I was afraid to go any farther along the path . . ."

"Same place as in the dream with the corpses?"

She nodded without speaking. "I remember thinking in the dream that the path led to them." Placing her spoon in the bowl, she rose and carried it to the sink. "Next thing I know, I was awake. The woods and Walks Quietly were gone," she said, dumping the cereal down the garbage disposal.

I watched her with concern. If Tink didn't start eating more, she'd lose weight. And she didn't have it to lose. I needed ways to improve her appetite.

"Hey," I said throwing an arm around her shoulders. "Isn't the Farmer's Market tonight?"

"Yeah, Nell's coming to the greenhouse this afternoon to help pick sweet corn and fresh tomatoes. She'll set up the stand with us."

I noticed her pink shoulders. "If you're working outside all day, you girls make sure you wear sunscreen."

"Okay," she answered, rolling her eyes.

A thought suddenly occurred to me. "How much does Nell know about Aunt Dot?"

Tink gave a small snort. "Don't worry, I told her Aunt Dot was kind of eccentric."

I guess that was one way to describe her.

"Nell thinks it's cool. Said she wished she had someone in her family who was different." Tink chuckled. "She said all her aunts do is crochet."

Darci joined me after work at the Farmer's Market, and as we strolled around before joining Abby at her stand, she peppered me with questions.

"How did you like Gertrude Duncan?" she asked.

"I think she'll be okay," I said, picking up a muskmelon and sniffing it. Not as good as Abby's, I thought, setting it down and moving to the next table. "I feel kind of sorry for her. Sounds to me like the salary isn't important to her. She sees the job as her chance to get away from her mother for a couple of afternoons a week."

Darci tapped her chin. "Hmm, I haven't heard anything about her mother."

"From what Gert said, I got the impression that they haven't lived in the area very long."

"I'll have to check Gert and her mother out with Georgia."

I laughed. "It doesn't make a difference what Georgia

thinks, Darce. I'm sure the library board will be calling her tonight and offering her the job." I turned to Darci and gave her a questioning look. "Do you think you'll be able to work with her?"

"I guess," she replied in a neutral voice.

"Hey, what's the deal? Don't you like her?"

"I don't know. There seemed to be something familiar about her. Like I've met her before." She stepped away from me and over to the next stand.

I hurried after her. "Like what?"

"Hard to say," she replied, shrugging off my question. "Oh well, I'm not the psychic. Maybe it was just some kind of déjà vu. I read somewhere when you have that kind of re-action to a person it means you knew them in a past life."

I laughed. "So you think you knew Gert in a previous incarnation?"

"Maybe," she said, grinning. "It could have happened."

"Darci, you've been hanging around Abby too long!" I exclaimed with a smile.

"No more about Gert . . . let's talk about something im-portant. What are you wearing tomorrow night?"

"Tomorrow night?" I asked perplexed.

"Yeah, silly, the speed dating—"

"Wait a second," I interrupted. "I told you I wasn't going."

"Oh sure you are," she replied with a careless flip of her hand. "I've already paid the fee. And no, you don't have to thank me—"

I stopped in my tracks and cut her off again. "I wasn't planning on thanking you because I'm not going."

Darci tossed her blond hair and said, "You wouldn't want a struggling college student to waste her money, would you?"

"That's the struggling college student's choice. And

you're not going to use money to guilt me into going," I replied heatedly.

She ignored my objections as she strolled over to a table with fresh baked pies lined up in a neat row.

"Yum, these look good, don't they?" she asked, holding one up. With a smile at Mrs. Simpson sitting behind the table, she dug a couple of dollars out of her pocket and handed them to her. Pleased with her purchase, Darci sauntered over to me.

"I don't understand why you're so dead set on doing this," I commented with a frown. "I would've thought after what happened with Danny, the last thing you'd want right now is to get involved with someone else."

"You mean because he lied and played me for a sucker?" she asked in a light voice.

"Well . . . *yeah*," I replied with a tinge of sarcasm.

She tucked a strand of hair behind her ear. "Just because one relationship was with a louse, it doesn't mean the next one will be. I learned from my experience with Danny that I'm okay alone, but that doesn't mean I don't want to find someone special." The corner of her mouth lifted in a grin. "After all, you know what they say. 'Men are like buses, if you miss the first one, there's always another one coming along.'"

"Ha! I've heard that's what men say about women."

"So? The same applies to men."

I thought for a moment. "That may be fine for a woman your age, but at mine, the next 'bus' usually has a few parts missing."

"Very funny," she said over her shoulder. "You're not that much older than I am." She stopped and faced me. "I can tell you this—if you don't ever step out of the nice comfortable little rut that you're in, you're never going to know if any parts are missing or not, 'cause every single 'bus' is going to drive right by."

"I'm not in a rut," I said defensively.

Darci gave me a knowing glance.

"Okay, maybe a little—"

She walked up and threw an arm around my shoulder. "It'll be a new experience for you," she said with a shake. "We'll have fun, even if we don't meet anyone interesting."

Maybe she was right. Lately it had been one thing after another—and most of it not too pleasant. Murder and mayhem were like that. Maybe if I focused on something positive, like a little fun, it would draw more positive things into my life. Help me deal with whatever situation I might be facing with Tink.

Darci sensed my hesitation and pressed home her advantage. "Seize the day, Ophelia. Step out of the rut—"

"Okay, okay, I'll do it," I said, finally giving in.

"Good," she said with a squeeze. "I'll come over early to help you. I'll do your makeup and hair; I'll pick out something for you to wear . . . " She paused, and I could almost see her going over my wardrobe in her mind. "On second thought, I'll bring clothes from my closet."

"I'm not your dress-up doll, you know," I grumbled, stepping away from her grasp.

Darci opened her mouth to reply but was cut short by Tink and Nell tearing over to where we stood.

"That creepy guy we saw in the woods is here," Tink said, her eyes wide.

My eyes traveled the crowd searching for him as Darci said, "What guy?"

"We were letting the dogs go for a run at Roseman State Park when this man startled us," Tink explained excitedly.

"What was his name?" Darci asked.

"Silas—" She broke off and pointed. "There, he's over at the table next to Abby's."

Darci's eyes narrowed when she saw the man in the slouched hat buying fresh-picked green beans. Her nose wrinkled.

"You know him?" I asked, watching her expression.

"Yes," she replied, her lips tightening. "He runs Green's Crematorium."

"I didn't know there was a crematorium around here," I said in a shocked voice.

"It's not really in Summerset, and it's a small one. He only does business with a few funeral homes in the area." Darci stared at him as she spoke. "He also owns land over by the state park. One of the guys I dated a couple of years ago rented it from him."

I nodded. "He said he was checking fence—" I stopped abruptly as Silas Green, feeling our eyes on him, turned and caught us staring at him.

With a smile, he tugged on his hat, acknowledging us, and then moved away.

As he'd stretched his mouth back from his crooked teeth, I noticed the way the late afternoon sun seemed to glint off his long incisors, and a chill ran through me.

# *Nine*

Friday night Darci had arrived as early as promised. As I sat in her car hurtling toward Des Moines, I wondered for the millionth time why I had agreed to do this. Even preparing for the event had been a strain. I'd been curled, powdered, and primped until I barely recognized the face staring at me from the bathroom mirror.

Tink had gotten into the act, too, by giving her opinion on the different outfits Darci had brought from her own closet. Darci's pants were all too long, so it was a struggle matching my slacks with her blouses. Once she and Tink came up with the coordinating ensembles, they insisted that I model each combination of shoes, tops, and dress pants while they picked apart how the clothes looked.

As a result, I learned that my favorite pair of linen slacks made my hips look too big, I did not own a decent bra and really, really needed to shop at Victoria's Secret. I also learned that three-inch heels, even though they pinched, gave me the stature my five-foot four-inch frame was lacking. Finally, my stylists decided on pants the shade of dark chocolate—darker hues are slenderizing, don't you know—and a camisole with a matching ivory top of georgette that draped softly over my shoulders and tied at the waist. The clothes, according to my personal fashion consultants, "rocked" and I looked "awesome."

In my opinion, it was Darci who was amazing. She didn't have to worry about clothes adding too many pounds. Her fitted black slacks hugged in all the right places, and her shirt was exactly the right shade of blue to bring out her eyes. She wore her hair in a tousled twist that gave her a "come hither" look without being obvious. I didn't doubt that every man there would be fighting for her phone number.

It was good to see Tink smiling and laughing. And it was one of the reasons that I allowed them, with as much graciousness as I could muster, to treat me like a life-size Barbie doll. I still feared what the runes had predicted.

Abby pointed out that maybe the course had been set, but it didn't mean that I couldn't alter the degree of negativity. If I stayed sharp and kept my senses alert, I could still do damage control. Worry would only cloud my judgment and make me ineffective, so I buried my concerns in the back of my mind.

A jab in the ribs brought me out of my reverie.

"Quit stewing about this," Darci chided.

"I'm not. I'm only doing this to humor you," I replied empathically.

Darci shot me a glance. "No butterflies?"

"Of course not," I lied, ignoring the knots in my stomach and the cold sweat threatening to break out at any minute.

"How bad can it be?" she asked, lifting her chin a notch. "What did the handout say? Six minutes talking with each guy. What's six minutes?"

A lifetime if you're sitting across the table from a complete stranger, with your mind a mass of jelly and your mouth feeling like it's stuffed with cotton.

I kept my sarcasm to myself. Instead, I asked, "What do I talk about?"

In the dim light of the dashboard, I saw Darci roll her eyes. "Here's a flash—how about Ophelia Jensen?"

"Uh-huh," I answered wryly. "Do I tell them at the beginning of the six minutes about the witch thing, or leave it until the end?"

She chuckled. "Ahh. I think it would be wise not to mention you're a psychic." Tapping the steering wheel she thought for a moment. "Everyone likes talking about themselves, surely—"

"I don't," I answered quickly.

"Let me rephrase that—*most* people enjoy it. But if you don't want to tell them about yourself, try asking questions."

"Like what?"

"Jeez, I don't know. Try, 'What's your idea of a perfect date?' Or, 'What hobbies do you enjoy?' And there's always, 'Describe your sense of humor.'"

"Wait a second." I grabbed my purse and began to rummage.

She took her eyes off the road for a second. "What are you doing?"

"Looking for a pen," I answered, my hand digging around in the bag.

"Why?"

"I'm going to write what you just said on my palm. You know, like when you were a kid at school?" I said, pleased at my cleverness. "If I get stuck, I can subtly glance at my hand—"

Darci reached over and yanked my purse away.

"What?" I asked in an injured voice.

"You're not going to write stuff on your hand," she huffed.

"It would be the same as hanging a sign around your neck, 'I haven't had a date in five years.'"

I crossed my arms over my chest and sank back in the seat. "Have, too—I went out with Ned a year ago."

I heard a snort.

"Right. The only reason you went out with him was because he was safe. You knew it wouldn't go anywhere," she said, whipping her car into the parking lot.

Gosh, we were here already. The knots tightened.

Seeing the expression on my face, Darci gave me a wink. "Enough about Ned. Come on, let's go."

I exited the car with about as much enthusiasm as a prisoner facing the hangman.

Darci noticed. With a sigh, she grabbed my arm and hurried me across the parking lot. Inside the building, an equal number of men and women milled around excitedly. All appeared eager and happy to be there. Next to me, Darci twitched with anticipation.

Panic hit. "I can't remember those questions," I hissed. "You should've let me write them down."

"You'll be fine," she assured me. "If all else fails, just smile and lean forward—"

"What! Why?"

"Trust me . . . works every time." She walked up to the registration table and signed us in. Handing me my name tag and score sheet, she pointed me toward my table. "Go get 'em, killer," she said with a slight shove. "Oh, and if you do remember the questions, try not to ask them like you're a prosecutor grilling a hostile witness."

"Funny," I replied over my shoulder as I tottered on my three-inch heels over to my assigned seat. Once there, I glanced back at Darci. She gave me a thumbs-up.

Yeah, right. Tiny beads of sweat broke out on my forehead. Peachy. How would I wipe them away without appearing nervous? I pretended to fluff my hair and at the same time brushed away the moisture.

*Get a grip, Jensen. Think—how important is this? One— you didn't want to come. Two—you're not looking for Mr. Right. Three—you're simply here to have fun. What do you care what these guys might think?*

The bell rang.

I watched as the first man took his seat across the table from me. The pep talk worked. I shoved away my anxiety.

*What the hell?* I smiled and leaned forward.


The first guy's idea of a perfect date was watching Green Bay play the Vikings.

*No, thank you.*

The second guy described his sense of humor as slapstick. He went on to relate his favorite Three Stooges' movie complete with the "nyuck, nyuck, nyuck."

I like the Three Stooges as well as the next person, but that didn't mean I wanted to date Curly.

*Next.*

When the third guy arrived, my first remark was, "Hi, how are you?" He told me. During the following six minutes, I learned about his recent breakup, in minute and boring detail. It was her fault of course, and he had done nothing to precipitate the split. He couldn't help all those women coming onto him.

*Hmm—read between the lines—this one has a problem with monogamy. Don't call me, I'll call you.*

The fourth guy? I smelled him before he even made it to the table. The scent of English Leather, the same cologne my dad wore, swirled around him in a toxic cloud, announcing his arrival. I tried the ol' "smile and lean forward" thing to cover my discomfort, but the strength of his cologne had me inching my chair back in an attempt to get away from the overpowering aroma.

The fifth guy had a comb-over that started about an inch above his left ear. Not a good look for him.

The bell rang. I spent the seconds between candidates by staring at my blank score sheet. So far I hadn't been impressed, but I had a hunch none of the men that I'd met were exactly swept away by me, either. It was an even wash.

"You're not having fun, are you?" said a deep voice to my right.

My eyes traveled from the sheet of paper to the man taking his seat across the table from me.

He looked sharp. The way he wore his dark hair, cropped fairly short, suited his strong features and high cheekbones. His soft brown eyes held a hint of humor. He was dressed in a white shirt, open at the neck. No gold glittered from around his throat. A definite plus as far as I was concerned.

"What makes you say that?" I tilted my head.

He gave me a big grin and a conspiratorial wink. "You have this tight look around your mouth."

I instinctively touched my fingertips to my lips. "It's that obvious?"

He chuckled. "No. I'm just good at reading people. It's a hobby of mine," he said with confidence.

Darci was good at reading people, too. My eyes darted over to her. This man was her type. I wondered if she'd zeroed in on him yet.

His eyes followed mine. "Is she your friend?" he asked, jerking his head in her direction.

"Yeah. She was the one who convinced me to come tonight."

"Pretty." He returned his attention to me as if he were dismissing Darci. "I'm glad she did. I'm Christopher," he said, extending his hand.

"I'm Ophelia," I replied as I pointed to my name tag and shook his hand.

His grip was warm and firm. I felt a tingle of interest.

"As in *Hamlet?*" he inquired, releasing my hand and folding his on the table. "You don't look like an Ophelia."

"Really?" I relaxed against the back of my chair. "How's an Ophelia supposed to look?"

"Wispy." His smile widened, "There's nothing wispy about you. You strike me as a woman who's independent and knows what she wants. I like that."

Christopher laughed at my shocked expression.

"I also think you don't take compliments easily."

My eyebrows scrunched together as I fiddled with my pen. "You know that how?"

"You have a transparent face. Hope you don't play poker," he teased.

I smiled. "No. You'd be more likely to find me curled up with a book than sitting at a card table."

"Another thing I like. What do you read?"

"Everything."

"Same here. I suppose you've read *The Da Vinci Code* like everyone else*?"*

"Of course," I answered with a self-satisfied grin.

Talking about books—we were on my turf now. Much better than football, comedies, and past relationships.

"Have you read *Angels and Demons,* too?" he asked.

I nodded. "I enjoyed it more."

"Me, too," he answered, leaning closer. "What else do you do for fun, Ophelia?"

*Ooh, tough question. What did I do for fun?*

A thought occurred to me. "Hiking in the woods with my dog—"

"I love animals," he said. "What kind of dog do you have?"

"She's a German shepherd and wolf mix. Do you have pets?"

"No, I wish I did. With my work schedule, I'm not home a lot, and I don't think it would be fair to leave a pet alone for long periods of time."

Compassion toward animals. Christopher's stock went up another notch.

I was so wrapped up in my conversation with him that the next few minutes flew. And when the bell rang, I watched with reluctance as he stood to leave.

"It was really nice meeting you. I hope we can talk again," he said, looking down at me.

"I would like that," I replied honestly.

Quickly, before the next candidate arrived, I scribbled Christopher's name on my sheet. Well, at least I had one, I thought. Maybe this wasn't a total bust.

I met two more nice men and added their names to my list, and soon the event was finished.

It took time to leave the building. Several guys stopped Darci on the way out the door. While she chatted and flirted, I hung back and scanned the room for Christopher. No luck. Evidently he'd left.

A little disappointed that I didn't get the opportunity to speak with him again, I followed Darci to the car. We were almost there when a voice called my name. I turned to see Christopher hurrying toward us.

"I'll wait for you in the car," Darci said with a smirk.

I shifted nervously from one foot to the other until he reached me.

"Thanks for waiting," he said in a rush. "I know we're not supposed to do this." He reached into his pocket, drawing out a small card. "I got the impression the only reason you were here tonight was to humor your friend, and I was afraid you'd handed in a blank list." He flipped the card over and over in his fingers. "I really did enjoy talking to you, so if it's not too presumptuous on my part, I'd like to give you my business card."

Taking it from his hand, I read his name <u>in</u> the dim light of the parking lot:

dr. chr ist opher ma son.

"You're a doctor?"

"Yes," he said with a shy smile. "I hope I'm on your list. If I am, the dating service will send me your email address. But if I'm not, please call me. I really would like to get to know you better, Ophelia."

"Ahh—"

He held up a hand, stopping me. "No, you don't have to say anything. Just call me and we'll get together." With that he turned and walked away.

# *Ten*

"Tink, I think the pole goes in that pocket," I said as I surveyed the mess littering the ground at our campsite.

"No, it doesn't," she replied. "It goes in this one."

I narrowed my eyes and watched as she tried inching the flexible pole into the nylon holder. "You're sure?"

She grunted. "Yes."

Tink ran the pole all the way in. It was six inches short of coming out the other end. "Well, maybe not." She grinned sheepishly.

"Here." I picked up a longer pole. "Let's try this one," I said, handing it to her.

"Shoot," Tink exclaimed, and dropped the pole.

"What's wrong?"

"The pole caught on the bracelet Nell gave me for my birthday," she said, holding up her wrist.

The gold heart, suspended on a thin chain around Tink's wrist, danced in the sunlight as she held up her arm.

I bent down to grab another pole. "You'd better slip it in your pocket for now. You don't want to break it."

With a sigh, Tink removed her bracelet before picking up the pole.

Finally, the tent lay on the ground in a big square. The poles made a big X in the center. Now all we had to do was lift the sucker and shove the poles into the soft dirt. A piece of cake.

Wrong. We raised the tent so the dome was off the ground, but the whole thing leaned dangerously to one side. And before we could straighten it, two of the poles popped out of the dirt and with a whoosh the tent sank to the ground.

Perspiration trickled down my back, and pieces of freshly mowed grass clung to my sweaty legs. For the umpteenth time I wondered at the wisdom of agreeing to this camping excursion. Frustrated, I felt like shoving the tent, the poles, the air mattresses, and all, back into the car and heading to town.

Lady and T.P. agreed with me. They had soon tired of chasing around the campsite, sniffing all the equipment as Tink and I hauled it from the car, and now lay out of the sun under one of the picnic tables.

I looked at the fallen tent, then at Tink. This overnight camping trip with Nell's family was important to her. We hadn't not spoken again of Buchanan's murder, but I knew it still lurked in the back of her mind. She needed this time to forget about her talents as a medium and just be a kid for a while.

Nell's family, the Johnsons, had been at Roseman State Park since last night. A fishing tournament brought many of the locals out for the weekend, and the campground was full. From a distance I heard the sound of a radio playing the latest country western hits. Wet bathing suits and towels dangled from lines stretched between trees at many of the sites, and the smell of wood smoke hung in the air.

Nell's site was neat and orderly, and reflected her mother's fondness for yard ornaments. A whirligig hung from a nearby branch, clacking away as the slight breeze spun it. The base of their tent was ringed with rope lights, and Tiki torches circled the fire pit.

Nell's father, Carl, had volunteered to help erect our tent before the family left for a late afternoon swim in the river, but I refused. I was an independent, self-sufficient woman, wasn't I? How hard could setting up one little tent be? Now I wished I'd taken him up on his offer.

By the time we finished raising the tent, Nell and her family were back from the river.

Now the campground came to life. Families lit grills and campfires, bustling about, preparing their evening meal. And the sound of children's laughter from the playground carried across the campground.

Carl lit the Tiki torches and started our fire in the pit. We didn't need a fire for warmth, but the smoke from the burning logs and the torches would keep bugs at bay once the sun went down.

Taking the dogs with them, Nell and Tink left to join Nell's little brother at the playground. While Carl grilled hot dogs and hamburgers, Chris busied herself by setting out paper plates, ketchup, mustard, and potato chips. I fetched my contribution to the evening's supper—Abby's homemade baked beans.

Soon all was ready, and Chris rang a huge cowbell to summon the three kids. After everyone loaded their plates with food, we gathered around the table to eat.

"Tink," I said between bites of baked beans. "Where's T.P.?"

"Over there with Lady," she replied, concentrating on her meal.

I turned to where Lady lay sprawled in the shade underneath a tree. "No, he isn't." Craning my neck, I glanced around our campsite for the puppy. "I don't see him."

With a groan, Tink set her hot dog on her plate and made a move to rise. "I'd better go find him."

Placing a hand on her arm, I stopped her. "No, eat your supper first."

Both she and Nell finished in record time, and left the table to find the errant puppy while Nell's mom and I cleaned up the campsite. Twenty minutes later they were back.

Concern etched lines on Tink's face. "We couldn't find him, and we looked all over the campground."

"Has anyone seen him?" I asked, shading my eyes against the setting sun.

"No," she replied as she scuffed the ground with the toe of her tennis shoe. "What are we going to do? Suppose he's lost in the woods?"

"Don't worry, Tink," Carl said as he got to his feet. "We'll all help look for him."

A sudden gust of wind sent the whirligig spinning, and with it came an awful smell.

"What is that?" I asked, wrinkling my nose. I turned to see T.P. gamboling across the field next to the playground, carrying a large ball in his mouth.

Great. He'd snitched some kid's toy. Irritated, I marched toward the puppy, with Tink right behind me. The closer we got to the dog, the stronger the odor became.

"Yuck." I covered my nose. "He's rolled in something rotten, Tink," I said over my shoulder. "You'll need to take him to the bathhouse and hose him off. We can't have him stinking up the tent tonight."

The words were hardly out of my mouth when T.P. ran past me to Tink and proudly dropped the ball at her feet.

I heard Nell's mother gasp, and I watched as Tink's face lost all its color.

"I knew it, I knew it," she said in a voice that carried over the campgrounds. "I should've warned Mr. Buchanan, and now I'm being punished."

Walking swiftly to her, I grabbed her arm and gave it a little shake. "Shh, everyone can hear you."

In horror I stared down at the ball at Tink's feet. Only it wasn't a ball. Two empty eye sockets gazed up at the summer sky, and crooked teeth protruded from what was left of the upper jaw.

T.P. hadn't fetched some kid's ball—he'd brought us a human skull.

When Bill and his deputy, Alan, arrived, they quickly dispersed the crowd gathered around the skull. T.P. was now safely tied to a tree, downwind, where he sat whimpering. Lady watched from a safe distance away. T.P. seemed perplexed as to why he was in trouble.

I'd insisted that even though it was hot, Tink go inside the tent, away from the curious stares of the other campers.

"So, Ophelia, now the bodies come looking for you?" Bill said as he strolled over to where I stood guarding the entrance to our tent.

I didn't appreciate his macabre sense of humor.

"That's not funny, Bill," I replied, stepping away from the tent. "Tink's had quite a shock."

"That's what I heard." He removed his hat and mopped his head with his handkerchief. "Someone told us she made a remark about 'being punished'? What did she mean by that?"

I gave a nervous laugh and walked farther away from the tent. "Oh, you know how teenagers are. It's always about them." I shoved my hands in my pockets and turned. "I suppose she feels guilty because it was her dog that found the skull."

His eyes grew thoughtful as he scanned the woods beyond the playground. "Any idea where the dog found it?"

Breathing a sigh of relief that he hadn't pursued his line of questioning about Tink, I said, "T.P. disappeared while we were eating supper." I gestured toward the other campsites. "The girls searched for him with no luck. Nell's parents and I were ready to join the hunt when he came running up with the skull."

"From what direction?"

"Over there," I said, and pointed.

He wiped his head again and shoved the handkerchief in his back pocket. "Lotta acres out there."

"Did you notice the way he smelled?"

Bill grimaced. "Kinda hard to miss, Ophelia. Wherever he went, he rolled in something foul."

He didn't need to spell out what "something" foul meant.

Bill glanced over his shoulder at the dog. "The medical examiner might want to check him over and take some hair samples." His eyes traveled back to me. "I need to talk to the girls while we're waiting for the M.E. to show up."

"Right now?"

"Yes."

Bill joined Nell, Chris, and Carl at the picnic table. I fetched Tink. Once we were all seated, he smiled kindly at Tink and Nell. "Did you girls go for a walk earlier?"

Nell spoke up. "Just over to the playground."

"The dogs went with you?"

"Yes," she replied.

"Then Lady came back to the campground, but not T.P.?"

"I guess." Nell lifted a shoulder. "Ophelia noticed her under the tree."

"But the puppy wasn't with Lady?"

They shook their heads.

"Did either one of you see T.P. run off into the woods?"

"No," they replied in unison.

Tink raised her head. "It's all my fault, Sheriff Wilson . . . "

"How's that, Tink?" he asked in a soft voice.

I held my breath waiting for her reply.

"We were playing on the swings, and I forgot all about the dogs." She dropped her head again, as I sighed in relief at her answer. "I didn't think about T.P. until Ophelia said he was missing."

Bill's eyes darted to me, then returned to Tink. "That's okay," he said. "In a way, your dog did us a favor—"

I doubted that, but let the comment pass.

"How?" Tink cut in.

"We can't have any poor souls lying around in the woods. This way, hopefully, we can find him and give him a proper burial."

Bill didn't mention they might also learn if the person in question had met with foul play.

Straightening his hat, he watched the sun sinking lower on the horizon. "It's going to be dark soon. Too late to start a search tonight, but we will in the morning."

The sound of a car slowly approaching had us all turning toward the lane. We watched as it stopped and the medical examiner, carrying a bag, got out.

Bill rose and approached the M.E. The two men talked for a few moments as Bill gestured toward the tree where T.P. was exiled.

The puppy immediately perked up and stopped his whimpering. As the two men approached, T.P., sensing liberation at hand, began to wag his tail. He was disappointed when the M.E. opened his bag, removed four plastic sacks, and systematically scraped the dirt off each paw into a bag. T.P. was further distressed when he noticed a pair of scissors headed his way. He tried to scramble out of the M.E.'s reach, but he was grabbed by the scruff of his neck. Snip, snip, and clippings of his black and white fur fell into the fifth evidence bag.

Apparently satisfied with his samples, the medical examiner followed Bill over to where the skull rested in the grass.

"Well," I said, rubbing my legs and watching Tink. "Do you want to go home now? I can come out in the morning and get our stuff."

Tink and Nell exchanged a look Chris caught. Reaching out, she took Tink's hand in hers. "Don't worry about the other campers. I bet T.P.'s going to be a hero before this story is finished making the rounds," she said with a smile. "Why don't you still stay the night, Tink? All the excitement's over."

Tink's eyes darted back to Nell.

"Come on," Nell said with a playful jab. "Mom's brought marshmallows, and we can make s'mores."

"Ophelia?" Tink asked with hesitation.

I glanced at Chris. I appreciated her kindness to Tink and decided I should make more of an effort to know her better.

"Sure," I replied with a grin. "Whatever you want to do, sweetie. Only wash the dog first. I'm not sleeping with a smelly puppy."

The girls ran off to wash the stinky puppy.

Chris was wrong about the excitement being over. Later that evening, after a relaxing evening roasting marshmallows and making s'mores around the campfire, and right before the witching hour, Tink's nightmare screams echoed through the campground.

# Eleven

Tink and I were up at dawn to break camp. I wanted her out of there before the campground came to life. She didn't need to endure the stares of the other campers. As we pulled down the tent, a much easier job than erecting it, we tried to be as quiet as possible. Nell's family still slept in their tent, and I didn't want to wake them. I decided I'd give Nell's parents a call later that evening and make my apologies for our hasty departure. Tink's nightmares should be easy to explain, right? She was a sensitive fourteen-year-old, and who wouldn't be freaked over her dog bringing home a human skull?

Before pulling onto the blacktop leading back to Summerset, I cast a worried glance at Tink. She sat slumped in the passenger seat with her baseball cap pulled low on her forehead.

Focusing my attention back on the road, I thought about how to frame my question. I didn't want to upset her any more than she already was, yet I needed to know the details of her nightmare.

"Want to tell me about the dream?" I asked, keeping my voice low.

She turned toward the window and watched the early morning landscape fly by.

The sun was higher in the hazy sky now, indicating the day would be a hot one. Low trailing fingers of fog reached across the green pastures and settled in the gullies. Outside the car window, I heard the calling of the crows as they circled on the horizon.

A peaceful summer morning.

I sensed the opposite in Tink. Distress resonated around her like an energy field.

"Well?" I insisted.

With a sigh, she tipped her head back against the head rest and pulled a tan leg underneath her. "It was sort of the same dream as before. I was walking down the path in the woods when I noticed a terrible odor—"

I cut her off. "The same way T.P. smelled?"

"Yeah," she replied hesitantly.

"What happened next?" I prodded.

She shuddered, obviously recalling the dream. "The corpses came out of the woods, just like before, only this time some of them were missing parts of their bodies." Tink shuddered again.

I sensed her reluctance to continue. Reaching out, I laid a hand on her bare knee. "If you don't want to talk about it, that's okay."

"No, it's better if I tell you about the dream. Maybe you can figure out why I'm having them." She sat up tall in her seat and I felt her eyes on me. "As some of the spirits reached out to me, I saw they had no hands. Just raw stumps. And the expression on their faces was awful."

"In what way?"

"Like they couldn't figure out what happened to their hands." Out of the corner of my eye, I saw Tink's face twist into a frown. "Like they expected me to explain it to them. Dumb, huh?"

I shook my head. "No, it's not dumb, but I don't get it."

"Do you think it was a dream or a vision?"

The same question that she'd asked me before, and I caught the hopeful note in her voice. I knew she wanted reassurance that the dream was nothing more than a nightmare triggered by T.P.'s little present. However, the more often these dreams occurred, the more convinced I became that someone or something was trying to tap into Tink's skills as a medium.

"I'm sorry, Tink, but I think your dreams are probably some kind of vision," I said as gently as possible.

"You or Abby aren't sensing anything?" she asked, picking at the seat upholstery.

I glanced at her. Should I tell her about the rune reading? I saw the lines of worry on her normally smooth forehead and decided not to. If I told her, it might only add to her unease.

"No. Neither Abby or I have picked up anything unusual."

Tink noticed the delay in my reply, and I felt the weight of her stare. "You sure?" she asked skeptically.

"Of course I am," I replied with a bravado I didn't feel.

"You're not hiding anything from me?"

I shook my head emphatically. "No. If I knew what was going on, I'd tell you."

"Even if you thought not telling me was for my own good?" she persisted.

This kid was really putting me on the spot. The rune reading had been ambiguous at best, and until I knew I'd interpreted them correctly, I intended to keep my mouth shut.

"Look," I said in an effort to change the subject, "when we get home, I'll call Abby. Maybe she and Aunt Dot can come over. We'll have lunch or something—"

Tink's snort stopped me. "You'll have to cook."

"Okay, so I have to cook," I replied with a wave of my hand. "I can surely come up with something. And while Abby and I are talking, it's going to be your job to keep Aunt Dot busy."

"How am I supposed to do that?"

"I don't know . . . take her out in the backyard and search for fairies."

Tink nodded. "I can do that." She paused. "You don't think Aunt Dot could help?"

"Oh boy, I don't think we want to go there." I gripped the steering wheel tighter at the thought of getting Aunt Dot involved in this mess. She might see it as an opportunity to pull us into Buchanan's murder investigation.

I had no intention of allowing that to happen.

True to her word, Tink kept Aunt Dot busy while I talked to Abby. The fairy-seekers made a lazy circle around the edge of the backyard. Aunt Dot clung tightly to Tink's arm as she walked over the uneven ground. And with her other hand, she waved her gnarled cane as she pointed to the trees and flowers ringing our yard. Tink would nod her head wisely, as if everything Aunt Dot told her made perfect sense. T.P. followed close on their heels, and for once he wasn't running madly through the grass. It was almost as if he were listening to Aunt Dot, too.

Abby sat on the patio in one of the lawn chairs and kept one eye on them, while I stood in front of the barbecue, grilling steaks. Lady lay curled up at her feet.

"What's wrong with Queenie?" Abby asked, pointing to where the cat sat a short distance away and stared at me with pure contempt.

"She's mad," I said, flipping one of the steaks. "We've

been gone so much, and Her Majesty hasn't been receiving the attention she thinks she so richly deserves."

As if to prove me wrong, Queenie rose and sauntered over to Abby. With a leap, she settled herself on Abby's lap and began to purr, rubbing her face against Abby's. And as she did, the cat's expression seemed to say, *I like your grand-mother best.*

Shaking my head, I picked up the conversation we'd been having. "You agree? You think the spirits are reaching out to Tink. They want her help."

"Yes," Abby replied as she stroked Queenie.

That wasn't the answer I wanted. I wanted her to tell me that I was wrong—that Tink's dreams were only nightmares. Frustrated, I jabbed one of the steaks with a meat fork and flipped it over.

"Why aren't we sensing anything?"

"This has to do with spirits, and we're not mediums," Abby said in an even tone.

"But we're psychics. Shouldn't we *know* what this is all about?"

Abby sighed. "You'd think so. There could be various reasons why nothing has been revealed to us. Maybe it's not our portion, maybe it's Tink's destiny to—"

"Hold on," I exclaimed, stopping her. "Tink's just a kid. She can't handle—"

"Ophelia, Tink may be young, but she *is* a medium. You can't protect her from her gift," Abby said gently. "All you can do is teach her how to use that talent."

"How do you suggest we do that, since, as you pointed out, we aren't mediums?"

"We can guide her . . . " Abby's voice trailed away as she focused on Aunt Dot and Tink. "We could ask the spirits what they want."

I shivered in spite of the heat. "No, we're not having a séance."

"We'd be there to protect her. To shield her."

"Ha," I said, shutting the grill lid. "Remember last time we had a séance? A ghost haunted my house for two weeks. That's all I need—a bunch of them taking up residence now. Especially ones that reek of rotting flesh. I might not be able to see them, and I sure as heck don't want to smell them."

Abby's face lost some of its color at my statement. "I see what you mean." She thought for a moment. "We could hold it in my summerhouse."

For fifty years Abby's summerhouse had been her private place of magick. It would be tough for any ghost to overcome all that accumulated energy.

"I don't know," I said with hesitation. "I still don't like the idea of putting Tink through that."

"They won't leave her alone, you know." Abby studied Tink carefully as she escorted Aunt Dot around the yard. "Is it better for her to be tormented by nightmares?"

Good point. "No."

Abby shooed Queenie off her lap and joined me at the grill. "We don't need to hold a séance right this minute, but we do need to consider all our options," she said as she put her arm around my shoulder.

"I know." A feeling of hopelessness nagged at me. "I don't want to keep going over this, but I can't get past why we're not picking up on the problem. We both love Tink—we should be able to sense the reason these spirits are zeroing in on her."

"It's not so unusual," she said with a squeeze meant to reassure. "There have been times in your life when you were in danger and I didn't realize it. You were the original target when Brian was killed, but I missed it."

"Why is that?" I asked, my forehead creasing in a frown as I opened the lid of the grill.

"It's the way it works sometimes," Abby replied with a shrug. "We're not supposed to be 'all-knowing.'"

"Well—"

Before I could continue, Abby looked up at the sky and shook her head. "Don't fight it, my dear. Accept it. The only thing you can do is use your gift to try and pierce the veil that surrounds her."

"I've already done a rune reading. At first I thought it meant the course was set, but now, the more I think about it, I think the reading pertained to the adoption."

"You didn't ask about the adoption."

"I know," I replied with confidence, "but I'm sure that's what the runes were showing me."

"Are you?" She lifted an eyebrow.

"What do you mean?"

"Are you seeing what's truly there, or just what you want to see?" Abby dropped her arm from my shoulder.

I pursed my lips in a stubborn line. "I'm seeing what's there."

The doubt was apparent on Abby's face.

"I am," I replied defensively as I slid my attention to the steaks on the grill.

A nudge stopped any further conversation. Aunt Dot and Tink were making their way to the patio.

"This girl's got talent," Aunt Dot said, hugging Tink to her side. "The fairies like her. It won't be long until she sees them, too."

I exchanged a look with Abby.

Great, first ghosts and now fairies. Boy, was my house going to be crowded.

Placing the steaks on the meat platter, I handed them to

Tink. "That's interesting, Aunt Dot. Food's ready, so let's eat," I said.

I had enough on my mind without listening to any more of Aunt Dot's theories about Tink's talents.

Abby understood. As we all took our places around the patio table, she chose a new topic.

"How was the speed dating?" she asked.

In all the excitement, I'd forgotten about Christopher. I hadn't been online since before we left for the campground, so if he'd tried to reach me, I'd missed his message. Dang.

"I don't have time to date," I replied, covering up my disappointment.

"Then why did you go?" Abby persisted.

I cut my steak. "Because Darci wouldn't take no for an answer, and—"

"She met a doctor," Tink teased.

Abby cocked her head and eyed me with interest. "Really?"

"Yeah, so?" I gave a nonchalant shrug.

"Well, if he asks, I definitely think you should go out with him," Abby announced.

"Why?"

"It will do you good." She gave a quick nod. "Stepping back from a situation and having a little fun can often help you see things more clearly."

I opened my mouth to reply, but Aunt Dot didn't give me a chance.

"Did you read the Sunday paper?" Her voice quivered.

"No, why?"

"Mr. Buchanan's funeral is tomorrow afternoon."

Tink's fork stopped halfway to her mouth. Without a word, she laid it on her plate.

"Aunt Dot, let's not talk about funerals while we're eating," I said with a nod toward Tink. Aunt Dot knew of Tink's reaction to Buchanan's murder, and after the nightmares last night, I didn't want her upset again.

"Don't see why not." Her lip came out in a pout. "Death's a part of life, girl."

"Yes, but . . . " I jerked my head again, trying to get Aunt Dot to pick up the hint.

Finally understanding, she waved her fork, dismissing my concern. "Oh that. I've got a plan," she said in a way that reminded me of Darci—a way that usually boded ill for me.

*Ignore her, ignore her,* said a voice inside my head. *Change the subject.*

But before I had a chance, Tink folded her hands in her lap and focused on Aunt Dot. "What plan?"

Aunt Dot turned toward Tink, her eyes wide with excitement. "On *Law and Order* the cops always stake out the funeral. So all we need to do . . . "

Abby and I both winced.

" . . . is go to the funeral," she announced with satisfaction.

# Twelve

As I walked into the viewing room at the funeral home in Aiken, the overpowering smell of carnations assaulted my senses. Mr. Buchanan's casket had to be surrounded by at least thirty different floral arrangements. And the spray on top of the open casket was elaborate, to say the least. It contained roses, carnations, lilies, and mementos of his life. I spied several fishing lures attached to the ribbon that said *Beloved Husband* in scrolled gold letters. A beat-up hat with more hooks and fishing flies fastened to the crumpled crown lay propped up against the coffin's lid. Evidently, Mr. Buchanan liked to fish.

The first two rows were empty—waiting for the family to join the group. With a hand firmly on Aunt Dot's arm, I hurried her to the back row. The last thing I wanted was for her to peer down at the deceased Mr. Buchanan as if she could detect a clue to his murder. If we had to be there, we could at least be as unobtrusive as possible.

She'd selected her purple pantsuit to wear today. Her purse was gripped tightly in one hand, and I eyed it with skepticism. It had taken a lot of persuasion to convince her that including a camera to snap pictures of the mourners would be inappropriate, but I wasn't so sure she'd listened. Oh well, Abby could sit next to her, and if a camera popped out, she could wrestle it away from her.

Abby looked classy in her black suit and her pale rose-colored blouse, but I knew by her expression that there were a million places she'd rather be.

Tink was the one who really concerned me. I hadn't wanted her to come. I suggested that she spend the day with Nell, but she insisted that she be here. When Abby weighed in on Tink's side, I caved in. I still questioned the wisdom of allowing a fourteen-year-old medium inside a funeral home, but Abby thought that leaving Tink out would only add to the guilt she still felt.

After taking the chair next to Tink, I squirmed uncomfortably. The tag at the collar of my white shirt seemed to make the back of my neck itch. Or maybe it wasn't the tag that was making me twitch. Maybe it was the idea of horning in on a complete stranger's funeral.

I cast a side glance at Tink. Abby held her hand tightly, and I knew she was adding her energy to Tink's to prevent any unwelcome messages from beyond to filter through.

I shifted my attention to the crowd filing past Mr. Buchanan's casket. I'd been so intent on getting Aunt Dot as far from the body as possible that I hadn't noticed the young man who was standing at the foot of the coffin with his hands solemnly folded in front of him. It was the same young man who had picked Buchanan up at the airport. Couldn't be a son, I thought. If he was a Buchanan, he'd be with the family gathered in another room as they waited for the service to start.

His role in Buchanan's life became apparent when I saw him hand one of the funeral programs to someone as they moved away from the casket. He worked here.

He caught me staring at him, and a flicker of surprise showed in his pale blue eyes. He bobbed his head slightly in recognition.

Kid's got a good memory, I thought.

Returning my concentration to the crowd filing into the room, I scanned each face, searching for a sign of remorse, a fleeting expression of guilt, anything unusual in their demeanor that might indicate they were hiding something.

Nope, no one looked like a killer to me. But then again, I knew from experience, they never do. Even the most innocent face can hide a monster willing to take another's life. In fact, in the past I'd even sat down to dinner with a murderer, never knowing that he'd killed my best friend. So much for being a psychic, and I knew under these circumstances, if I tried using my talent now, all I'd pick up would be a bunch of jumbled emotions and thoughts. There were too many people in the room to home in on just one person.

Turning my head, I checked on Tink. She sat with her head lowered, staring at Abby's hand holding hers. Abby caught my eye over the top of Tink's head and gave me a reassuring smile. I wondered if she remembered the young man from the airport. I'd ask her after this ordeal was over.

"Psst, Ophelia," hissed a voice from my right.

I was shocked to see Christopher Mason standing in the aisle next to our row.

My brow wrinkled in a frown. What was he doing here? He knew Buchanan? What a coincidence.

He motioned for me to join him in the back of the room. Mumbling my apologies, I carefully made my way over to where he stood.

"Hi," I said, keeping my voice low.

"I'm surprised to see you under these circumstances," he whispered back.

Not wanting to explain that the reason we were there was based on my great-aunt's half-baked notion that she'd be able to spot Buchanan's killer, I ignored his remark. "You knew Mr. Buchanan?" I asked.

"Yes. I was his mother's physician before she passed away . . . and we've had some business dealings." His gaze darted to the front of the room. "This is such a tragedy. Raymond was a very nice man, and I don't know what Kevin's going to do now."

"Kevin?"

"His assistant. Raymond took him under his wing after Kevin flunked out of medical school. And the last time I spoke with Raymond, he said he was trying to get Kevin into mortuary school."

"Really?" I eyed the young man with interest.

Christopher noticed my expression. "Yes. Nothing unusual about that; many former medical students wind up in the funeral business."

"And now he's out of a job?"

"Yes, unless he can find another funeral home that will take him on."

Before I could ask more questions—like what kind of "business dealings" would a doctor have with a funeral director—the organ music began and the family made their way quietly into the room.

"I'll talk to you later," Christopher said softly, laying a hand on my arm.

I returned to my seat and watched the family. It was obvious who the widow was. She clung tightly to Kevin's arm as he escorted her to her seat in the front row.

To call her flamboyant would be an understatement. She was obviously several years younger than what Buchanan had been, and even from my chair in the back row, I could see the sparklers on both hands. And I would have bet they weren't cubic zirconia. Those diamonds had to be several carats each.

In addition to the diamonds, she wore a black suit and black hat. Appropriate attire for a widow, except her hat, suit, and shoes were trimmed with leopard print.

I shook my head. Darci would have a conniption over an outfit like that. Even I, with my lack of fashion sense, thought the widow's dress was cheesy beyond belief.

Abby cleared her throat and drew my attention away from the grieving widow. Her eyes widened as she flashed a look that said she shared my opinion.

Two men followed Mrs. Buchanan at a respectful distance. From their resemblance to Mr. Buchanan, I guessed them to be his grown children, and based on their obvious age, the widow was *not* their mother. Everything about them told me they were glad she wasn't. They held their bodies stiffly, and with every move, I sensed their disapproval of their father's wife.

Hmm. I wondered whose name was on the life insurance policy. Maybe Aunt Dot's insistence at attending the funeral wasn't so half-baked after all.

Aunt Dot wasn't satisfied just going to the funeral. Oh no, we had to go to the graveside service, too. Abby marshaled her over the rough ground of the cemetery while Tink and I brought up the rear. Even though the weather had been dry and hot, the spikes of my low heels sunk into the sod as I followed Abby.

We were hanging at the back of the gathering when Kevin spotted Aunt Dot. He made his way to her and offered her his arm, and before Abby or I could protest, he led her to the folding chairs lined up by the open grave. I suppose he thought, because of her age, she should be seated during the service.

And she was—right next to Buchanan's widow.

I observed her bright eyes taking in the grieving family. Peachy. Aunt Dot was out of our sphere of influence, and we had no way of controlling what she might decide to do. Hopefully, she wouldn't pull out the camera I still suspected she carried and start snapping away.

From where I stood, I saw her lean to the side until her shoulder was touching the widow's. She said something, but I was too far away to catch her words.

The widow sniffed delicately into a white handkerchief as she listened intently to Aunt Dot. Well, at least the cloth wasn't trimmed in leopard, I thought unkindly.

I shifted uneasily throughout the service, nervous over what Tink's reaction to the cemetery might be and waiting for the opportunity to get Aunt Dot away from the family. Finally it was over, but before I could make my move, Kevin walked down the line of chairs, shaking each person's hand and murmuring what I presumed were words of condolence. When he reached Aunt Dot, again he offered her his arm and brought her back to where Abby, Tink, and I stood.

Smiling, he extended his hand to Abby. "It's a pleasure to meet you, Mrs. McDonald, but I'm sorry it's under such sad circumstances. I'm Kevin Roth."

Shock registered on my face. How did he know Abby's name?

Catching my surprise, he explained, "Ray told me all about his plane ride with Miss Cameron." His blue eyes twinkled as he glanced at Aunt Dot.

I dropped my chin and stared at a spot on the ground. *Gee, wonder if Mr. Buchanan shared Aunt Dot's tales of her fairies, too?* This kid had to think we were all nuts.

"And this must be Titania," he said, shifting his attention to Tink.

He even knew Tink's real name. I raised my head and saw Tink preen with pleasure. She suddenly had more color in her face than I'd seen all day. My eyes narrowed, gauging her reaction to Kevin, and I felt an instinct that I didn't know I had. I went on alert.

A good-looking guy and a young girl just beginning to notice the opposite sex. Not a good combination. And no doubt about it—Kevin was cute. Blond hair, blue eyes, a little short, but built well. If he were taller, he could be a model. How many years separated them? Six? Seven? Not many if you're an adult, but for a teenager it was too wide a gulf as far as I was concerned. I resisted the urge to tug Tink to my side.

Kevin's eyes moved to me. "And you're Ophelia."

"You have a very good memory, Kevin. To remember all our names," I replied.

Kevin's smile brightened. "It's easy. Ray was thoroughly entertained by your aunt's stories. He talked of nothing else on the way home from the airport."

I just bet he was, but before I could make a polite reply to Kevin's remark, Christopher came up from behind and clapped a hand on Kevin's shoulder.

"How are you doing?" he asked.

The smile left Kevin's face. "Okay," he answered with hesitation. "I'm going to miss Mr. Buchanan, and I'm—I'm worried about what Mrs. Buchanan will eventually do with the business. For now, another director from Taylor is going to take care of things, but I don't know how long that will last." He sighed. "I feel guilty for thinking of it at a time like this, but . . . "

"You need the job," Christopher finished for him.

"Yeah." He picked at his sleeve. "I've got all those school loans to pay off, and then there's the money I send Mom."

"Would you like me to ask around at a couple of places in Des Moines? See if they have any openings?"

Kevin's face brightened. "Would you? That would be terrific, Dr. Mason. Mrs. Buchanan said I could stay in the apartment at the funeral home for at least a month." He cast a nervous look over one shoulder. "I'd rather not if I can help it."

Christopher's eyes followed Kevin's and came to rest on the grieving widow. "I'll see what I can do," he said shortly.

We'd turned and begun to walk to our cars when Tink tugged on my sleeve. "There's that guy that runs the crematorium."

"Where?" I asked, scanning the departing crowd.

I was busy searching for Silas Green and didn't see what happened next. All I knew was one minute Aunt Dot was digging in her purse, and the next she was falling. Maybe she stepped in a gopher hole. Maybe she tripped on a fallen branch. As she pitched forward, she struck her wrist on a headstone. Christopher managed to grab her and keep her on her feet, but the damage was done. Her wrist was bent at an unnatural angle.

# *Thirteen*

As I walked into the library Tuesday morning, Darci hurried toward me, leaving Gert standing by one of the bookshelves with a perplexed look on her face.

"What happened to Aunt Dot?" she asked, twisting her hands.

I rolled my eyes. "How did you know anything happened?"

"It's all over town. One story has her breaking a hip, another her arm." She dropped her hands and gave me a sly glance. "It's also been said you were accompanied to the hospital by a doctor."

"Jeez," I said, marching to the counter and stowing my backpack underneath. "Are there no secrets in this town?"

"Not many. The doctor was Christopher, right?" She tossed her head. "I can't figure why you picked a funeral as your first date—"

I grasped the edge of the counter. "It wasn't a date," I exclaimed. "Christopher knew Mr. Buchanan, so he came to his funeral. It was a coincidence that we ran into each other—"

"Abby says there's no such a thing as coincidence," she replied in a smug voice, interrupting me.

"Well, this time it was," I said, shoving back from the counter. "And, before you say it, there's no mystery brewing, either, Darce. Aunt Dot tripped as we were leaving the cemetery and hit her arm on a headstone. Her wrist broke."

She opened her mouth, but I held up a finger, stopping her.

"Christopher specializes in geriatrics, so he helped the emergency room doctor treat Aunt Dot. End of story."

Darci cocked her hip and watched me with a speculative gleam in her eye. "Did you get a date?"

I tipped my head back and stared at the ceiling. "You are impossible. My ninety-one-year-old aunt was in the emergency room, for Pete's sake . . . not exactly a time for romance," I finished and busied myself with the stack of books sitting on the counter.

Darci strolled over, took the books away from me, and walking over to Gert, handed them to her. "Here," she said, "why don't you place these on the shelves, Gert? I've showed you how." She wagged a finger at her. "Remember, we can't let them pile up."

I snickered. Like that ever mattered to Darci in the past. She hated putting books away and was notorious about letting them sit gathering dust on the counter.

She returned to where I stood, leaned back and crossed her arms. "Okay, so if he didn't ask you out while you were at the hospital, when did he?"

"Ahh . . . " I felt the heat creep up my neck and into my face. "Last night, after we returned home, he called," I muttered.

"I knew it," she said, smacking her hand on the countertop. "Good. You need to get out."

Frowning, I picked up the pens lying scattered about and returned them to the cup holder. "I don't know . . . there's a lot of stuff going on right now."

She quickly checked over her shoulder to see if Gert was still occupied filing the books. Satisfied, she pulled me off to the side, out of Gert's line of vision.

At the same time, I noticed Edna Walters lurking near the counter. She pretended to study the back cover of a paperback, but even from where I stood, I saw she held the book upside down.

Darci spotted Edna, too, and tugged me back to the far corner.

"What happened Saturday night?" she asked in a hushed tone.

"You know about that, too?"

With a jerk of her head, she motioned toward Edna. "She's here now, and Agnes was in earlier. All morning the town gossips have been circling the library, waiting to pounce on you." Her eyes traveled to Edna, who was easing her way closer to where we stood. "If I were you, I'd spend most of the day in your office."

"What's the rumor going around?" I asked with a grimace.

"A skull was found at your campsite. Georgia tried pumping Alan about it, but for once he won't talk."

"I wonder if Bill knows he's got a major leak in his office, thanks to Alan?"

"Who cares—tell me what happened," Darci insisted.

I pulled a hand through my hair. "T.P. fetched a skull out of the woods. That's it."

"What does the skull have to do with Buchanan's murder?" she asked with eyes narrowed, as if she thought I was holding out on her.

"Nothing," I said, spreading my hands wide. "It's probably the remains of some poor soul who died in the woods. And the death doesn't have to be something sinister. Maybe it's a hunter who died in a hunting accident. Maybe an elderly person wandered off. Maybe an indigent died from the elements."

"But no one's been reported missing," she argued.

"Got me, Darce. All I know is we're staying out of the investigation."

"Why did you go to Buchanan's funeral if you're staying out of it?"

"We were trying to placate Aunt Dot. It was her brilliant idea." I gave Darci a narrow look. "If I didn't know better, I'd swear the two of you were related. You both like to go looking for trouble."

"Very funny," she said with a pout. "Why does Tink think the skull has something to do with Buchanan's death?"

"What?" I exclaimed.

"Shh," she whispered, glancing past me to Edna. "Keep your voice down. Edna's soaking in our conversation."

I stepped closer to Darci.

"The story's going around town that Tink must know something about Buchanan's murder," she said.

I groaned, remembering Tink's remarks at the campground. She'd mentioned Buchanan when T.P. dropped the skull at her feet. And thanks to the way people embellished rumors, it now sounded like she was some kind of material witness. Not good.

"What else are they saying?" I asked in a tired voice.

Darci shrugged. "That your family sure has a knack for turning up dead people."

I gave a soft moan, but before I could speak, the door of the library swung open and Bill marched in. He didn't look happy.

He walked with purposeful strides toward the counter, and without preamble said, "Ophelia, may I talk to you in your office?"

"Sure," I replied, trying to hide my trepidation.

I reluctantly led Bill down the stairs and into my office. After shutting the door, I took my place behind my desk and gestured to the chair across from me.

"What's this about, Bill?"

Removing his hat, he got right to the point. "Is there something you're not telling me?"

"Absolutely not," I replied heatedly.

"I heard you went to Buchanan's funeral."

I decided the best defense was a strong offense. "Last time I checked, it's a free country and I can go where I want."

"Why did you want to attend the funeral?" Bill asked, not giving up.

"Aunt Dot had met Mr. Buchanan on the plane and they hit it off. When she learned he'd passed away, she wanted to go to his funeral to pay her respects."

I wasn't lying—she had wanted to go. I didn't need to mention the main reason was that she thought she could spot his killer.

"Why didn't you mention that Miss Cameron knew Buchanan?"

"You never asked."

From across the desk, Bill glowered at me.

"Honestly, I never thought about it." I picked up a pen and tapped it on the desk. "And what's to tell? My elderly aunt met a man on a plane and they talked. That's it."

"He might have said something to Miss Cameron on the plane." Bill wiped his bald head. "Did he act afraid, worried, distracted?"

I tossed the pen down. "I don't know. As far as I know, they had a pleasant trip, he helped her off the plane when it landed. It's happenstance that someone Aunt Dot met wound up a victim of a violent crime."

"Your family seems to attract these 'happenstances,'" he muttered. "Let's talk about the skull—"

"Hey," I interjected. "I can't help that Tink's dog found a skull."

Bill spun his hat in his hands. "No, but Tink said—"

"Come on, Bill," I said, interrupting him again. "She's a teenager and it freaked her out. She can't be held responsible for her babbling."

"I know that, you know that, but this is a small town, and stories change as they make their rounds."

Something in Bill's eyes frightened me.

"Tink's a good kid, and I hate to see anything happen to her because of a rumor," he continued.

My hand flew to my throat. "Is she in danger?"

"I don't think so, but Buchanan didn't hook himself up to the embalming machine. A killer's still out there, and I don't want a rumor causing him to think Tink's a risk to him."

I grabbed the phone and, in a panic, began to punch in Abby's number. I'd dropped Tink at the greenhouse before work. Abby had to know about this. She had to make sure Tink stayed safe.

"Hold on," Bill said, taking the receiver from my hand and placing it back on its base. "I said she's not in imminent danger—"

"No," I exclaimed, shaking my head back and forth. "You said the murderer might—"

"The point I was trying to make is these rumors *could* compromise Tink's safety." He gave me a hard stare. "So if you know anything, Ophelia, you'd better come clean and tell me."

"I don't, really I don't," I stuttered. "I know in the past I haven't always been completely honest with you, but I swear, this time—" I clamped my mouth shut to stop my blathering.

"Okay." Bill gave me a kind smile. "I believe you." He stood and settled his hat back on his head. "Just keep an eye on her, and to be on the safe side, I'll ask the chief to send a patrol car by every so often in the evenings."

"O-o-kay," I bumbled.

Pulling his hat low on his forehead, he exuded confidence. "Don't worry. We'll catch whoever's responsible for Buchanan's death."

I stood in shock, staring at Bill's back as he left the office.

Was Tink not only going to be haunted by ghosts, but by a killer, too?

# *Fourteen*

I examined my face in the mirror on my vanity table. Lines of tension crossed my forehead and creases bracketed my mouth. Even Darci's makeup tips weren't going to hide those suckers.

"I don't think this date is such a good idea, Darci," I said as my eyes moved from my face to her reflection hovering by mine in the mirror.

"Yes it is." She moved to the side of the table and, resting a hip on the edge, stared down at me. "Bill told you that he didn't think Tink's in danger. She's staying with Abby tonight, so I don't see what the problem is."

I brushed the hair away from my face. "Come on, Abby's in her seventies and Aunt Dot's in her nineties. How much protection can two senior citizens provide?"

"Bill was only warning you to be careful, not suggesting that you call out the militia to protect her."

"And Aunt Dot has a broken wrist," I said, ignoring Darci's statement. "She couldn't even protect herself."

She chuckled. "I'm not too sure about that," she exclaimed. "I bet she can be really wicked with that cane of hers." She straightened and stepped behind me. Laying a hand on my shoulder, she pinched the muscle.

"Ouch," I said, batting her hand away.

"You're so tense those muscles are in knots. If you don't do something to relax, you're going to crack."

"I know." I stroked my forehead trying to ease the lines away. "When I came home this afternoon, I let my guard down to summon a vision. It didn't work. I couldn't focus."

"Did anything come to you?"

I stood and walked back to my bedroom with Darci following. "No, not really. All I saw was a bunch of random images—"

"Such as?" Darci asked, butting in.

"From the past . . . mainly from our trip to Minnesota when we first met Tink." I stretched my neck trying to ease the kinks.

Leaning back, Darci tapped her chin thoughtfully. "That makes sense, since you're concerned with her safety."

Taking a seat next to her, I slipped on my sandals. "I suppose, but I didn't find anything enlightening about what I saw."

"Quit worrying," she replied, poking me in the ribs. "Go have fun. Set the problems aside for tonight. Maybe if you do, it will help clear your mind and you'll be able to see things more clearly."

"You're right," I agreed reluctantly, and stood. Holding my arms out to the side, I watched Darci's face. "So? How do I look?"

She squinted and eyed me from head to toe.

Suddenly self-conscious, I smoothed my hands over my navy blue sundress. "Well?"

"Turn around slowly," she instructed.

Making a small pirouette in the center of the room, the hem flared around my knees.

"Hmm," she said. "The wider straps are flattering, and it fits well around the bust line. A little cleavage—"

My hand flew to my chest in alarm. "Too much?"

Darci laughed. "No, it's just right. The dress shows your curves, but it doesn't look like you're advertising, if you know what I mean."

"Are you sure?" My eyes narrowed in doubt. "I don't want Christopher to get the wrong idea."

"I'm sure." Darci tapped her watch. "If you don't hurry, you're going to be late."

Grabbing my purse, I flew down the stairs and out of the house, leaving Darci to lock up behind me.

When I arrived at the restaurant, Christopher was waiting for me by the hostess station.

"You look lovely," he said with a smile.

He wasn't a slouch in the looks department, either. He wore camel-colored pants with a light blue shirt and a navy sport coat. There was a definite style about him that spoke of his success.

Nervously, I fiddled with the gold chain I wore around my neck. "Thanks. You look nice, too."

His smile broadened, and placing a hand in the small of my back, he guided me after the hostess.

Once seated, the hostess handed us our menus. "Would you care for anything to drink?" she asked.

"Would you like a glass of wine?" Christopher asked me.

I blanched at his question, remembering my last experience with the stuff. "No, I'd rather have a beer."

The hostess rattled off a list of what the bar had on tap.

"I'll have a Bud Light, please."

Christopher's eyebrows shot up. "They have imported beers."

"No, Bud's fine." I picked up the menu and studied it

while Christopher ordered what sounded like a very expensive glass of wine.

A few minutes later a waitress came with our drinks and took our orders. I selected a small steak, while Christopher ordered the lobster. He tried to convince me to order the same, but I declined.

He picked up his glass and held it toward me. "Here's to new friendships," he said in a warm voice, and clinked his glass against mine.

I sipped my beer and felt the tension ease out of my shoulders. Maybe Darci was right—this was a good idea after all.

Setting down my glass, I leaned forward and crossed my arms on the table. "Do you mind if I ask you a question?"

He hooked an arm over the back of the booth. "Of course not. You can ask me anything."

How did I ask without sounding like a snoop? I wondered. "Umm, well," I said, playing with the silverware, "you said you had business dealings with Mr. Buchanan, and I—"

"Wondered what kind of business would involve a doctor and a funeral home director," he said, finishing for me.

"Yes."

He traced a finger down the stem of his wineglass. "I'm a co-owner of a biomedical supplier."

"Biomedical? As in 'organ donations'?"

"No." He gave a nervous laugh. "I'd explain, but I don't know if it's proper dinner conversation."

I remembered Aunt Dot's remark about death being part of life. "Don't worry about it," I replied, waving his concern away.

"Okay, without going into details, the best way to describe it would be to say we harvest tissue from the deceased."

I winced a little at the mental image.

He caught my reaction and patted my hand. "It's then

used for bone transplants, joint replacement, skin grafting, that kind of thing."

"I didn't know people did that."

He patted my hand again. "Yes, and it not only saves lives, but can improve the quality of someone's life, too. Burn victims, children with heart problems, patients with deteriorating disks in their spines."

"It's good people are willing to be donors."

He smiled. "I think so. Of course, there are guidelines to be followed—and it's done only with the consent of the family—but as I said, the gift of tissue can really make a difference in someone's life." He squeezed my fingers. "Now let's talk about something more pleasant."

And we did. Through the salads and the main course, Christopher told me amusing stories about his patients, his days in medical school, and his various interests.

By the time I'd finished my second beer, I had the courage to ask him the other question that I'd been pondering.

"At the speed dating event, I think you were the only man there who didn't try and contact Darci. Why?"

It wasn't a very subtle way to ask, but he didn't seem to mind.

Pushing his plate to the side, he held my hand, making lazy circles with his thumb on the inside of my wrist. It made it hard to focus on his answer.

"In my experience, I've found brunettes to be more sophisticated."

Gently pulling my hand away, I leaned against the back of the booth. "That's a stereotype."

"Maybe it is, but I'm involved in several business associations, the hospital guild, fund-raisers, and so on. And I do a lot of entertaining. I need a partner who can fit into that kind of life."

My eyes widened. "And you thought I could?" I asked in shock.

Christopher chuckled. "Yes, that surprises you?" he continued before I could answer. "Whether you know it or not, you strike me as a woman with class, Ophelia."

"Th-thank you," I stuttered.

"You're educated, well-read, and can discuss a number of topics with intelligence."

"Kind of you to say so," I mumbled.

Glancing at his watch, he signaled the waitress for our check. Turning to me, he said, "I know you have a drive back to Summerset, but could we continue this conversation at my house? I'd love to show you my home . . . "

"Ah, gee, ah . . . " I stumbled trying to think of a proper response. Did I want to go to his place? I didn't know him that well, but I had enjoyed our conversation up to this point. I was interested. He'd been so kind to Aunt Dot that evening in the emergency room. He was a respected doctor and a businessman and I sensed he was "safe." Oh, what the heck, why not? Darci had said I needed to get out of my rut. Well, going back to Christopher's would certainly be out of character for me.

"Okay," I said, picking up my purse.

"Great," he replied with a huge grin.

I followed Christopher back to his house, and as I did, left a voice mail on Darci's cell letting her know where I was going. I might be willing to try something new, but I wasn't stupid. It was never a good idea to go off with someone you barely knew without telling someone where you were.

After we arrived, he gave me a tour of his house. It was gorgeous—spacious rooms, tall windows overlooking a creek running through his backyard, and a stone fireplace big enough to roast a cow.

He offered me a glass of imported beer, and we settled on the large couch in front of the fireplace. With the touch of a remote, soft music filled the room.

I had a feeling Christopher had done this before.

Smiling to myself, I sipped my beer as I watched the flames leap.

"Why are you smiling?" he asked.

"I think you're a little better at this than I am, Christopher," I said, placing my beer on the coffee table.

He moved closer to me. "Better at what?"

"This dating thing," I answered succinctly.

"I have had practice," he replied, and laughed softly. "A year ago, I finally realized what I've missed in my life. I've been so focused on establishing my career as a doctor that I didn't take the time for home and family." His eyes traveled around the room. "I bought this house and started devoting more time to dating." He took my hand in his. "But it's hard finding the right person."

"I think it takes time, don't you?"

"Yes, but at our age, I feel like the clock is ticking." He turned to face me, and reaching up, took a strand of my hair in his fingers. "You have beautiful hair, Ophelia."

"Umm, thanks," I said, glancing away.

No one had ever told me that before, and I didn't know how to take the compliment.

Sensing my discomfort, he gently touched my chin, turning my head toward him, and placed his other arm around me. The next thing I knew, his warm lips were on mine.

Wow, the tingle I'd felt when I first met him shot through me again. Only this time it was way more than a tingle. And as the pressure of his kiss increased, I felt my nervousness melt out of my body. It had been so long since I'd felt the comfort of a man's arms around me, and this felt so good.

My body relaxed against his and I let myself drift on the pleasure of Christopher's kiss.

A smooth palm stealing up my leg brought me out of the moment and back to reality.

I broke off the kiss and removed his hand from my leg. "Whoa," I said, still a little befuddled by the intensity of his kiss. "We need to slow down." I moved away from him.

Without speaking, Christopher raised my hand to his mouth and touched his lips to the soft skin on the underside of my wrist. The feelings flamed again.

"We really don't know one another, Christopher," I stammered.

"This is a good way to get acquainted, don't you think?" he said as I felt his lips move against my wrist.

Man, this guy was good! He had the sparks shooting through me.

Gently, I withdrew my hand. "Christopher, I—"

"Shh," he said, leaning in to kiss me again. "You are so lovely. Stay the night," he murmured against my mouth.

Stay the night? Wait a second—how did we go from "let's get acquainted" to "let's sleep together"?

Pulling away, I slid farther away from him. "I'm not a booty call," I exclaimed indignantly.

An injured look appeared on his handsome face. "That's not what I meant. You've been drinking and I don't want you driving home."

I eyed the unfinished beer sitting on the coffee table. "I've had two beers over the course of the evening. It would take more than that for me to cross the legal limit. I'm fine," I said with determination.

He raised his hand to touch my face, but I put more distance between us.

"You're just the kind of woman I've been looking for."

"You don't know that." I picked up my purse, just in case I needed it.

"Yes, I do. I can sense these things."

Yeah? Well I sense things, too, I thought. And I sensed it was time to get the hell out of there.

I stood and looked down at him. "Thanks for the lovely dinner—"

"Don't leave like this." He reached for my hand, but I placed it behind my back. "Stay."

I gave him a tight smile. "Trust me, you'll respect me more in the morning if I don't."

He sat back against the couch and frowned. "That's an old cliché."

"Right. Funny thing about old clichés—they're old clichés because they're true."

I spun on my heel and left.

# *Fifteen*

"How was your date?" I heard Tink ask through the receiver of my cell phone.

My lip curled in a silent response. No way would I tell her about Christopher and his grand seduction scheme. "He's not my type."

"Really?" she said in surprise. "He was nice to Aunt Dot at the hospital."

I drummed my fingers on the steering wheel, thinking of how to reply. "Ahh, he's looking for the perfect wife, and I'm not it."

"Too bad. Abby's going to Aiken. May I go?" she asked, shifting the conversation away from Christopher to her.

"Sure. I guess. Why's Abby going there?"

"Mrs. Walters asked Abby to drive her to the nursing home in Aiken so she could visit her sister." She took a deep breath. "Something about Mrs. Walters's car's in the shop. Aunt Dot's going, too."

Hold on, Edna around Aunt Dot? And Tink? Edna would be trying as hard as she could to get the latest dirt out of them.

"You want to spend the afternoon with Edna?"

"Not really . . . Mrs. Walters sure asks a lot of questions . . . but Abby's going to drop Aunt Dot and me off at the bookstore while they're at the nursing home. We're supposed to meet them at the ice cream shop."

"Do you have any money?"

"A little, but some extra wouldn't hurt," she said with a giggle.

"Okay, do you have time to stop by the library on your way?"

"I don't know."

"If you don't, ask Abby if you may borrow some cash from her. I'll pay her back when I pick you up . . . but Tink?"

"Yeah?"

"Don't spend it all at the bookstore. Save some for ice cream."

"Okay."

"Speaking of the library," I said as I parked my car, "I'm at work now, so I've got to go. I'll see you when you stop by."

"Gotcha. Love ya."

"Love you, too, sweetie," I said, and flipped the phone shut.

I unlocked the door of the library and breezed through. I stopped in my tracks as my eyes skimmed over the room.

All the returned books were put away, no paper from various notes littered the counter, and all the pens were neatly placed in the pen holder. Maybe Aunt Dot's fairies had paid a visit during the night and straightened the place up. The library never looked this good first thing in the morning, especially after Darci had worked the afternoon shift the day before.

"Good morning." The words echoed in the quiet.

Startled, I watched Gert come around the corner of the mystery section. Placing my hand on the reading table, I leaned against it. "You scared me to death."

A sheepish grin flitted across her face as her fingers curled around the chain at her neck. "Sorry."

"The door was locked," I said, pointing to it. "I didn't think anyone was here."

"I came in early, but I locked it behind me." Gert gazed down at the floor. "I wanted to tidy up before we opened. I hope you don't mind."

"No, that's fine." I walked behind the counter and dropped my backpack. "Place looks nice, Gert."

She smiled with pleasure and joined me. Picking up a pile of sticky notes, she handed them to me. "These are for you. Nothing important—just requests to order books from the regional library. I didn't want to bother you with them yesterday."

I took the notes and flipped through them. Hmm, she was correct, nothing important. Funny thing, Darci never worried about interrupting me with requests from patrons while I was working in my office. I appreciated Gert's consideration.

"There aren't any hold orders here?" I asked.

"No." Gert shifted self-consciously. "I may be exceeding my authority, but I took the liberty of making up a chart." She reached under the counter and picked up a clipboard. "It's in alphabetical order by title." She handed it to me. "Each sheet lists the names of the patrons wanting to check out that book when it becomes available."

"My," I said studying the pages. "I'm impressed."

Gert's color deepened.

I turned to the clock. "Darci won't be here for another thirty minutes—can you handle the counter by yourself, or do you want me to stay with you?"

"No," she said, shooing me toward the stairs. "I'm sure you have paperwork to do."

I thought of the mound of unfinished reports sitting on the corner of my desk.

"Okay, if you're sure," I replied, placing the clipboard on the counter. "If you need anything, just holler."

The rest of the morning flew by quickly. With both Gert and Darci manning the counter, no one disturbed me. It was a welcome change to be able to concentrate on unfinished business, and I plowed through the reports in record time.

About one-thirty I heard a short knock on my office door, followed by Darci barging in.

"What's up?" I asked, pausing over the financial report.

She flopped down in the chair across from me. "Can I have the rest of the day off?"

"Why?" I laid down my pen. "Aren't you feeling well?"

"I'm fine." A sullen expression tightened her face. "I'm bored out of my mind."

"Why? Aren't we busy today?"

"Yes," she answered with a pout. "But every time I go to do something, Gert's already done it."

I grinned. "I'd think you'd like that. You've never been fond of all the filing and returning the books to the shelves. You've always preferred helping the patrons."

"She's beating me to that, too," she exclaimed, her pout changing to a frown. "Agnes was in looking for the latest romance. I've been helping her for six years—I know exactly what her tastes are—but before I could make my suggestions, Gert butted in."

"She likes romances, too."

"Humph," Darci snorted. "She rattled off a list from our most recent shipment." She jiggled one knee in irritation.

"You should've seen Agnes's face. She was *so* impressed. She's never acted that way when I helped her."

Leaning back in my chair, I placed my feet on the edge of my desk. "You're jealous."

"I am not," she huffed. "I don't know how this Gert thinks she can learn everything in one day when it's taken me six years."

Lowering my feet, I sat forward. "I don't think it's like that, Darce. I think Gert may be a little overanxious to please—"

Darci cut me off. "Well, it's driving me nuts. And she's always messing with that necklace of hers. What's up with that?"

I'd noticed that, too.

"It's a nervous habit, I think." After a glance at the clock, I returned my attention to Darci. "It's only about three hours until we close. Gert should be okay, so if you want to leave, you may."

"Thanks." Darci appeared to be pacified. "Hey, you've been hiding out down here all day, and I haven't heard about your date." She leaned forward in anticipation. "How did it go?"

I eyed the dwindling stack of paper on the corner of my desk. It would be nice, for once, to finish them. And I knew if I started telling Darci about Christopher, I'd never get them done.

"I don't have the time to talk about it right now. Let's just say Christopher isn't the guy I thought he was. Can I call you tonight? I'll give you the details then."

Disappointment flared in her eyes. "Okay," she said with reluctance and rose.

"I'm sorry." I motioned to the pile of papers. "I need to clear my desk, but I'll call you tonight, I promise."

"It's okay." Her voice was full of resignation. "I'm going

home and eat a dozen chocolate chip cookies." She jerked her head in a nod. "That'll make me feel better."

"It'll be okay, Darce. Once you start school, you won't be working with her that much." I tapped my pen on the desk. "Plus, she'll settle down and quit trying so hard."

Darci paused at the door. "I hope so." She gave me a wicked grin. "I hate to have to hurt her."

Hooray, the stack of papers was gone, and it was closing time. Shutting off the lights, I made my way through the children's section and up the stairs. Once again the library was neat and tidy. Not a single checked-in book in sight.

"Nice job, Gert," I said, crossing to the counter. "Did you have any problems?"

"Oh, no," she said with a wave of her hand. "I had a wonderful time, helping people, filing. My, there's a lot to do, isn't there?"

I smiled. "On some days."

"That's the way I like it. I don't like being idle."

Jeez, I thought, she must be a workaholic. For someone like her, living out there in the country with her mother would have driven her batty. I only hoped Darci would quit feeling threatened by Gert. I decided to include that thought in our conversation tonight, too.

"Why don't you leave, Gert? I'll lock up."

She drew her purse out from underneath the counter, and I realized I'd forgotten my backpack. "Dang," I muttered. "I left it down in my office."

"What did you leave in your office?" Gert inquired.

"My backpack," I said, heading toward the stairs.

"The black with a Star Trek emblem on it?"

"Yeah," I said, flushing pink. "Darci bought it for me as a joke."

"It was on the shelf."

I ran around the end of the counter. I could've sworn I'd taken it with me to my office. The shock at seeing the library so neat must've broke my routine and I'd forgotten to grab it when I went downstairs.

Great. My backpack was gone.

"It's not there?"

"No. Did you see anyone go behind the counter?"

Gert pulled on her bottom lip. "I don't think so. We were really busy, and I spent a lot of time helping patrons find the books they wanted."

I shoved my hands onto my hips as I scanned the library. Spying a black strap at the end of one of the bookcases, I hurried over to it.

"Here it is." Quickly, I unzipped the front pocket. Whew, my wallet was still there. I pulled it out and examined the contents.

"Is everything there?" Gert asked.

"Looks like it," I said with relief.

"Good, I'm so glad you found it," she said, as she fiddled with her necklace. "Well, I'd better be off. Mama's going to be expecting me, and she hates tardiness."

"You go," I said. "I'll lock up."

"Have a nice evening," she called out in a cheery voice.

"You, too," I said distractedly as I went back to checking my billfold.

Yup, driver's license, money, my ATM card. Thank goodness. Shoving the wallet back in the front pocket, I zipped it. The rest of the bag was empty, so I didn't stop to go through all the numerous pockets. I needed to get to Abby's to pick up Tink. I hoped she had a good time browsing the bookstore with Aunt Dot, I thought as I hurried out the door, locking up as I went.

When I reached Abby's, she was waiting on the front porch.

That was odd.

I threw the car into park and got out, and as soon as my head cleared the door, Abby called out.

"Get in here now," she exclaimed.

I scrambled up the walk and up the steps with my heart thudding all the way. "Tink? Is she okay?"

Abby squinted, and I didn't know if it was against the rays of the sun or at me. Her mouth settled in a thin line. "That remains to be seen," she said cryptically through clenched teeth.

# Sixteen

Confused, I followed close on Abby's heels as we walked down the hallway and into the kitchen. Tink and Aunt Dot sat at the table. One was the face of youth, the other the face of the aged, but they both wore the same expression. That of two chastised children.

Relieved to find Tink safe and sound, I still regarded them with bewilderment. "What's going on?"

"Who wants to go first?" Abby asked in a voice heavy with the sound of the South.

When Abby's accent became pronounced, it was a sure sign she was upset.

Both Aunt Dot and Tink hung their heads and didn't speak.

Abby blew a strand of silver hair out of face and watched the two of them in annoyance. "No?" She moved to the table and took a chair, her eyes never leaving them. "These two decided to play detective while we were in Aiken."

As if we didn't have enough problems, I thought, joining them at the table. "What did they do?"

Abby arched an eyebrow. "Aunt Dot pretended to be a customer—"

I broke in. "What kind of customer?"

"At Buchanan's Funeral Home. She pretended she wanted to preplan her funeral." She grimaced. "And while Aunt Dot," she said, pointing a finger at her, "kept the funeral director busy, this one," she moved her finger to Tink, "snooped through the files."

"Tink! You're grounded!" I exclaimed.

"Figures," she grumbled.

I flashed a look at Aunt Dot. Unfortunately, Abby couldn't ground a ninety-one-year-old.

Abby followed my thoughts. "Oh, don't worry, she's not getting out of my sight again," she said with certainty.

Returning my attention to Tink, I scrubbed my face with my hands. "What would you have done if you'd gotten caught?"

"Told them I was looking for the restroom?" she replied hopefully.

"Uh-huh. And you just happened to decide to go through the files while you were at it."

She lifted a thin shoulder and didn't answer.

"Did anyone suspect what they were doing?" I asked Abby.

She shook her head. "No, I think Holmes and Watson here pulled off their little caper without anyone the wiser."

"How did you find out about it?"

"We left the nursing home early. Edna's sister had to go to physical therapy, so we cut our visit short. We saw these two coming out of Buchanan's as we were driving down Main Street."

"Edna knows that they were snooping around the funeral home?"

"Not exactly. Aunt Dot made a lame excuse that she'd stopped by to visit Mrs. Buchanan."

"Edna go for it?"

"Not really. She was the one who spotted them walking out of Buchanan's. She became so excited she couldn't wait for them to get in the car so she could start pumping them for information."

"And whatever they didn't tell her, she'll fill in the blanks with suppositions . . . "

Abby nodded. "Yes, and by this time tomorrow those suppositions will be going around town as facts."

"Bill isn't going to like this," I stated with a sigh.

"I should say not." She sat back and crossed her arms. "And right now, if he did want to make the two of them overnight guests of the county, I wouldn't lift a finger to help them."

"Sheriff Wilson can't arrest a kid," Tink pointed out logically. "And Aunt Dot—"

Tink's next remark was interrupted by a knock on Abby's screen door.

Shifting in my chair, I looked over my shoulder. "Who's that?"

Abby rose. "Didn't I tell you?" She cast a derisive look at Aunt Dot. "*She* invited Mr. Buchanan's assistant, Kevin, here for dinner."

A couple of minutes later Abby escorted Kevin into the kitchen. He greeted everyone, and when he smiled at Tink, I noticed her face flush before she ducked her head in response.

Aunt Dot's expression took on a transformation, too. She eyed Kevin with avid interest, and I had the distinct impression that Abby's earlier scolding about her snooping had absolutely no effect on her. She intended to have an adventure regardless of what anyone said. My only hope was that it wouldn't compromise Tink's safety.

"How old are you, Kevin?" Aunt Dot asked.

"Ahh, twenty-one," he replied.

"Would you like some wine?" Aunt Dot stood, but before she could toddle over to the cupboard, Abby placed a hand on her shoulder and gently pushed her down to where she'd been seated.

"No," Abby said, her voice brooking no opposition. "In this heat, ice tea is much more refreshing."

After serving everyone ice tea, Abby and I set about preparing a light supper—ham sandwiches, pasta salad Abby had made that morning, and some leftover chocolate cake for dessert. At first an awkward silence hovered over the room as we sat down to eat, but then Kevin broke it.

"You have a nice home, Mrs. McDonald." He took in the kitchen with a wandering glance. "I don't think I've ever seen a kitchen quite like this one."

"It's patterned after the one in the cabin where I grew up," she said, smiling fondly, "in Appalachia."

"And you live there now, Miss Cameron?" he asked.

"Call me Dot, please," she said with a pat of her hand. "Yes, my sister Mary and me live at the old home place now."

Kevin tugged on his lip. "I don't mean to be nosy, but if you live in Appalachia, why were you interested in a pre-planned funeral here in Iowa?"

I sat back in my chair and crossed my arms. This ought to be good. I wondered how Aunt Dot was going to explain it.

She appeared unshaken by Kevin's question. "Ack, I'm an old lady and you never know what's in store. What if I would cross over on this visit? Without a little planning," she motioned toward Abby, "my poor niece here would be left to make the arrangements on her own. Sister always says plan for the worst and it never happens."

Humph, pretty thin excuse if you would have asked me, but Kevin seemed to accept her logic. I suppose he thought her merely eccentric.

Changing the subject, he glanced at the bundle of plants drying overhead. "What are those, Mrs. McDonald?"

"Herbs. I like to grow my own. They—"

Aunt Dot interrupted. "She uses them for healing. We—"

She broke off when I nudged her foot under the table. "Abby's a master gardener," I said before Aunt Dot could start blabbing secrets. Uncertain as to how much Kevin knew about our family, I had no intention of letting her give any more information away.

"Umm," Kevin said as he pushed his plate to the side. "Ray mentioned that you've also helped the police with their investigations."

I exchanged a look with Abby. How did we explain that away?

"No," I exclaimed. "Not really. We've had the misfortune of being in the wrong place at the wrong time."

Jeez, my excuse sounded as lame as Aunt Dot talking about planning her funeral.

"You're not unofficial private investigators?" He sounded disappointed.

"Oh gosh, no." I assured him.

"That's too bad." Kevin sagged a little in his chair. "I'm afraid the police aren't going to solve Ray's murder. I was going to ask if you'd look into it for me . . . " His voice dropped. "I don't have much money, but I'd pay you whatever I could," he finished, his voice rising on a hopeful note.

"No, no, I'm afraid Aunt Dot misled Mr. Buchanan when she related some of our experiences to him," I said in a rush.

"This kind of thing should be left up to people who *know what they're doing.*"

I stressed the words as I gave Aunt Dot a steely look.

She suddenly found something very interesting about Abby's tablecloth and ignored me.

"But the investigation isn't moving forward," he argued. "The longer it continues, the less chance Ray's killer will be brought to justice."

"Don't worry, Kevin. Sheriff Wilson is good at his job," I said, trying to reassure him. "He'll make an arrest."

"If only I'd stayed home that night."

"You live in the apartment above the business, don't you?" I asked.

"Yes. It'd been Ray's until he married Mrs. Buchanan." His face twisted with distaste. "She said living above a funeral home gave her the creeps, but she sure didn't mind the money the business brought in."

"Was this Mr. Buchanan's second marriage?" Abby questioned.

"Yes. After his divorce, he tried one of those online dating sites. That's where he met Mrs. Buchanan. And once she got her hooks into him, that was it."

"I don't mean to be personal, but I take it you don't care for his widow?"

He made a derisive sound. "To be honest? No. She's caused trouble between Ray and his sons from his first marriage, she went through money like no other, and was always pressuring Ray for more." He halted for a moment. "I question how committed she was to Ray."

My eyebrows shot up after a quick glance at Tink, who sat soaking the conversation in and then said, "An affair?"

Kevin's gaze slid to Tink and back again. "There've been rumors."

Aunt Dot leaned against the back of her chair and watched Kevin with narrowed eyes. "Young man—" she began in a frosty voice.

"Did her husband know?" I asked before she could finish.

"He never mentioned it, but I think he'd heard them, too, and chose to ignore them."

"Kevin," I said, choosing my words carefully, "have you told Sheriff Wilson any of this?"

He dropped his head. "No. I didn't want to falsely accuse anyone."

I chewed the inside of my lip. I'd heard of women wanting to do away with their husbands, but embalming one alive? Pretty cold.

"Do you know if she has an alibi for his time of death?"

"Supposedly she was home waiting for him. He'd stayed at the funeral home to go over the books." He shrugged. "From what I've heard, the medical examiner has had trouble establishing the exact time due to the way Ray was killed."

He didn't need to say any more. I got the picture, and it was an unpleasant one. Since the body was preserved, there wouldn't have been any decomposition to indicate how long he'd been dead.

Pursuing that line of thought, I asked another question. "Would she know how to work the equipment?"

"Even though she's always avoided coming there, probably. It's not that hard. And she'd been a nurse when Ray met her, so she'd have knowledge of anatomy."

"I'm sure Sheriff Wilson's uncovered all of this," I said distractedly as I went over the possibilities in my mind.

Motive? A boyfriend and maybe a nice fat life insurance policy with her as the beneficiary. Means? That was obvious—the equipment was on site. But Mrs. Buchanan wasn't a very large woman. How would she have restrained

Mr. Buchanan long enough to hook him up to the machine? Maybe the phantom boyfriend helped her? Maybe she'd knocked him out first? Hmm, but then she'd have to find a way to get him on the table. Opportunity?

I shook the thoughts away. *No, Jensen,* I told myself, *You are not going to get involved. Plus, you're beginning to sound just like Aunt Dot—no more TV for you!*

# Seventeen

"Kevin's nice, isn't he?" Tink commented when we arrived home later that night.

"Yes, he is," I replied, following her into the living room.

"Abby and Aunt Dot like him, too, don't they?"

I thought about our conversation with Kevin, and I remembered Aunt Dot's reaction when he mentioned Mrs. Buchanan's possible affair. Her voice had gone cold and she didn't seem as friendly to him as she had in the beginning. Maybe she didn't approve of discussing illicit romances in front of a teenager?

"I don't know about Aunt Dot, but personally, I feel sorry for him. It sounds like his future is pretty undecided right now."

"That would suck," she said, falling into one of the wing chairs. "Wait until Nell hears that we had dinner with him. She'll die. Don't you think he's hot?"

Hot? Oh yeah, that meant attractive. Sometimes talking to a teen was like speaking in another language. "Chillin' with your bros"—spending time with friends. "You're straight up" is a good thing. "You're lame" isn't a good thing. Evidently in Tink's eyes Kevin was "straight up" and not "lame."

"Kevin is a nice-looking young man." I stressed the word "man." "And he's several years older than you."

"Duh," she said with a roll of her eyes, even though her face tinged pink. "It's not like I have a crush on him, or anything."

I chuckled as I sat on the couch. "It's okay to have crushes, just don't act on them." Lifting a shoulder, I grinned. "I had a crush on my girlfriend's older brother."

Surprise registered on her face. "You?"

"Don't be so shocked. I was your age once, too. I dated in high school."

"Humph," she said, as if the concept of me having a life as a teenager was new to her.

My eyes locked on her face. "Enough about Kevin, let's talk about you and Aunt Dot instead."

"You've already grounded me," she groused as she plucked at the arm of the chair.

Leaning forward, I clasped my hands on my knees. "Tink, what you did was really wrong, and I don't understand what you hoped to find."

"Oh," she exclaimed, sitting forward. "I found a map."

"A map? What kind of map?"

"Not like a treasure map or anything. It was in with a bunch of stuff about fishing."

Fishing? I remembered Buchanan's funeral, the hat, the lures.

Tink continued. "The map had little X's on it, marking streams and rivers. There were also notes with dates and numbers and names of fish."

Buchanan not only loved to fish, he sounded organized about his hobby.

"He'd actually taken the time to write down where he fished and what he'd caught?"

"Yeah." Tink chuckled. "Can you believe that? From the map, it looked like he did a lot of fishing around Roseman State Park."

"That's not unusual. Roseman is a popular fishing spot. I think they catch catfish, walleye, and bluegill out at the river."

"Mr. Buchanan sure did. From the dates, he went out there two or three times a week."

Tink was distracting me from the original subject—a lecture on *not* snooping in people's private papers. Maybe I wasn't the most qualified, given some of the things I'd done, to be the one to deliver such a talking-to, but I wasn't going to let it stop me. If she brought up any of my experiences, I'd fall back on the old "Do what I say, not what I do."

"Forget about the fishing, and let's get back to what you and Aunt Dot did . . . " My voice trailed off when I saw the scowl on her face. "Tink, you need to be careful—"

"We didn't break any laws," she said defensively.

"I'm not too sure about that one, but that's not what I meant." I stopped again, uncertain how to continue. I didn't want to frighten her, but she needed to be aware of the rumors.

I took a deep breath. "Bill stopped by the library. He told me there are stories going around that you have inside information about Buchanan's murder—"

"I don't," she exclaimed, interrupting me. "Just those creepy dreams."

"I know that, but people in town are saying that you do, whether it's true or not."

She shoved back in the chair. "That's crazy."

"I agree, but it's not like we can take out an ad in *The Courier* announcing that you don't know anything. And your little trick this afternoon, visiting Buchanan's, isn't going to help quash the rumors." I nibbled on my lip. "Someone killed Mr. Buchanan, and if they believed you knew something—"

"They might come after me," she said with finality.

"Yes, that's why going to the funeral home wasn't a smart move. We all need to stay as far away from the investigation as we can."

"But what about those dreams and the skull T.P. found?"

"Bill's going to have to deal with the skull and figure out that one without our help." I let out a long sigh. "And the dreams . . . I don't know what to do. Abby and I have talked about it." I hesitated. "We might try a séance."

Tink's face blanched. "I don't like that idea."

"Don't worry, we certainly wouldn't force you to do one. Abby only brought it up as an option." I gave her a reassuring smile. "We'll get to the bottom of it, sweetie."

She gave me a doubtful look.

"Right now, though, my main concern is your safety. I don't want you going off by yourself—you stick close to Abby or me," I said, shaking a finger at her. "Be alert to your surroundings, don't let any strangers approach you—"

"I know, I know," she replied in a weary voice. "They talk about this stuff at school."

"Then remember what they've said." Satisfied that she took me seriously, I changed the subject. "Did you borrow money from Abby today?"

"Yeah."

"Did you spend it?" I asked, sitting back against the couch and letting Queenie jump on my lap.

"Yeah," she said with a small smile.

"I'd better give you the money now, so you can pay her back when I drop you off in the morning." I motioned toward the hallway. "I think my backpack is by the door."

She shoved out of her chair and crossed to the hallway.

I smiled to myself as I stroked Queenie's black fur. Tink got the message. She was a smart girl. She'd outfoxed her aunt Juliet when Juliet tried to keep her doped up. I scratched Queenie's ears. I swear, she and Aunt Dot were quite the pair, and if the situation hadn't been so serious, one would have to admire their nerve and resourcefulness.

Looking over my shoulder, I wondered what was taking her so long. My billfold with the money was in the front pocket of the bag.

"Tink, did you find the money?" I called out.

No answer.

"Tink," I called again.

Silence.

I moved Queenie off my lap and went to find her.

She sat in the hallway with her back against the wall. Her knees were drawn tightly to her chest, and her blond head rested on them. Lady and T.P. lay by the kitchen door, staring at her.

I looked down to see papers scattered across the floor.

Taking a step toward her, I reached out my hand. "What's wrong?"

She lifted her head. Tears ran down her face and terror filled her eyes. "I've got to get out of here," she shrieked, and scrambled to her feet.

I grabbed her arm before she could dart up the stairs. "What on earth is wrong?"

Jerking away, she whirled on me. Anger had replaced the terror in her eyes. "You weren't going to tell me about the letters, were you?"

My forehead wrinkled in confusion. "What letters?"

"Those," she said, pointing a trembling hand at the papers lying jumbled on the floor. "I found them in your backpack.

They're from Juliet," she said, her voice frantic. "She's coming for me."

Tink watched, curled up in a tight ball in the wing chair, while I read the typed sheets of paper. Now my hands were trembling as I flipped each page. The messages sounded like they were from Juliet, but it was impossible. She was still locked up in the mental hospital in Minnesota. She couldn't have planted them in my bag at the library that day.

But the letters? They mentioned Tink's childhood, her mother who'd died when Tink was little, and Tink's special gift. They went on to say my adoption of Tink was wrong, and that she, Juliet, would never allow it. Tink belonged with her and she had no intention of ever letting Tink go.

Whoever wrote those letters knew a lot about Tink.

I placed the letters on the coffee table and rubbed my palms on my jeans as if I'd handled something dirty.

"Have you told anyone about your past?"

Her eyes refused to meet mine. "Nell. A little." She swiped at her nose with the back of her hand. "But Nell's my best friend, and she wouldn't rat me out to anyone."

"Someone knows about your life before you came to Iowa." I rubbed my forehead trying to organize the thoughts bouncing around in my brain. "I—"

Tink's attention turned to the hallway. I glanced over the back of the couch in time to see Abby striding across the room followed by Aunt Dot. I blew out a shaky breath. Abby would be able to make sense of these letters.

Aunt Dot hobbled over to Tink and tugged her to her feet. "Come, child, let's make you a cup of nice hot tea."

Ah, yes, tea. Our family's first line of defense when meeting a disaster, I thought sarcastically. A cup of tea wasn't going to solve this problem.

Sitting next to me, Abby picked up the papers and swiftly read through them. When she finished, she placed them back on the coffee table.

"They're not from Juliet." Her voice sounded convinced.

"How do you know? She could have somehow sent someone down here to plant them."

"Who?"

"I don't know." I ran a hand through my hair in frustration. "Maybe she smuggled them to Jason—"

"Jason's willing to give up legal custody of Tink."

"Okay, so not him. How about one of the other cult members?"

"First of all, most of the members dispersed before Juliet put on her show at the old cabin, so I doubt if they even know what happened that night," Abby said, stroking the hair away from my face.

"Winnie did. And she escaped into the woods as the cabin burnt to the ground." I felt a prickle of fear. "Winnie was devoted to Juliet. She'd do anything for her."

"I imagine Winnie's too busy avoiding the warrant out for her arrest to worry about Juliet right now." She took my hand in hers. "And even if she did try and contact Juliet, it would be improbable she could get in to see her. Juliet's only visitor is Jason."

"Maybe Juliet mailed them," I said, trying to come up with an explanation for the letters.

Abby shook her head. "All mail is monitored before it's sent."

"You seem awfully convinced Juliet didn't write these. Did you pick anything up from touching them?"

"No, I didn't sense anything, but there are several incorrect statements in them."

"Such as?"

"Tink's age when her mother died—the reference is off by two years."

I frowned. "I missed that."

"I'm sure you'd have caught it if you weren't so upset," she said, squeezing my hand.

"What else?"

"The letters mention Frederick Von Shuler as a great magician—"

"He was at one time," I broke in.

"Yes, and he was also Tink's great-grandfather. Wouldn't Juliet have referred to him as such?"

"I suppose," I replied. "How did someone learn all of this about Tink?"

"Has Tink shared her past with anyone at school?"

"Nell, but she swears Nell wouldn't divulge her secrets." I leaned back against the couch and stared at the ceiling. "This information had to be leaked by someone close to us—"

The doorbell interrupted my next remark.

"I'll get it," Aunt Dot called from the kitchen.

Minutes later Darci strolled into the living room. "Hey, having a party?" She looked first at me, then at Abby. "Guess not. What's going on?" she asked, taking the spot where Tink had sat.

Abby quickly told Darci about the letters.

Her mouth opened as a strange expression flitted across her face. Closing her mouth, she chewed on her bottom lip.

"You were at the counter today," I said. "Did you notice any strangers hanging about?"

"I don't know." Her eyes darted to the side. "We were busy . . . " Her voice trailed away and her face twisted.

"You were complaining that you didn't have anything to do—Gert was taking care of everyone—"

"Well, ah, I . . . " Darci squirmed.

My eyes narrowed as I watched her. She knew something that she wasn't telling me. For some reason she looked guilty as hell.

"Spill it, Darce," I commanded.

"I don't know anything, honest. It's—" She stopped.

"It's what?" I persisted.

She exhaled slowly. "I wasn't at the counter the whole time. I got bored, so I went to the bathroom and called Georgia on my cell phone."

An awful thought occurred to me. Georgia was one of Darci's closest friends, and I knew they shared information with one another.

"Did you tell Georgia anything about Tink's past?" I asked, putting my thoughts into words.

"No, of course not," she huffed. "If you must know, I was whining about working with Gert. That woman drives me bonkers."

"You've never told Georgia about what happened in Minnesota?"

"Ophelia." Abby touched my arm in warning.

"What are you saying?" Darci's voice tinged with temper.

"Only someone close to us knows about Tink's past—"

Darci jumped to her feet. "Are you accusing me of writing these letters?"

I stood. "I'm not saying that, but what if you did let something slip about Tink, and Georgia repeated it. She does love a good story, and what happened in Minnesota was a dinger—"

"I'd never do anything to hurt Tink," she exclaimed, her voice rising.

"I'm sure you didn't mean to, but someone heard the story and used it to write that trash. You're the only one who knows what happened, and if you told Georgia—"

"Ophelia Jensen, that's the rottenest thing you've ever said to me!" Her eyes were shooting daggers at me.

Mine shot them right back.

"I didn't accuse you of telling on purpose, but we both know you like to talk—"

"We both should also know that I can keep my mouth shut, too." She glowered at me.

Abby rose as if to separate us. "Girls, girls," she exclaimed. "Simmer down."

We ignored her.

Darci shoved both hands on her hips. "I can't believe you'd think I'd betray your secrets—"

I shifted to one foot. "You had a guilty look on your face when we were talking about the letters," I countered, my voice ringing in my own ears.

"I felt guilty because I wasn't at the counter where I should've been, not because I've spilled my guts to Georgia about Tink!"

"How was I supposed to know that?" I said, taking a step back.

"Because you're my best friend and you ought to trust me," she cried with a stamp of her foot. She spun away and strode out of the living room. Seconds later I heard the front door close with a bang.

Slowly, I sank to the couch. "I didn't need that," I said in a tired voice.

"You shouldn't have accused Darci of giving Georgia information about Tink," Abby said, standing above me.

I winced and drew a hand across my forehead. "You're right. I kind of lost it." I rose on stiff legs. "I'd better talk to Tink."

Aunt Dot stood at the kitchen sink, washing two cups.

"Just put those in the dishwasher, Aunt Dot," I said, joining her at the sink. I glanced over my shoulder at the table. "Where's Tink?"

"She heard shouting and went in the living room," Aunt Dot replied in a perplexed voice.

"No she didn't." I ran from the kitchen and up the stairs. Lady followed close behind me, but I didn't see T.P. in my rush. I flew down the hall and into Tink's room.

Clothes lay scattered on the floor and across the bed. Her closet door was swung wide open and her duffel bag was gone. T.P.'s leash, usually hanging on Tink's doorknob, had disappeared.

Suddenly, my legs couldn't hold me. I grabbed a bedpost to steady myself.

"Abby! Abby!" I hollered, my throat clogged with unshed tears. "Tink's run away!"

# Eighteen

"Quit pacing, Ophelia. It won't bring Tink home any sooner," Abby said calmly from her place at the kitchen table.

Three steaming mugs of hot tea sat there. Mine untouched.

I peered out the kitchen window into the darkness. "We should've gone looking for her, too."

"Bill will find her. She can't have covered much distance on foot." Abby came and stood next to me at the window. "We need to be here in case she comes home on her own."

I rubbed my arms. "What *was* she thinking?"

Abby drew me close to her side. "I don't imagine she was."

"A killer's out there." I leaned my head on her shoulder. "Someone's trying to scare her—" Stopping short, I raised my head. "You don't think it's him, do you, the one who wrote the letters? He heard the rumors, heard about her past, and is coming after her?"

"My dear—"

I walked away from her and circled the room. "What if he's out there? What if he's been watching the house, waiting for a chance to get her alone? What if—"

"Ophelia," she said in a stern voice. "Cease the 'what ifs' immediately."

Halting, I stared at her with fear in my face. "Do you think Bill believed our explanation about the letters?"

She shrugged. "I don't know if he believed someone had taken rumors and twisted them to frighten Tink. I did hear him tell Alan to have another deputy put a call into the mental hospital. They'll find out what Juliet's condition is and whether she could've somehow sent those letters."

"What if she's escaped? People do, you know."

Abby walked up to me and gave me a shake. "Knock it off. Your worrying isn't helping anyone. If Bill isn't back in fifteen minutes, we'll go to Tink's room and I'll use a personal item to try and sense where she is."

"You don't see anything when it's a member of the family," I said, hugging myself tightly.

"Maybe this time I will. It's worth—"

The front door slammed.

We all rushed into the hallway.

Bill stood in the doorway, and right next to him, Tink.

I didn't know whether to shake her or hug her. The hug won.

"You scared me to death," I whispered in her ear as I held her slight body close to mine.

"Sorry," she replied in a muffled voice.

I stepped back and laid my palm on her smooth cheek. "Don't you ever run away again."

Tink gave a bob of her head.

Abby and Aunt Dot were next in welcoming back the prodigal. Aunt Dot gave a loud sniff as she pulled a hanky out of her pocket and wiped her eyes.

Hooking my arm through Tink's, I led everyone to the living room. When we were all seated, I gave Bill a big smile. "Thanks."

"I'm glad we found her," he replied.

"Where was she?"

"Hitchhiking along Highway 169."

I clutched Tink's arm. That's it—I was locking this kid up until she was at least twenty-five.

"You're—"

"I know," Tink said with reluctance. "Grounded."

"Right!" I exclaimed. Taking a deep breath, I continued in a calmer voice, "Where were you going?"

"Minnesota."

"To do what?" I asked, my voice rising again.

Abby gave me a nudge to the ribs.

"Were you going to see Juliet?" I asked in an even tone.

"Are you kidding?" she asked in disbelief. "I figured I'd hide out at Walks Quietly's until the adoption was all set."

"Running away isn't going to help the adoption. What do you think a judge would say about you taking off like you did?"

"I hadn't thought about that," she replied, bowing her head.

Satisfied my words had made an impression, I sat back. "Well—"

"Actually, Tink leaving town might not be a bad idea," Bill interjected with a smile at her before turning his attention to me. "It would get her out of harm's way and give these rumors a chance to die down."

"Are you suggesting that I send her back to Minnesota?"

"No, but don't you have family she could visit?"

I exchanged a look with Abby. "Aunt Rose in Cedar Rapids?"

Abby turned to Bill. "My sister-in-law," she explained. Tapping her chin, she thought about the possibility. "If I can find someone to look after the greenhouse, I could take Aunt

Dot and Tink on a visit to Rose's." She cast a glance their way. "It would keep them both out of trouble."

"'Both' out of trouble?" Bill said in a wary voice. "What does that mean?"

"Just a figure of speech, Bill." Standing, Abby placed a hand on my head. "Are you going to be okay?"

"I will be now," I said, squeezing Tink's hand.

She moved her hand from my head to Tink's. "And you, young lady, no more foolishness."

"I'd best be going, too," Bill said, standing. "I couldn't persuade you to go with them, could I, Ophelia?"

I held up my hand, palm forward. "I'm not going to muddle in your investigation this time, Bill. I promise."

At the library the next morning, I was surprised to see Gert behind the counter instead of Darci. To be honest, I was relieved. I knew I'd eventually need to talk to her and resolve the fight we'd had, but I wasn't prepared to face it today.

"Hi, Gert," I said, holding my backpack firmly to my side. After yesterday, I intended to keep it within eyesight at all times. "Darci isn't coming in?"

"No, she called me late last night and asked if I could work for her this morning. She sounded like she has a cold."

Raising an eyebrow, I said nothing.

"Ah, about Darci . . . I know the two of you are good friends—" She hesitated.

Humph, good friends? Right now I questioned the depth of that friendship.

"Darci doesn't like me," she blurted. "I seem to annoy her."

"It isn't that," I lied. "She's not used to having new staff at the library. You're the first employee we've hired since I've been here."

Gert watched me with a thoughtful expression. "How long has she worked here?"

"Over six years. Why?"

"Oh, no reason." She ran her fingers up and down the chain holding her pendant. "I would've thought her tenure a lot less."

"Really?" Picking up a stack of phone messages, I thumbed through them. "What makes you say that?"

"It's not for me to criticize," she replied, turning to the bookshelves behind us, "but I would've thought someone with that amount of time on the job would have a higher level of performance."

Okay, I *was* mad at Darci at the moment. And I did think that somehow she'd let information slip to Georgia. But my current feelings didn't mean I would join in knocking her.

"Darci has her own skills that are an asset to the library," I said in a curt tone.

Gert swiftly laid a hand on my arm. "As I said, I don't mean to judge her. After all, I really don't know her that well."

"Once you do, I'm sure you'll get along fine," I said, putting an end to that line of conversation. "I need to return these calls. Can you handle the counter?"

Gert smiled. "No problem."

Later that morning, after I'd returned my calls, I was back at the counter when Abby and Tink arrived, but without Aunt Dot.

"Where's Aunt Dot?" I asked after hugging them both.

"She's home packing," Abby said.

Glancing over my shoulder, I noticed Gert standing a couple of feet away.

"Gert, this is my grandmother, Abigail McDonald, and my daughter Tink. Abby, our new employee, Gert Duncan."

"Very nice to meet you," Abby replied, grasping her hand. "Ophelia told me that you're new to Summerset?"

"Yes, ma'am. Mama and I are renting a house just outside of town," she answered pleasantly. "Mama loves it in the country, but it's a little isolated for me." Gert gave me an ingratiating smile. "This job is a real blessing."

Abby smiled in return. "I hope you enjoy working here."

"Oh, I surely do," Gert exclaimed with passion.

"Gert's the master of organization," I explained to Abby and Tink.

Gert preened at my compliment.

"Good," Abby said. "My granddaughter could certainly use some help in that area." Her eyes traveled to the pendant Gert always wore. "My, that's a lovely piece of jewelry. Is it an heirloom?"

"Oh, no. Just something I picked up on the Internet. Gets in the way sometimes." She tucked the pendant inside her blouse and turned her attention to Tink, who'd remained silent during the introductions. "I understand you help your great-grandmother at the greenhouse?"

"Yes," Tink said with a cheeky grin, "but I'm not very good at keeping the plants alive, so I do a lot of weeding."

Abby chuckled. "She's getting better. At least now she knows the difference between a velvet leaf and a dahlia." She patted Tink's arm. "She also has a very good eye for color and has been very helpful to customers in their selection of plants for their gardens."

"Your aunt isn't with you, Mrs. McDonald?" Gert asked, looking over Abby's shoulder.

"No, she stayed home this morning to pack."

"Oh." Gert sounded disappointed. "I'd hoped to meet her during her visit. I've heard so much about her."

"She'll be here for a while longer. Right now, we're taking a short trip to visit my sister-in-law in Cedar Rapids."

"Are you going, Ophelia?" Gert inquired.

"No, I didn't feel now was a good time to leave the library. I might drive up next weekend."

"You'll be gone that long, Mrs. McDonald?" Gert's face mirrored her surprise.

"We're not sure."

"Who's going to take care of the greenhouse, Abby?" I asked.

"I talked to Arthur last night. He thinks, with Michael Nolan's help, they can manage. He understood our need to get away," she answered cryptically.

Gert shot her a questioning look but didn't comment. "It was lovely meeting you, but I must get back to work." She motioned to the pile of books sitting at the edge of the counter.

Drawing Abby toward the door and out of earshot of Gert, I said, "So the trip's all set?"

"Yes, I've talked to Rose and we can stay as long as we want. I'm planning on leaving first thing in the morning."

I exhaled a long breath. "I wish there was another solution."

"I do, too, but for now, this is best." She glanced at her watch. "I'd better get home . . . I've lots to do. Come on, Tink."

I kissed Tink's cheek and stepped back. "You'll pack tonight?"

"Yeah."

"Plenty of clean clothes?"

"Yeah."

"Okay, I'll see you after work."

As they were leaving, I overheard Tink.

"Are you sure I can't bring T.P.?" she pleaded.

Abby's laugh drifted through the open door. "Aunt Rose doesn't tolerate animals in the house."

A sense of loneliness flooded me as I watched the library door swing shut. I didn't know how long Abby and Tink would be gone, and Darci and I were fighting. For the first time in a long time, I'd be well and truly alone. Once, I'd have welcomed the solitude, but now the idea left me with an empty feeling in the pit of my stomach. How and when had my attitude shifted? What happened to the wall that I'd so carefully built to isolate myself? I knew. It lay in rubble.

"You look sad," Gert said, slipping next to me.

I shrugged. "I was thinking about how much I'll miss Abby and Tink."

"She's a lovely girl. You must be very proud of her."

Smiling, I turned and walked back to the counter. "I am."

Gert followed me. "The name Titania suits her. There's a regalness about her, even at this age."

"There is, isn't there." I stopped suddenly. "How did you know her real name is Titania?"

"Oh, Darci mentioned it," Gert replied with a wave. "She said her real mother nicknamed her Tinkerbell because she was so tiny."

I winced at Gert's term "real mother." "Did Darci say anything else about Tink?" I asked suspiciously.

Gert appeared astonished at my sudden change in demeanor. "No. Why?"

"No reason," I answered, blowing her off.

My mind whirled with suppositions, and my churning stomach drove the empty feeling away. If Darci talked about Tink to someone she barely knew, and someone she wasn't sure she liked, how much more would she tell her close friend, Georgia?

\* \* \*

Gert left after lunch to take her mama to a doctor's appointment, so Brenda and I manned the counter. The traffic through the library was light. It was a beautiful day—moderate temperatures and, for once, low humidity. Unusual for Iowa at this time of the year. I imagined most people were spending the day outside, enjoying the weather.

"Brenda, I'll be downstairs. I'm going to look over the last catalog we received containing the new releases. See if there's anything we want to order."

I'd reached the top of the stairs when the phone rang. I heard Brenda answer it.

"Ophelia, it's Abby!" she called out.

Rolling my eyes, I crossed to the telephone. She probably had some last minute instructions for me.

"Hi, Abby," I answered brightly into the receiver. "What's—"

Abby's shrill voice broke off my question. "Come immediately. We can't find Tink."

# *Nineteen*

The scenery flew by the car window, but my unseeing eyes didn't notice the green fields of corn, the huge round bales of hay dotting the hillsides, or the slender stalks of oats blowing in the summer breeze. My entire focus was on reaching Abby's.

Had Tink run away again? My heart said no.

I took a curve too fast and felt the tires slide in the loose gravel. Madly steering out of the skid, I whipped the car back to the center of the road.

Maybe this was all a mistake—when I reached Abby's, Tink would be sitting at the kitchen table, drinking ice tea and getting a good scolding from Abby for scaring us so.

The tears in my eyes made the road ahead shimmer. I blinked them away. Until I knew exactly what was going on, I didn't have the time to cave in to emotions.

As I tore up Abby's lane, my worst fears were confirmed. I wouldn't find Tink inside—Bill's sheriff's car sat in the driveway. Barely coming to a stop, I threw the car into park, grinding the transmission. I bolted from the vehicle and rushed into the house.

Abby and Aunt Dot sat closely together on the couch in the living room. They held each other's hands in a tight grip, as if clinging to a life raft. Every line, every wrinkle on Abby's face, stood out in the late afternoon sunshine that poured through her lace curtains. The braid she wore twisted around her head looked bedraggled, and strands of silver stuck out in every direction.

Aunt Dot watched her with eyes full of concern and fear.

Bill sat in a chair next to the couch with a pen and notebook in hand. Tiny beads of sweat had gathered on his shiny bald head, but he appeared too intent on listening to Abby to take notice.

I paused at the doorway, and as I did, three somber faces turned to me at the same time.

Without a word, Bill stood, walked over to me, taking my arm, and guided me to a chair.

"You haven't found her?" My voice rose on a hopeful note.

"No," Abby gasped while her eyes flitted away from mine as if she couldn't bear to look at me. "I'm to blame. It's such a nice day . . . we were busy . . . Tink asked if she could fetch the mail. Without thinking, I said yes." Her voice cracked. "The mailbox is only down at the end of the lane. You can see it from the house—" She ended with a sob.

Each word Abby said was like a knife twisting in my heart, but I couldn't stand to witness her pain.

"Abby, it's not your fault—"

Her eyes flew to mine. "Yes, it is. We'd agreed to not let Tink out of our sight."

"You couldn't have known someone would have . . . have . . ." I couldn't say the word. Turning to Bill, I swallowed hard. "Is the mail gone?"

"No." He glanced at Abby. "After they realized Tink had disappeared, everyone started searching. When they couldn't find her, Abby called me."

"Bill—" I began, not hiding the fear in my eyes.

"We've contacted the highway patrol, deputies are organizing a search party, we've talked to Nell and her parents to see if they know anything, and we've called the sheriff's department in Crow Wing County, Minnesota. He's going to contact Tink's friend, Walks Quietly."

"She didn't run away," I said with conviction.

"Ophelia, we have to examine all the possibilities. She ran last night," he pointed out.

"She was afraid. She thought Juliet was coming for her—" I stopped and leaned forward as a thought occurred to me. "Is Juliet—"

"We've talked to the hospital. She's still incarcerated and not had any visitors other than Jason." He paused. "What's more, she's delusional, and the doctor said half the time she doesn't even know where she is."

"She didn't write the letters," I stated in a flat voice.

"No, the doctor said it was impossible." He turned his attention to Abby. "Did Tink seem frightened today?"

Abby silently shook her head.

Bill looked at me. "Was she resisting the trip to Cedar Rapids?"

"No, no. The last thing I heard her say—" My throat tightened, making it difficult to speak. "She was begging Abby to take her dog with them." I cleared my throat. "Bill, she didn't run away."

He bowed his head.

"You warned me she might be in danger—the letters—someone was targeting her," I insisted. "Was there any sign of a struggle at the end of the lane?"

"No."

Defeated, I leaned back. "You *do* think she ran, don't you?"

Bill picked at the cover of his notebook. "I don't know.

Like I said, there isn't a sign of a struggle, which might indicate she left of her own free will." He wiped his head. "Or it could mean she knew the person. Or it happened so fast that she didn't have time to put up a fight."

A tear leaked down my face.

"I don't want to make the wrong call, so I am treating this as a kidnapping."

There—it was said. The word everyone had been avoiding. Kidnapped. I didn't want Bill to think she'd run away, but somehow saying the word made it all real.

I swallowed the bile suddenly rising from my stomach.

Aunt Dot's shoulders shook as she silently cried, while Abby sat there looking shell-shocked. How were we ever going to get through this ordeal?

Wiping the tears away, I took a deep breath and exhaled. "What happens now?"

"I'm going to post Tink's picture and description on a website dealing with missing and exploited children." He flipped open his notebook again. "I'll need to know what she was wearing."

What she was wearing? How was she dressed at the library? I tried to remember, but my brain felt like a congealed mass of nothing. I couldn't remember. I told myself I *should* remember. Shorts—she was wearing shorts. What color? Blue. No, red with a white strip down the side. Wait a minute—that's what she wore yesterday.

"I can't remember," I said in a plaintive voice.

Aunt Dot wiped her eyes. "She had on dark pink shorts with a light pink top."

Bill scribbled in his notebook. "Anything else? Shoes? Cap?"

"A pink baseball cap and white tennis shoes," Aunt Dot answered.

"Abby . . ."

She looked at Bill as if his voice was coming from far away.

" . . . I need a list of everyone who was at the greenhouse today. Maybe someone saw something," he said gently. "And I'll need a list from you, Ophelia, of everyone who might have had access to your backpack at the library."

"I spent the day in my office. I don't know who came in."

"Who worked upstairs?"

"Darci and our new employee, Gert Duncan."

He wrote their names in his notebook. "You have a number and an address for Ms. Duncan?"

"The Duncans are renting the old Blunt place, and I have her number at the library. But she's new to the area, and she wouldn't know if a patron lived in Summerset or if they were a stranger."

"I'll send one of the deputies out to talk to her anyway."

"What can I do?"

A sad expression marked his face. "Nothing."

"Can't I join the search party?"

"It wouldn't do any good, Ophelia."

I stared at him with resignation. "You don't think you'll find anything, do you?"

I got my answer when he looked away.

"The best thing you can do to help is go home, in case either Tink, or the person who grabbed her, tries to contact you." He got to his feet and watched Abby with kind eyes. "I know you're upset, but the sooner I get that list, the better."

Abby released Aunt Dot's hand. As she wiped the tears from her cheeks, she lifted her chin and straightened her shoulders. Her face settled into an expression marked with steely resolve. Slapping her legs, she rose to her feet. "I'll make that list now. Today's receipts should help." She crossed to me, pulled me to my feet, and grabbed my upper arms. "We *will* find her," she said with a shake. "You go home. Aunt Dot and I will join you later." She glanced back at Bill. "I'm closing the greenhouse until this is over."

Bill nodded in agreement. "That's a good idea. Once word gets out, there'll be curiosity seekers showing up, and maybe the media."

"The media?" I said, startled. "Newspaper reporters?"

"Yes, and probably a TV crew, but you don't have to talk to them. Let our office handle them."

I groaned. Last thing I needed was a bunch of people camped out on my front lawn.

"Media attention isn't always a bad thing, Ophelia," Bill said. "The more people who know about Tink's disappearance, the bigger the chance someone might step forward with a lead."

"I suppose you're right," I mumbled.

I guess I didn't care how many reporters tramped over my yard as long as their attention helped locate Tink.

"Do you need one of my men to drive you home?" Bill asked.

I shook my head. "No, I can manage."

"Good," he replied with satisfaction. "The next few days are going to be tough on you, but you can't give up hope." He settled his hat on his head. "Don't worry—we'll find her."

The drive home from Abby's seemed like the longest one in my life. No one followed, and I arrived home without incident. With heavy steps, I exited the car and walked up the steps to the porch. I unlocked the door, crossed the threshold, and let the door swing shut behind me.

Lady and T.P. came scampering toward me, anxious to get

outside. Like a robot, I walked through the house and let the dogs out into the backyard.

I wandered back to the kitchen and put out fresh food and water. From her perch on the windowsill, Queenie watched me with interest. A scratching at the back door, followed by a short bark, let me know the dogs were ready to come inside.

The animals tended and happily gobbling down their supper, I pulled out a chair and collapsed. My eyes traveled the empty room.

No rock and roll blared from the stereo in Tink's room. No chatter relating the day's events sounded in my ears. The silence in the house pressed down so hard, it felt like it was crushing me. The control that I'd maintained the last few hours slid away under its weight.

My head sank lower and lower, until my forehead rested on the kitchen table. Covering my head with my arms, my insides cracked. Hot tears formed a pool beneath my face.

I took a deep breath, and all the pain poured out of my soul in one ear-shattering wail.

# Twenty

The phone began ringing at 7:00 A.M. Throwing off the covers, I rushed to look at the caller ID. The number wasn't familiar to me.

Did I answer or let it ring? It could be Tink, or it could be a nosy neighbor. I answered.

"Ophelia, I'm so sorry to hear about Tink." It was Edna Walters.

"I'm sorry Edna, but Bill said to keep the line open." With that I hit End.

Grabbing the robe from the foot of my bed, I made my way to the kitchen for a cup of coffee. Abby had made sure it was ready to go in the morning, so all I had to do was flip on the switch.

I waited, coffee cup in one hand, drumming my fingers with the other, for the pot to eke out at least enough for one cup. Satisfied I'd have at least a few sips, I poured the black liquid into the cup.

It had been a short night. Abby and Aunt Dot arrived late in the evening, bearing food and groceries. I shuddered as I sipped the hot coffee. The thought of braving the stares of the curious at the store made me physically ill. Right now, thanks to them, we had enough food to last a week. By then maybe Tink would be found.

I had slept, but not much. If I remembered correctly, the last time I'd looked at my alarm clock the time had read 3:00 a.m. I glanced at the phone on the kitchen counter and chewed on my bottom lip. How were we going to handle the calls? We had to answer all of them, just in case a call came from Tink or—I shuddered again—the person who held her captive.

I was so lost in my thoughts that Aunt Dot tottering into the kitchen surprised me.

She gave me a hug, and stepping back, looked me up and down. "How are you this morning? Did you sleep?"

I lifted one shoulder. "A little. Did you?"

"A little," she said with a small grin.

"How's Abby?"

"Ack," Aunt Dot said with a wave of her hand as the grin fled her face. "Still blaming herself."

"It's not her fault."

"Well, maybe you can convince her, because she wouldn't listen to me."

"Aunt Dot, you know about the family's history. Why can't we see each other's future?"

"These gifts that have been handed down are sometimes hard enough to bear." She rubbed her cast absentmindedly. "Sister thinks it's a way our sanity is protected. A body would never know a moment's peace if we saw all of life's troubles. Especially when it comes to our loved ones."

"I know you love Tink, too, but you're a little more removed than Abby and me. Have you sensed anything?"

Aunt Dot removed the eggs and milk from the fridge with her left hand. After setting them down, she moved to the cupboard and brought out a box of pancake mix and a bowl.

Placing the bowl on the counter, she began cracking eggs into it.

I assumed she hadn't heard me.

I repeated my question louder. "Aunt Dot, do you sense anything?"

She paused. "I heard you the first time."

"Well? Do you?"

Placing the shells on the counter, she turned and faced me. "I was up before dawn, and I went in the backyard to find the fairies. They like Titania, you know. They'll guard her."

Number one—I didn't believe in fairies, and even though I loved Aunt Dot to death, I thought she was a little addled around the edges. Two—if they did exist as she claimed, it would take more than a fairy to protect Tink from a kidnapper.

But I was desperate, and willing to listen to even the craziest of theories. "Did they tell you anything?"

"She's not going to be hurt," she replied, pouring milk into the bowl.

"You're certain?" I asked, my voice skeptical.

"Yes. The one who took her sees her as a prize."

"I don't suppose the fairies gave you any names, did they?"

Aunt Dot picked up a whisk and beat the eggs and milk. "No, but they will keep her from harm."

I wished with every part of me that I could believe her, but I didn't.

"Aunt—"

The phone ringing interrupted me. I made a move to answer it, but Aunt Dot got there first.

She listened for a second. "No, I'm sorry. No comment." Slamming the phone back on its base, she returned to the counter. "Why don't you take your coffee out on the patio while I make the pancakes? You'll go crazy if you stay cooped up inside all day."

Calling the animals, I did as she suggested.

Another nice day. The birds were singing and the air was full of the smell of flowers and fresh cut grass. Across the yard, Lady and T.P. rolled with delight in the morning dew.

How could the day be so peaceful, so beautiful? It wasn't right. It should have been bleak and gray. As bleak and gray on the outside as I felt on the inside.

Was Aunt Dot right? Was Tink unharmed? Was she terrified? Did she know we were searching for her?

For what seemed the millionth time I wondered about the gifts our family possessed. Tink wasn't my biological child, but I loved her as much as if she were. And don't all mothers feel a bond with their child? If I added to the bond that, according to Abby, I was a talented psychic, then why didn't I have a sense of where and how Tink was?

*Because you haven't tried,* said a voice inside my head.

A new thought occurred to me. What if Abby, Aunt Dot, and I joined our energy together and tried to reach out and touch Tink with our minds? To comfort her, to protect her. Maybe, if we were successful, we might learn who held her and why. We could use Abby's books—the journals that had been written by the women in our family and handed down generation to generation—to help us. Surely one contained a spell of protection. We could do the ceremony in Abby's summerhouse.

The idea was worth a shot. At least I'd be doing something instead of waiting helplessly for the phone to ring.

The back door slammed shut, and I twisted in my chair, expecting to see Abby.

Gert Duncan.

"I hope you don't mind—I called Claire for your address. I wanted to stop by and see how you were faring. I don't mean to intrude," Gert said, toying with her pendant.

"It's okay." I pointed to the empty lawn chair. "Have a seat."

"I wanted to tell you not to worry about the library. I spoke with Claire last night, and we'll manage."

I didn't want to ruin her thoughtfulness by telling her that with Tink gone, not once had the library crossed my mind in the past few hours.

"Thanks, Gert. I'm sure it will be in good hands," I replied a little tersely.

Gert leaned forward, her eyes scanning my face. "How *are* you?"

*Get used to it, Jensen, until Tink is found, that's a question you'll be asked a hundred times.*

Should I tell her how I really felt? Like my heart had been ripped out of my chest and tromped on by a herd of elephants.

*No, I'll save my pain for when I'm alone.*

"I'm hanging in there," I replied politely.

Gert sat back and crossed her legs. "This is the most awful thing. A lovely girl like Tink . . . " She abstractedly fingered the silver charm. "She must be beside herself with fear. Humph, God only knows what that poor child is going through."

I knew Gert was only trying to commiserate with me, but her words were like a stick poking a raw wound. I had to put an end to the conversation.

"I appreciate your concern, Gert, but I'd rather not discuss Tink right now."

"Oh, I'm so sorry," she said as a funny look flashed across her face. "Here you are, beside yourself with worry, and I'm rambling on and on. I just wanted you to know that I understand."

I doubted if she truly did understand. How could anyone understand until it happened to their family?

Gert stood. "I'd best be going." She patted my arm sympathetically as she passed by. "You take care, you hear?"

I nodded without answering.

Thankful she'd finally left, I stared out over the yard. I'd been through some tough times—Brian's murder, Grandpa's sudden death of a heart attack—but I'd never felt anything like this. This sense of total, utter uselessness.

I heard the door slam again and a familiar voice came from behind me.

"Are you just going to sit there, or are you going to do something to find Tink?"

Glancing over my shoulder, I saw her standing by the door, her hand fisted on her hip and a challenge in her eyes.

Darci.

After Darci and I were done crying and apologies were made—mine—we set about making plans.

"I'll stay here at the house to answer the phone while the three of you go to Abby's," Darci said.

"I need to run this plan by her," I replied with hesitation. "She's not thinking straight right now."

"Why?"

"She blames herself."

"She shouldn't."

"I know. Aunt Dot tried to convince her, but it didn't work. I hope I can."

"Hmm . . . " Darci thought for a moment. "What's Plan B if the ceremony doesn't work?"

"Plan B?" I blew out a breath. "I don't have a Plan B. Do you have any ideas?"

She pursed her lips. "Not at the moment." Her eyes widened and she snapped her fingers. "I'll make a list."

I made a derisive sound. "What kind of list?"

"Oh, you know, one with all the suspects, a timeline, everything weird that's happened, that kind of stuff," she said with a wave of her hand.

"Darce, that only works on TV shows and in the movies."

She arched an eyebrow. "You got a better idea?"

"No, I don't," I said with a sigh. "Go ahead, make your list. At this point, it can't hurt, and who knows, maybe you'll be able to make some sense out of this tangled mess."

"Listen to me." She leaned forward, her face intense. "I have a lot of faith in our ability to figure things out. And I think we've been pretty successful for a couple of amateurs—"

"It was blind luck."

"So? Who cares how we did it? We still solved the crimes." She tossed her head. "I know you didn't want to get involved in this investigation, that you promised Bill—"

I held up a hand, cutting her off. "All bets are off now." I stared at her with a glint in my eye. "I *am* involved. Whoever took Tink made this very, very personal. I'm going to use every means at my disposal to hunt them down." I pushed myself out of the chair. "Whether Bill likes it or not."

# *Twenty-One*

We escorted Aunt Dot across the yard to the summerhouse. It had been Abby's private space since Grandpa brought her to Iowa. Inside, Aunt Dot seated herself in the old rocking chair, while Abby and I examined the rows of old journals contained on the bookshelves.

"Aunt Dot," Abby said as her eyes traveled down the row of worn books. "Whose journal do you think might have the spell we need?"

"Ack, I don't think we've had this happen before in the family." She slowly rocked back and forth. "The closest thing would be when cousin Edgar ran off and joined the circus at the age of ten."

"Who was Edgar's mother?"

"Minnie." Aunt Dot shook her head. "I don't know what his mother did to that boy when she found him, but Edgar feared clowns for the rest of his life."

"Did she use a spell to locate him?" Abby asked, taking one of the old journals in hand.

"I'm sorry, I can't remember."

"Hmm." Abby thumbed through the pages of the book. "Ophelia, you start at the other end. Look at each journal and see if you can find anything about searching for lost children."

I did as she asked. I found remedies for easing childbirth, curing a child of the croup, protecting yourself from gossip, but nothing about missing children.

Finally, Abby slammed one of the books shut. "This is taking too long. We're just going to wing it."

She walked to the cupboard and took out two blue candles and a silver one. Placing them on a small table in the center of the room, she then removed five stones from a drawer—four blue lace agates and an amethyst. After lighting a small ball of sage contained in an abalone shell, she passed the candles and stones one by one through its purifying smoke. Once she finished with the candles and stones, she set a bowl of water and a bowl of sea salt next to the candles.

Stepping back, she eyed the table. "Do you have the picture of Tink?"

"Here," I said, reaching in my backpack and pulling out Tink's most recent school photograph.

Taking it from me, she laid it carefully on the table in front of the three candles now safely secured in metal candlestick holders. The top right corner of the picture pointed to the north, and she began there, laying the blue lace agate at each point. She laid the amethyst at top center directly in line with Tink's face.

I didn't need to ask what she was doing. The blue lace agates and the blue candles were for communication, to help us in our quest to reach Tink. The positioning of the stones represented the four elements—to the north, Earth; to the west, Air; to the south, Fire; and to the east, Water. The very top stone—the amethyst—represented the Spirit, and, along with the silver candle, would help increase our psychic energy. And if Abby drew imaginary lines between the five stones, it would form a pentagram over the picture of Tink.

Satisfied that all was as it should be, Abby crossed to a small closet and handed both Aunt Dot and me a white cowled robe.

Since Aunt Dot was several inches shorter than Abby, the sleeves of her robe hung down her sides while the hem puddled at her feet. She reminded me of a child playing dress-up in her mother's clothes.

Abby walked back to the table and, picking up the smoking shell, wandered about the room wafting smoke into the corners and around the doors and windows. Then she returned to where Aunt Dot and I stood and did the same to us. We hadn't taken the time to purify ourselves in a saltwater bath, so using the smoking sage was the next best thing.

Together we moved to the table.

Abby picked up the bowl of salt and, walking clockwise, sprinkled a circle around us on the worn floorboards. She joined us at the table, and after adding a pinch of salt, dipped her fingers into the water. Again, moving clockwise, she flicked the water in a circle around us. She lit the candles.

Holding each other's hands, we began.

Staring at Tink's picture, I conjured each of the elements in my mind. Rich black dirt warmed by the summer sun. I inhaled and imagined I caught the scent of lavender and lilacs drifting on a light breeze. I saw logs blazing on the hearth, the heat radiating out from them and chasing away the chill I'd felt since Tink had disappeared. From outside the summerhouse, I heard the whispering of a gentle stream as the water tumbled over rocks in a riverbed.

Finally, the Spirit—Tink's spirit. Her humor, her grace, the way every day was an adventure as she stood poised at the threshold of becoming the person she was meant to be.

My throat tightened as sadness gripped my heart. I felt the

warmth fade and my concentration slip. Worry ate at me.

I scrunched my eyes shut. *Deep, slow breaths, Jensen*, I told myself while I fought to regain control.

Abby sensed my distress and her hand gripped mine firmly. I felt her energy pour into me, strengthening me. A slight squeeze of my own hand let her know that I'd won the battle.

Opening my eyes, I focused on Tink's picture and let all the love I had for her rush out. Her face shimmered in the flickering light as irritation and frustration niggled at me.

Irritation? Frustration? Those feeling weren't mine—they were Tink's.

I stared harder at her picture, and in my mind I flashed back to the night Tink and I had walked in the woods, talking about the adoption.

As in reality, Silas Green suddenly appeared, only in my mind he held a pile of bones in his arms. I gasped in horror as I noticed a shiny gold bracelet dangling from one of the bones. Tink's bracelet. Did it mean Tink was dead? No, she stood next to me, as she had that night in the woods.

I focused again on Silas.

Specters floated around him, their faces angry. Their mouths moved in silent curses. I cocked my head to listen, but the words sounded like static on a radio. Turning, I looked at Tink, only to see her being pulled away from me by invisible hands.

Shock registered on her face, and as she faded in the distance, the sound of a woman's maniacal laughter overrode the static in my head.

I pivoted back to Silas and saw Walks Quietly standing behind him, watching me with disappointment in his eyes.

The spirits swirled and twisted around both of them as images spun through my mind.

Tink, the first day I'd met her at Gunhammer Lake in Minnesota. The awful night at the abandoned cabin when Juliet had tried to use Tink as a vessel to summon a demon. Winnie slinking off into the woods as the cabin burned to the ground. Tink playing with T.P. at Roseman State Park the night of the ill-fated campout.

The images came faster and faster until it felt like my brain was in overdrive.

Panting like a dog, I tried to draw air into my lungs, but I couldn't seem to fill them. My body began shaking so hard, it made my head rattle—

As if someone flipped a light switch, the images ended.

I opened my eyes, not realizing that I'd closed them, to find Abby standing in front of me, shaking me for all she was worth.

"Ophelia!" she exclaimed.

I clenched her arm to stop the shaking. "I'm okay," I said, my voice trembling. "Man, I *hate* it when that happens."

Abby led me over to the rocking chair. "When the images take over?"

"Yeah, this experience was like the one at Darci's when I tried to tune in on the murder this spring." I rubbed my face with my hands. "There's got to be an easier way to do this."

Aunt Dot sat next to me and patted my knee in sympathy. "You're getting your color back now."

Abby handed me a glass of water. "Drink this."

I drained the glass and passed it to Aunt Dot. Resting my head against the back of the rocker, I watched as Abby closed the circle in silence.

She snuffed out the candles, and walking counterclockwise, seemed to drain the energy from the room. After picking up the blue lace agates, she pulled up a chair next to the rocker. She handed one of the stones to Aunt Dot, set aside one for herself, and held out the last two to me.

"Place these in your left pocket," she said as she pressed them into my open palm. "I'm leaving the amethyst by Tink's picture until she comes home." Settling back in her chair, Abby studied me. "How are you feeling?"

"A little shaky."

"Aunt Dot, there's a notebook and a pen on the stand next to you . . . would you please give them to me?"

Aunt Dot did as Abby asked.

"What did you see?" Abby asked then, poising the pen over the blank paper.

Quickly, I related my vision to her, and she scribbled my words down.

Abby nibbled on the end of the pen. "You saw Silas Green? And he had Tink's bracelet?"

"Yeah. I never met the man until a week or so ago. Now, lately, I've run into him at Roseman State Park, at the Farmer's Market, and at Buchanan's funeral."

"You ran into him three times before Tink's disappearance?"

I nodded. "Is that significant?"

She doodled on the paper as she thought about my question. "The number three has a lot of power associated with it."

"What about the bracelet?"

"I don't recall seeing it the day she disappeared. Do you?"

"I couldn't even remember what she had on," I said, scrubbing my face with my hands. "Let alone whether or not she was wearing the bracelet."

"What about Walks Quietly? He was in the vision, too?"

"Uh-huh. He looked disappointed that I'd failed to protect Tink like I'd promised."

"I wonder if Bill has contacted him yet?"

"I need to," I said, rocking back in the chair.

"I think he'll be calling you," Abby said, tapping the pen on the paper, reviewing her notes. "Most of the images were of Gunhammer Lake?"

I puffed out my cheeks and exhaled slowly. "Maybe my subconscious was just reliving our first meeting with Tink." I sat forward, facing her. "Did you see the same things?"

"No, mine were more of the future." A smile broke out. "I saw Tink home safe."

I clutched her hand as I felt a burden lift. "That's terrific, Abby!" I exclaimed.

The smile dropped from her face. "That's the good news . . ."

Why does the good news always have to be followed by bad news?

" . . . the bad news is there seemed to be a wide gulf separating Tink from us—"

"Let me guess," I said, holding up my hand to stop her. "I'm the one that gets to cross it?"

"Yes." She shuddered. "Tink stood on its banks while enraged spirits floated around her." Abby rubbed her arms as if fighting away a chill. "Some were missing appendages."

"That's what Tink's been seeing in her dreams." I thought for a moment. "Tell me more about this gulf. Did you recognize any landmarks?"

"No. All I saw was Tink on one side and you on the other. You were running back and forth trying to find a way across." She frowned. "There was a man standing in the shadows—"

"Silas Green?"

"No, and not Walks Quietly, someone else, but I couldn't see his face. The only other thing that seemed important—a hawk and an eagle circled above you." She watched my reaction. "Does that mean anything to you?"

"No . . . wait, the hawk does. I've seen them before. Remember the time that I felt like I was flying with one?"

"Ophelia," she said sternly. "Apparently the hawk is one of your animal guides, and when you see one, it's significant. You need to pay more attention."

"Got it—watch for hawks. Anything else?"

"No, at that point I noticed you were actually vibrating. My concern for you broke my focus."

I turned to Aunt Dot. "What did you see?"

"Fairies."

I grunted. *Go figure.*

Aunt Dot ignored me. "Two fairies are guarding her."

"That's it?"

"Umm-hmm. In a bedroom with big pink roses on the wall. Tink was pacing back and forth while the fairies watched. One perched on the bedpost." Aunt Dot's eyes glazed over. "She was beautiful—I think she's a wood fairy—she wore a green dress with a crown of oak leaves on her head. The other one—"

"Okay, Aunt Dot, we get the picture. Did you get a sense of where this room was?"

"No, only that she's safe for now."

I put aside my disbelief and asked the question. "Would the fairies tell you where she is?"

"No, they will only protect her. You must find her on your own."

Peachy. And all I had to do was cross a gulf full of danger. Simple.

If I failed, would Tink still make it home safely or would she be lost to us forever?

## Twenty-Two

We removed our robes for Abby to wash later and left to return to the main house.

The experience had raised more questions than answers. I felt relief to know that Tink was safe and waiting for us to find her, but puzzled because I hadn't sensed any fear.

Tink was ticked off, not terrified. Not a normal emotion for one who's been kidnapped and held against her will by a killer. Maybe she hadn't figured out her abductor was a murderer? Maybe they'd made promises not to hurt her if she cooperated with them?

Lost in my thoughts, I rounded the corner of the summerhouse and bumped straight into a solid body. My gaze traveled up his chest, shoulders, neck, until I found myself looking into a pair of very familiar gray eyes.

I took a step back. "Cobra . . . err, Ethan! What are you doing here?" Peering over his shoulder, I noticed Bill standing behind him.

"Hi, Ophelia," Ethan replied with concern. "I heard about your daughter. I'm sorry."

I introduced Abby and Aunt Dot, then eyed him with suspicion. "Are you here officially? Did Bill uncover evidence that the DEA is interested in?"

"No, I'm on a sabbatical, so to speak." He glanced over his shoulder at Bill. "I called him just to see how things were." Looking down at the grass, he grinned. "I wanted to see if you'd mentioned running into me at the airport. He filled me in on what had happened to Tink. Thought maybe I could help," he finished, his eyes meeting mine again.

"How?" I asked, crossing my arms over my chest.

"I know how the system works . . . unless evidence suggests foul play, or a kidnapping, law enforcement assumes the kid ran away—"

"She didn't run away," I said hotly, cutting him off.

"I believe you." Again he looked over his shoulder. "So does Bill. Look, Tink seemed to be a nice kid, and I've got contacts that Bill doesn't. Maybe I can shake loose a lead from one of them."

I'd narrowed my eye as he made this explanation.

"You doubt my motives, don't you?" Ethan asked.

Before I could answer, he shoved his hands in his back pockets and continued. "Do you think I'm still afraid that you'll curse me with those boils?"

Bill went on alert and stepped forward. "Boils? What boils?"

The subject needed to be changed. "Never mind," I said, and resumed walking to the house. "How did you find us?" I asked as Ethan fell into step next to me.

"Darci told Bill when we stopped by your house."

I did a swift calculation on the time. Thank goodness they hadn't showed up thirty minutes earlier or they might have seen more than they bargained for.

Once we reached the house, we all gravitated to the

kitchen. Abby pulled a pitcher of ice tea out of the refrigerator and offered Bill and Ethan a glass.

Still parched from my experience in the summerhouse, after serving them, I swiftly downed my own glass and poured another. Leaning against the counter, I watched them. My level of trust in Ethan left a little to be desired, and it was hard to believe he'd take time off from the DEA to help us.

"Are you sure the DEA isn't involved?" I asked. "Tink's not in the hands of a drug dealer?"

"No, we're not involved, and no, she isn't being held by a drug dealer," he replied with a grin as he stole a glance at Bill. "Whether Bill likes to admit it or not, you did help us put a crooked cop and an escaped felon behind bars." He traced over the wet circle left by his glass. "I figure I owe you, and I like to pay back my debts."

That, I could understand far better than his desire to help out of the goodness of his heart. I didn't like feeling beholden to anyone, either. It had always been easier for me to give than receive graciously, but for Tink's sake, I'd suck it in and accept his offer.

"Okay, fine," I said setting my glass on the counter. "Any leads?"

"No," Bill answered reluctantly. "I've entered her picture in the National Crime Information Center's Missing Person File, plus the National Center for Missing and Exploited Children." He shook his head sadly. "I hate to say this, but until someone steps forward, it's a waiting game."

"Did anyone call Jason Finch?" Abby asked from her spot next to me. "He's still Tink's legal guardian."

"Yes," Bill replied. "I thought maybe he'd want to come down to Iowa, but he said he couldn't leave Juliet."

Course not, I thought. Jason hadn't gone to jail because of his involvement with Juliet. They'd never proved he was aware of what she'd done, but he was in a prison of his own making. Bound by his obsession with his wife. To him, no one would ever be as important, not even his missing fourteen-year-old niece.

Bill moved his chair away from the table and looked at the three of us. "You all seem calmer today. That's good to see." He drained his glass.

Aunt Dot jumped up from her place at the table and bustled over to the counter for the pitcher of tea. Filling Bill's glass, she smiled down at him. "Tink's safe—"

His glass stopped halfway to his lips. "What?" He stared at me with squinted eyes. "Did you get a phone call and decide not to tell me?"

I stepped away from the counter. "No, no . . . nothing like that . . . " I shot a pleading look at Abby.

"We didn't get a phone call." The words rushed out of Aunt Dot before we could stop her. "We saw her."

Bill's gaze raked over Abby, me, and Aunt Dot.

Aunt Dot beamed back at him confidently.

Abby turned a bright shade of pink.

I tried to look innocent.

Ethan lowered his head, but not before I noticed a grin spread across his face.

Bill zeroed in on Aunt Dot. "Well?" he asked, his tone angry.

Her eyes widened in surprise, as if she couldn't understand why Bill was upset.

The clock above the stove ticked off the seconds as a sense of doom settled around me. Aunt Dot was going to spill the family secrets, I knew it. Where was the duct tape when you needed it? I thought. *Cold, Jensen, cold—contemplating taping your ninety-one-year-old aunt's mouth shut.* But if she started blabbing about the fairies . . .

"We're psychics," I blurted out.

Abby gasped, while Aunt Dot's smile returned as she nodded vigorously.

Ethan raised his head. "You left out the witch part," he said smugly.

Bill's jaw dropped. "All three of you?"

I bobbed my head once.

"Well, I'll be damned," he said, scratching his bald head as he soaked in the news. "I always knew there was something off about you, Ophelia!"

We joined Bill and Ethan at the table, while mentally I scrambled for a way to explain our family's talents and still maintain an ounce of credibility.

"See, it's like this—" I began, pulling out a chair.

Bill waved his hand at me. "Just a minute." He turned to Ethan. "You knew about this?"

"Sure," he replied, swirling the tea around in his half empty glass. "She's legit, Bill. She grabbed my arm once and started rattling off all kinds of things. If I hadn't broken contact, I think she'd have figured out who I really was." He grinned my way. "This was after she'd not only threatened me with her Louisville Slugger, but with a case of boils."

I groaned. "Is it necessary for you to keep bringing that up? I said I was sorry."

His grin spread as he enjoyed my discomfort.

Ignoring him, I looked at Bill. "Do you believe me?"

He scratched his head. "It would explain how you're always tripping over bodies," he replied almost to himself. "You said the word 'witch,' Ethan. What did you mean by that?"

Ethan leaned back in his chair and folded his hands behind his neck. "I'll let Ophelia explain."

"Folk magick, Bill," I said with a nasty glance at Ethan. "It's too long to explain, but one of the things we do is use crystals, herbs, candles, things like that, for healing. Nothing sinister," I assured him.

"Tink? What about her? Is she a psychic, too?"

"No."

Bill gave a sigh of relief. "That's good."

"She's a medium."

"Damn," he muttered again. "If you know she's unharmed, does that mean you know where she is?"

I made a derisive sound. "If I did, do you think I'd be sitting here now?"

"Having had experience with your meddling—no." His voice was curt. "What do you know?"

"Does that question mean you do believe me?"

"About being a psychic?" He made a clicking sound. "I don't know—going to have to think about it—like I said, it sure would explain a lot. I do know there are departments who use psychics when the case goes cold. They don't broadcast it, though." He gave his head a slow shake. "But you being a witch?"

"Forget the witch part," I said, trying to brush the subject away. "You asked me what we know . . . According to Aunt Dot, Tink's being held in a room that's papered with cabbage roses."

Aunt Dot scooted closer to the table. "That's right, and the f—"

Abby touched Aunt Dot's hand, silencing her. "Not now, dear."

I picked up the narrative. "She's not only unharmed, she's not afraid. Do you think that means she knows her kidnapper?"

"It might. Or her lack of fear might mean she's unaware

of the danger she's in. She is only a kid, she might trust that she won't be hurt."

"Tink's not that dumb," I argued.

"Ophelia, people who commit these crimes are really clever. It's as if they instinctively know how to manipulate their victims. They know just what buttons to push in order to control."

"What about the wallpaper?" Ethan asked as he sat forward. "Did any of you recognize it?"

"I did," Aunt Dot said, jumping into the conversation. "Twenty years ago, Sister and I had that same paper on the walls of the spare bedroom."

"I don't think that's what Ethan meant, dear," Abby said gently. "I think he wants to know if we've seen any like it around Summerset."

"Oh." Aunt Dot's shoulders sagged.

Ethan winked at her. "No, what Miss Cameron said is important. We know now that the paper's been around awhile and is most likely out-of-stock." He glanced at Bill. "An old farmhouse?"

Bill pursed his lips. "Probably. Problem is, which one? The area's scattered with old farmsteads." He rubbed his chin. "Did you see anything else?"

"Silas Green keeps cropping up," I said.

Bill shot forward in his chair. "Was he with Tink?"

"No, I saw him in the woods."

I decided to leave out the part about the angry spirits and the pile of bones in his arms. I suspected we'd freaked Bill out enough as it was.

"Silas? Hmm. We've never had any complaints about him. Only talk there's ever been about him was when his business ran into trouble a couple of years ago, but he managed to save it." His eyes traveled to each of us. "Anything else?"

"Just a bunch of jumbled images that don't make much sense," I answered.

Bill turned in his chair and looked at the clock. Standing, he nudged Ethan in the arm. "We'd better get back to the office. Thanks for the tea, Abby."

"Quite all right, Bill."

Ethan rose and followed Bill, but stopped when Bill paused at the kitchen door.

"Remember your promise, Ophelia," he cautioned, wagging a finger at me. "Don't go running off half-cocked based on some psychic vision."

"Sure thing, Bill," I said, and gave him a sweet smile.

As he followed Bill, Ethan shot a skeptical glance at me over his shoulder.

I smiled at him, too. And as they disappeared down the hall, I uncrossed my fingers.

# *Twenty-Three*

"Here, are these okay?" Darci asked, handing me a stack of papers when we entered my house.

Glancing down, I saw Tink's picture staring up at me. I quickly read the information listed below it, which contained her height, weight, what she'd been wearing, and where she'd last been seen.

"I found a website on the Internet—one listing missing and exploited children. It showed how to make a 'missing person' poster."

"Bill mentioned the site. He's posted Tink's picture on it," I murmured while I focused on the sheet in my hand. The same sense of hopelessness threatened to swamp me again, and I felt the tears gathering in my eyes as I looked at Tink's photo. I truly believed that she was unharmed. But for how long? And the dark gulf Abby saw—what if I failed in my quest to cross that gulf? Would my gift help me, or would my talent let me down as it had when I tried to save Brian?

A tear ran down my cheek.

Darci placed an arm around my shoulder and rested her head against mine. "It'll be okay," she said, gripping me. "I've called Arthur, and he's stopping by to pick these posters up. He's got people lined up who are going to plaster these all over the county. Mike's even taking a stack into Des Moines." She gave me a shake. "We'll find her."

"Thanks, Darci," I said, moving away from her and giving one of the flyers to Aunt Dot and Abby.

"Not a problem." She joined Abby and Aunt Dot at the kitchen table. "Did you learn anything?"

"The fairies are protecting her," Aunt Dot replied in a disgruntled tone.

Darci shot a questioning glance first at me, then Abby. "Ahh, that's good, right?" she said with hesitation.

Aunt Dot's eyes narrowed as she focused on me. "At least this girl understands."

"She's unhappy because we didn't give her a chance to tell Bill about the fairies," Abby explained as she rubbed her forehead.

"Ahh—well—" Darci stumbled over her words. "You don't want Bill finding out about your secrets."

"He knows," I replied.

Shock registered on her face. "What? You told him you were a psychic and a witch?"

"No, I only told him we were psychics." My lips tightened in a frown. "Co—er, Ethan, told him I was a witch. And—"

Darci raised her hands. "Hold on, hold on . . . I missed something. Cobra's here?"

"Uh-huh. Ethan. Didn't he stop by with Bill earlier?"

"Bill was here, but I didn't see Cobra—ah, Ethan."

"He was probably waiting in the car," I said with a shrug.

"Okay, let's go back here. You," Darci said, pointing at me, "told Bill you were a psychic, then Ethan," she moved her finger in an arc, "told him you were a witch?"

"Yup. Made the announcement, and let me explain."

"Did you?"

I shrugged again. "Sort of."

"How did Bill take the news?"

"Rather well, wouldn't you say, Abby?"

"Um-hmm," she said as she bent down to pet Queenie, who'd wandered over to where we sat at the table. "He seemed more concerned as to whether Tink was a psychic, too."

"And you told him what?"

"That she wasn't a psychic, but a medium," I replied.

Darci rolled her eyes. "I can see why you didn't want Aunt Dot mentioning the fairies—"

"Yeah, that might have bordered on 'too much information.'"

Queenie left Abby's side and strolled over to me. With a smooth leap, she landed on my lap. As I stroked her black fur, I noticed a notebook open on the table. "What's this?"

"A list of everyone I could think of associated with the funeral home." Darci leaned forward and pushed the note-book toward me.

Quickly, I read the names. Mrs. Buchanan, Buchanan's sons, Kevin Roth . . . I stopped. "Christopher Mason? Why him?"

"He knew Buchanan, had business dealings with him, and knows his widow."

"Okay." I continued reading. Silas Green; Gert Duncan. Gert?

Tapping the page, I focused on Darci. "Why Gert? She doesn't have anything to do with Buchanan."

"I don't like her," Darci replied succinctly.

I snorted. "That's not a reason to consider her a suspect."

Darci shrugged. "Reason enough for me. I don't like her and I don't trust her."

I rolled my eyes. Her attitude was childish. And I didn't need it, not now.

"You can't just point a finger at an innocent woman because you don't like her."

Darci huffed. "I can point a finger in any direction I want. I'm telling you—"

"Girls!" Abby interrupted us. "Is this really necessary?"

I caught the stubborn expression on Darci's face. No way around it, for some reason, she didn't like Gert and wanted Gert on her list. Her personal bias was overriding her judgment, but I knew I'd be fighting a losing battle trying to point that out. I dropped the subject.

I continued reading. Except for the inclusion of Gert's name, Darci had done a good job listing what we knew. In another column, she'd written: restless spirits, funeral home, crematorium, cadaver tissue, skull.

There was definitely a common theme here—death.

Darci pulled the notebook toward her. "See," she said, writing Buchanan's name in the center and drawing a circle around it. "Silas Green, Christopher, and Kevin were all business associates of Buchanan's." She wrote their names and drew a line from their names back to the circle. "And all benefited financially from Buchanan."

"Buchanan also did business with casket companies, flower shops—"

"But Tink's dreams were of restless spirits, not bunches of flowers. These three men, along with Buchanan, handle the deceased one way or the other." She tapped the notebook with her pen. "Did any of Tink's dreams ever take place in the funeral home?"

"No, in the dreams she was always in the woods," I replied, not getting her point.

"Like at Roseman State Park?"

"Could be. Tink never mentioned any landmarks, so I don't know."

Abby pulled the notebook away from Darci and studied it. "The first time you met Silas Green was at the park. It was also where the skull was found."

"You're right," I said, turning to her. "What are you suggesting? That we go tromping through the woods at the state park, looking for clues?"

Something Tink had said nipped at the corner of my mind. What was it? So much had happened over the past couple of days that I couldn't remember. Was it something that had happened in her dreams? Frowning, I searched my memory, but came up blank.

"Did you learn anything during your ceremony?" Darci asked Abby, shifting the subject away from the park.

Abby handed Darci her notes and quickly explained what had happened.

"Your vision took place in the woods," Darci said, a puzzled expression on her face. "You heard a woman laughing?"

"Yeah, can't figure that one out," I said. "No woman listed on your little web around Buchanan."

"Mrs. Buchanan."

"And why would she laugh?"

"Maybe she was laughing about all the lovely piles of money she'd be receiving from Buchanan's life insurance."

I shook my head. "You're making a supposition. We don't know for a fact that Buchanan left her anything."

"You saw Silas Green, too?" Darci tapped her chin. "I think we need to check out a connection between Silas Green and Mrs. Buchanan."

"He's her boyfriend," Aunt Dot chimed in.

"What?" I tried to picture the widow in her leopard-trimmed suit with the creepy Mr. Green. It didn't compute. "Ha, if she were having an affair with a business associate of her husband's, it's more likely it would be with Christopher, rather than Silas—"

"I agree," Aunt Dot said, nodding. "It makes more sense."

Darci's face lit with excitement. "Affair? What affair?"

"That young man, Kevin, said he suspected her of having a boyfriend," Aunt Dot said.

"But at the funeral, Christopher didn't seem to be too fond of her," I argued.

"Maybe it was an act," Abby interjected.

I thought about my date with Christopher. "Okay, he's a jerk, but I don't see him as a killer and a kidnapper."

"Aunt Dot has a doctor's appointment with him tomorrow," Abby said in a sly voice.

"Huh?"

"He's replacing her plaster cast with one made of fiberglass."

"We should take her," Darci said.

"Oh, no," I said, shaking my head. "I don't want to see him again."

"We'll sit in the waiting room." Darci's eyes sparkled. "I'll distract the receptionist while you sneak back and snoop through his office."

"Wait a second." I fisted a hand on my hip, disturbing Queenie. "Why am I the one who always has to do the sneaking and the snooping?"

"Okay," Darci said with a shrug. "I'll do it."

Trapped again.

# *Twenty-Four*

The Muzak version of the Beatles' "Paperback Writer" sounded softly from the speakers discreetly hidden in the ceiling. In a corner, a silk ficus stretched upward from behind a table littered with weeks-old copies of *Field and Stream, National Geographic,* and *AARPThe Magazine.* Walkers and canes lined the aisles as their owners waited patiently for their turn with Dr. Mason.

Darci and I settled Aunt Dot in one of the empty navy blue chairs, then took our place next to her.

Hmm, I thought, eyeing the pile of magazines, which one did I want to read? I didn't care for fishing, too young for *AARPThe Magazine,* so I guess I'd make do with *National Geographic.* I moved to stand, but Darci clasped my arm and forced me down.

"Psst," she hissed out of the corner of her mouth. "How are you planning on distracting the receptionist?"

"I don't know. Any ideas?" I whispered back.

Darci rolled her eyes in disgust. "Don't you think you should've thought of something by now?"

"Yes," I said in dismay. "I tried, I really did, but I'm not good at faking."

She poked her finger in my ribs, making me jump. "You'd better get good at it, and fast. Pretend you're having heart palpitations or something. That'd bring the doctors and nurses running."

"I'm not that good an actress. Can't you come up with another suggestion?" I complained.

"Okay, let's set off the fire alarm. We—"

"Darci, we can't do that," I muttered, clenching my jaw. "This room is full of senior citizens. One of them might have a heart attack for real if they think the building's on fire."

"Okay, we go with the next plan."

"Which is?"

"We'll have to go with Aunt Dot back to the examining room—"

"I said," my tone insistent, "I didn't want to see Christopher again."

"Tough, you'll just have to suck it up. You want to get to the bottom of this mess and find Tink, don't you?"

"Of course."

"Okay, then." She gave a satisfied nod. "Once we get back to the room, I'll make some excuse about using the phone and wander off. You keep Mason busy while I'm rummaging through his office."

"Do you have any idea what you're looking for?"

"I want to see if I can find anything about his business dealings with Buchanan."

"And if you can't?"

"We'll follow him," she replied with a shrug. "See if he does hook up with the widow."

"Are you crazy?" I sputtered. "We can't stalk him."

Darci exhaled in a huge sigh. "I said 'follow,' not 'stalk.' There's no law against following a person."

"What if he spots us?"

She dismissed my concerns with a flip of her hand. "He won't see us."

"What about her?" I asked, jerking my head in Aunt Dot's direction.

"She goes with us. I checked the office hours when we walked in. They close at noon. We'll hang around and tail him when he leaves."

"Darci—"

Before I could finish, a nurse in a pale blue lab coat called Aunt Dot's name. Darci rose gracefully and extended a hand to Aunt Dot before turning her attention to me.

"Show time," she said with a wink.

As we followed the nurse back to the examining room, my heart seemed to beat a little faster with each step. And it wasn't due to excitement at the thought of seeing Christopher again. Oh no, my racing heart was caused by full-fledged panic. We hadn't exactly parted on the best of terms. What would his reaction be? Would he be embarrassed? Condescending? Rude?

With a smile, the nurse motioned us into the room. After helping Aunt Dot onto the high examination table, she took Aunt Dot's vitals and asked questions concerning her general health. Shutting Aunt Dot's file, she again smiled and with a "the doctor will see you soon," left the room.

After waiting five beats, Darci slowly opened the door and peered into the hallway. Glancing at us over her shoulder, she flashed a broad smile. "Here I go."

A second later she disappeared.

"Do you think she'll find anything?" Aunt Dot asked in a loud whisper.

"Shh." I held a finger to my lips. "Your voice carries. Aunt Dot, you can't let on Darci's up to something. You have to act as if this is just a normal visit."

She snorted. "Don't worry about me. I'm not senile, you know. I can handle that doctor."

The door opening cut short my response, and Christopher strode into the room. He paused, momentarily flustered when he caught sight of me sitting in the chair next to the table.

"Ophelia," he said smoothly as his bedside manner slid on like a glove. "Kevin told me about your daughter. I'm so sorry. Has there been any word?"

I shifted in my chair uncomfortably. "No, but they're doing everything they can to find her."

He said nothing, but laid a sympathetic hand on my shoulder.

I scooted away from his touch.

"Miss Cameron, how are you feeling?" he asked loudly as he approached Aunt Dot.

"It's my wrist, not my ears, that are broke, so you don't need to shout," she answered with a scowl.

An ingratiating smile lit his face. "Quite right, Miss Cameron. Let's take a look."

It only took a moment for him to review Aunt Dot's chart and to examine her wrist. Satisfied, he patted her knee. "Everything's fine," he said. "My assistant will be in shortly to remove the plaster cast and fit you with a fiberglass one."

*No, no, no.* I peeked at my watch in apprehension. Only five minutes had elapsed since Darci had disappeared out the door. If he left the room now, he might catch her coming out of his office. What to do? What to do?

I opened my mouth to speak, but Aunt Dot beat me to it.

"Can't *you* take the cast off?" she said with a pitiful whine.

"Don't worry, my assistant is very qualified," he reassured her and began to step away from the table.

Aunt Dot's good hand shot out and grabbed the hem of his

lab coat, stopping him. "I know I'm just an old lady . . . my life will be over soon. What if your assistant makes a mistake and my hand is crippled? It'll take away my few pleasures left."

"He knows what he's doing, so you're not going to be permanently incapacitated," he replied as he tried to tug his coat from her grip. "It's only a small bone in the wrist."

Her fingers tightened. "What if he chips a bone taking the cast off? It could go to my heart and kill me."

"Miss Cameron, I have other patients waiting." His eyes flew to his watch.

"He's going to use one of those saws, isn't he?"

"Yes, and he's used them to remove hundreds of casts."

Aunt Dot pursed her lips in a firm line. "What if the saw goes too deep and he cuts my skin? It's fragile, you know."

"I know, but that won't happen."

"What if the saw slips and he cuts off a finger?"

Christopher, evidently moved by Aunt Dot's plea, sat next to her. "You're letting your fears get the best of you," he said gently. "My assistant will have the cast off in no time."

"Can't you remove the cast?" She held her broken wrist firmly to her chest and stared at him with tears in her eyes. "Please?"

With a sigh, Christopher stood and made his way to the door. Opening it, he stuck his head out and called to his nurse.

"Nancy, Miss Cameron wants me to remove her cast. Would you please tell the other patients that I'll be with them in a minute?"

From behind his back, Aunt Dot gave me a cheeky grin. However, when Christopher turned, her face instantly settled into that of a sorrowful old lady.

I hid my smile. Man, she was as good at manipulation as Darci. I wondered if Abby was on to Aunt Dot yet.

Soon the hum of the saw filled the room as Aunt Dot patiently sat and let Christopher remove her cast. He was so intent on his work that he didn't see the look of victory cross her wrinkled face.

Once the plaster was removed, it only took a moment for him to fit the fiberglass cast on her wrist. "There," he said with a smile. "All done. You'll be more comfortable now." He pushed back his sleeve and snuck a look at his watch again. "If you have any problems, give us a call."

Dang, he was leaving, and Darci still wasn't back. What was taking her so long?

"Ahh, ahh, is there anything special Abby and I need to do for Aunt Dot?" I stumbled, trying to delay him.

His brow creased in a frown. "Special? What do you mean?"

"Umm . . . well . . . vitamins? Are there any vitamins that would help speed the healing?"

"Calcium," he replied with another glance at his watch.

"Anything else?"

"No, it will take time for the bone to heal." Irritation laced his voice.

"What about pain? How should she deal with the pain?"

"Miss Cameron, are you in pain?" he asked, focusing on Aunt Dot.

Her eyelids drifted down. "A little," she said with a pathetic sigh, "but I don't like to complain."

He pulled a prescription pad out of his pocket and quickly wrote a script for medication. "She can take these as needed," he said, handing me the slip. He glanced back at her. "Is there anything else?"

The door swung open then and Darci strolled into the room. "Are you about finished?" she asked.

I tried to mask the relief I felt at seeing her. "I think we're done. Are we done, Aunt Dot?"

"Yes," she answered, and to Christopher's surprise, slid off the table with amazing agility.

With a shrug and a murmured "Thanks," I followed the two schemers from the room.

# Twenty-Five

We killed the hours between Aunt Dot's appointment and noon by eating lunch in the cafeteria.

"Anything interesting in Christopher's files?" I asked between bites of salad.

"I don't know—not much relating to his tissue supply business," she said with a shrug. "I suppose he keeps those records at the business." A speculative light shone in Darci's eyes.

"No," I whispered as I leaned in close. "We're not burgling his office."

She gave me an injured look. "I wasn't suggesting that we do."

"Good." I stabbed a piece of lettuce with my fork.

"But . . . taking a look at those files might be enlightening. I did a little searching on the Internet last night. Did you know that a body sold off in parts is worth thousands in fees?"

"Huh?"

She nodded. "Biomedical suppliers charge fees for storage and handling. There's a huge demand for various body parts at research facilities."

I laid my fork down. "That sounds like something out of *Frankenstein*."

"Not as long as ethics are observed. There are age limits to be followed; if the tissue is to be used for transplants, the health of the deceased prior to death is important—"

"Wait—what does their health have to do with it?"

"If they've tested positive for HIV or hepatitis, their tissue can't be used."

"That makes sense—might be a chance of spreading the disease."

"Exactly."

"You didn't find any paper trail leading from the biomedical company to Buchanan's Funeral Home?"

"No." Her eyes slid slyly my way. "I found something else interesting, though."

"What?"

"A love letter and a card. Recent, too."

"From Mrs. Buchanan?" Aunt Dot inquired in a hushed voice.

"How recent?" I asked, ignoring her.

"Last month."

"Evidently, last month he was involved with someone, but this month he's speed dating? He didn't waste much time jumping back into the dating pool, did he? Were the card and letter signed?"

Darci exhaled softly. "No, darn it."

I chuckled. "Did you think you'd find something incriminating signed, 'Love you madly, Mrs. Buchanan?'"

"Silly, she wouldn't sign 'Mrs. Buchanan,' she'd use her first name."

"Which, if I might point out, we don't even know."

"It's Barbara," Aunt Dot said, joining the conversation.

My face registered surprise. "How do you know?"

Aunt Dot looked at me as if I was an idiot. "I asked her at the funeral."

Darci stood and gathered up our trays. "We'd better get out to the car so we'll be ready when Mason leaves."

After a boring twenty minutes of watching people come and go from the building and listening to Aunt Dot softly snore in the backseat, Darci shifted around to face me. "You'll recognize his vehicle, won't you?"

"I think so." I eyed her speculatively. "You're sure you know how to tail someone?"

Her red fingernails fluttered in my face. "Of course I do. You can't believe the number of times when I was a kid and my brothers—"

"Good," I said, slumping down in the seat. "'Cause there he is."

Darci slammed her sunglasses on her face and turned on the ignition. "Keep an eye on him," she said, backing out of the parking space.

Christopher walked a few cars down from where we'd been parked and got in a white SUV. Darci hung back, allowing him to pull ahead of us. We watched as he slowly drove out of the lot and took a left onto the street. Darci followed suit.

"I can't get too close or he might spot us, so don't lose sight of him, okay?" she said, focusing on the traffic.

"Look." I pointed at the windshield. "He's changing lanes."

With a jerk of the steering wheel, Darci whipped her car to the left. A horn sounded from behind us.

Aunt Dot's snoring came to an abrupt halt. "What? What's going on?"

I turned and reached over the seat. "It's okay. We're following Dr. Mason."

"Shoot, he's turning at the light. I'm not going to make it," Darci exclaimed as she gunned the car.

"Might want to buckle up," I called to Aunt Dot. The soft *snick* of the clasp told me she'd followed my advice.

The car shot forward, and I grabbed the dash to steady myself. "You okay, Aunt Dot?"

"Yes," she whispered in my left ear. A quick glance over my shoulder showed her leaning forward as far as her belt would allow. Her face mirrored her excitement.

The light changed to yellow just as Darci approached the intersection where Christopher had turned. She pressed down on the accelerator. Tires squealed and horns blew as her car sped through the now red light.

As an apology, Darci waggled her fingers at the other drivers. One of them did return her wave, but with only one finger.

I craned my head to watch him as we whizzed by. "Man, you ticked that guy off."

"Tough," she replied, her eyes never leaving the white SUV pulling farther ahead of us.

"Running a light is a good way to have an accident. The other car had the right of way, you know."

"Oh pooh, who cares? We made it through the intersection, didn't we?" She increased her speed to close the distance.

I watched the needle of the speedometer inch past the legal limit.

"Aunt Dot, still buckled in?"

Her good hand clasped my shoulder, while her voice sounded in my ear again. "Hurry up, Darci, don't let the bastard get away!"

"Aunt Dot!" My eyes flew from her to the road. "He's slowing down and has his turn signal on."

Darci let up on the pedal, and the car slowed to the speed limit.

The SUV made a right turn into a business mall parking

lot and pulled into a reserved spot in front of one of the offices. Christopher exited the SUV and entered the office as Darci slowly drove by.

Her head turned to the right, then the left, looking for a parking space.

"One's open next to the SUV," I pointed out.

"Duh, we can't park there. He might see us. We need a spot where we can see the building and not be noticed."

"To your left, child," Aunt Dot said from the backseat.

A big smile crossed Darci's face. "Perfect," she replied, smoothly turning into the spot.

It was perfect. From that location we could see the office door yet not be obvious.

Still, I couldn't see the point of it. "This is a waste of time," I groused. "He's obviously not meeting Mrs. Buchanan. I can't imagine a biotech office would be a good place for a romantic rendezvous."

Leaning my head against the seat, I closed my eyes. "How long are you planning on sitting here? I do need to get home, call Bill, see if I can reach Walks Quietly . . . " My voice trailed away as I thought of all the things I could be doing to find Tink instead of following Dr. Christopher Mason around.

A jab in the ribs made me raise my head.

Darci jerked her head toward the SUV. "Look, a car's parking next to Mason's."

Maybe Aunt Dot and Darci were right and Christopher did have a meeting with Mrs. Buchanan.

Only it wasn't a woman who exited the late model car. A man, his face shadowed by the hood of a sleeveless sweatshirt, got out and walked to the rear of the car. With his back to us, he opened the trunk and removed two Styrofoam coolers by their handles. Setting them on the ground next to him, he closed the lid of the trunk. Then he picked up the coolers and walked to Christopher's office.

Pausing at the door, he turned and looked furtively around the parking lot.

I gasped.

It was Silas Green, making a delivery.

Once we arrived home, Aunt Dot steamrolled up the sidewalk and into the house, letting the screen door slam behind her. Darci and I hurried after her.

We entered the house in time to see her rounding the corner into the kitchen. In her wake, Queenie, Lady, and T.P. scattered to avoid getting their tails smashed by her cane smacking the hardwood floor with each step.

Darci and I skidded to a halt as we heard the words pouring out of Aunt Dot's mouth.

" . . . And then we ran a red light. You should have heard the tires squeal. We were almost hit."

With each word, Abby's eyes grew rounder with fear. They flew from Aunt Dot to Darci and then to me.

"Hey, I wasn't the one driving," I said, crossing to the counter, where I picked up a bag of chips.

Abby zeroed in on Darci. "What have you girls been doing? I thought you were only going to look around Dr. Mason's office."

Darci pulled out a chair and plopped down. "I didn't find anything, so we decided to follow him."

Abby glanced at me for affirmation.

I shrugged and popped a chip in my mouth.

"That junk's not good for you," she said.

"Honestly, Abby, Aunt Dot's exaggerating a little," Darci said. "That car missed us by this much," she added, holding her hands far apart.

Abby fisted a hand on a hip. "What did happen?"

Munching on the chips, I let Darci do the explaining. For once, it was nice for someone else to be in the hot seat.

When she'd finished, I closed the bag of chips and leaned against the cabinet. "Did Bill call?"

"No, but that nice young man Ethan stopped in." Abby shook her head. "I can't imagine how you ever suspected him of being a murderer."

Oh, maybe it was the tattoos, or the fact that he appeared to be a member of a drug-running biker gang, or because he threatened me whenever I ran into him? I kept my thoughts to myself.

"Abby you've lived in Summerset for a long time. Surely you knew Silas Green's family?"

Her brow wrinkled. "Not really. His mother, when she was alive, bought bedding plants occasionally. I think she mentioned Silas worked up north one time—"

"At a crematorium?" I interrupted.

"No, I don't think so, but right now I can't recall what his occupation was. I do know he came home when his father had his heart attack."

"He took over the business?"

"Yes, I believe so." She tapped her chin. "There was a rumor going around a couple of years ago that he might have to close the crematorium."

"Bill mentioned that. I wonder how long he's been providing Christopher with body parts?"

Darci sat up in her chair. "Do you think that's how he saved his business? Selling tissues from cadavers?"

I pulled a hand through my hair. "Could be, but as you pointed out at lunch, if he is receiving a fee from Christopher, it's not illegal."

"No, as long as he's following the rules," she said thoughtfully.

Pacing the room, I tried to shove all the pieces of the puzzle together. "Even if what they're doing is illegal, how does that connect with Tink?" I stopped in the middle of the room. "If there's as much money as you said, Darci, I can see how illegal tissue harvesting might have led to Buchanan's death. Maybe he was involved, or maybe he discovered what Silas was doing and threatened to go to the sheriff." I shook my head. "But do you think he snatched Tink?"

"If he heard the rumors," she suggested.

"He thought Tink was a loose end?"

"Possibly. You said Tink had dreamed of corpses missing body parts." She spread her hands wide. "That ties into what Silas Green is doing."

"Wouldn't he have to show Christopher the family consent forms and the death certificates?"

Darci nodded. "Yes."

"I don't think Silas Green is smart enough," Aunt Dot interjected.

"But, Aunt Dot, how do you know?" I asked. "Today was the first time you've ever seen him."

"The fairies mentioned it."

My eyes met Abby's from across the room. She gave her head a slight shake.

Aunt Dot picked up on our disbelief. "Well, they did," she replied defensively as her bottom lip came out in a pout.

"She has a point—" Darci began, then paused, catching the look on my face. "Maybe not about the fairies . . . sorry, Aunt Dot, I don't know much about them. You'll have to explain them to me sometime," she said, trying to placate her. "But she is right about Silas. I don't know him well, but he's always seemed a little odd, and it's hard for me to imagine he'd be clever enough to carry out this scheme."

"What about that young man, Kevin?" Aunt Dot asked.

"Might he be involved?" She clearly didn't suspect Silas.

"He's just a kid—only a few years older than Tink." I shoved my hands in my pockets. "With Buchanan's murder, he might be out of a job soon. From what Christopher said, that would put him in a financial bind."

"All right," Aunt Dot said, smacking the table. "It's the doctor and the widow. Dr. Mason's smart enough. And on *Law and Order,* it's always the wife and the boyfriend."

I rolled my eyes. I swear . . . that show must have been all she ever watched. Taking my hands out of my pockets, I paced the room again. No matter how I tried, I couldn't make sense of what was happening. At every turn, all I found were more questions—not answers.

"We're no closer to finding Tink than we were yesterday." I hugged myself. "Every day that goes by, the chances get less and less. We need answers."

"We need to take a peek at Silas Green's records," Darci pointed out with a sly expression.

I halted my steps and gave an exasperated sigh. "You know, your mind definitely has a criminal bent, Darci. I've got a feeling you'd make a great second story man."

She tossed her head. "Do we need answers or not?"

"Yes."

"Does Silas Green keep popping up, in your visions and in real life?"

"Yes."

She crossed her legs and leaned back. "Then I say we do a little more snooping and check out the crematorium."

Aunt Dot's pout faded and she watched us with bright eyes. "Can I go?"

*"No,"* Darci and I said simultaneously.

# Twenty-Six

It wouldn't do to leave Darci's car along the gravel road, where passing vehicles would be bound to notice it. We parked it at an abandoned farmstead near the road leading into Green's Crematorium instead and hiked the rest of the way.

We were dressed in black sweatpants and sweatshirts, and Darci wore her hood pulled closely over her blond hair, which would've shone like a beacon in the night if left uncovered. She'd wanted to camouflage our faces, too, but I'd drawn the line at rubbing dirt across my cheeks and forehead.

As we walked down the road leading to the crematorium, the beams from our flashlights danced over the gravel at our feet. The heat and humidity made the dark fleece cling to my arms and legs, and I felt perspiration run down my spine, dampening the waistband of my sweatpants. It felt like walking through a sauna.

Nerves fluttered in my stomach. Would we be able to find an unlocked door or window? Or would we truly have to bust a window to get inside the crematorium? Darci and I had done a lot of snooping in the past, but we'd never actually broken into a building. This would be a first.

We had no choice. I knew Silas Green was the key to finding Tink, but Bill couldn't execute a search warrant based on my hunch. We had to find proof first, then we could go to Bill. I snorted softly. That would be a fun conversation—I knew he'd object to our methods. Oh well, I'd worry about talking to Bill once we had something more concrete than just my feelings.

Darci and I rounded a corner and saw a low brick building ahead. Its smokestack loomed high in the night sky. The path we'd traveled widened and led around to the side of the building. Stopping, I took a deep breath of the heavy air and exhaled slowly.

We'd lucked out. We were alone.

"Okay, what's next?" My voice seemed to echo in the still night.

Darci pointed to her left. "Let's see if there's a door," she said as she made her way closer to the crematorium.

I followed in her footsteps until we reached the side of the building. Two large bay doors faced us, each wide enough for a hearse to enter. An entrance door was to the right. Silently, I motioned to it with my flashlight.

Darci crept over to the door and slowly turned the knob. It was unlocked. She smiled at me over her shoulder and disappeared through the dark doorway. I hurried after her.

Inside, we stood in a large room with concrete floors. To our right was a door leading to the rest of the facility. Opening it, we found ourselves in a hallway with another door to our left and one at the end. We picked the first door.

As I shone my flashlight around the room, my beam bounced back and hit me in the eyes.

"What's that?" I asked, keeping the light pointed down.

A huge metal box with stainless steel doors sat in the middle of the room. Attached to its side appeared to be some kind of control panel.

"It's the oven." The whites of Darci's eyes shone in the darkness. "I think they call it an oven . . . I don't know . . . I've never thought about it . . . "

I clasped my hand over her mouth. "Shh, you're babbling."

She blinked twice and nodded. I moved my hand away.

Shining my light around the room, I spotted another door. "Let's see what's in there."

Our tennis shoes squeaked on the concrete floor as we made our way to the door. It was unlocked, too.

"Silas isn't real big on security, is he?" I said as I swung the door open.

Our flashlights played around the room, revealing a stainless steel table along one wall. Next to the table, laid out with precision, were various instruments such as saws, knives, and forceps.

My stomach pitched. It was obvious the room was used for harvesting body parts. Yuck.

"Let's get out of here," I said, turning to Darci, to discover that she wasn't there. She was standing in front of two large upright freezers.

"What's in here?" she asked, grasping one of the handles.

"No!" I exclaimed rushing to her. "Don't open—"

Too late. Her scream reverberated off the walls of the cavernous room.

Her knees started to bend as she made a retching sound deep in her throat.

I grabbed her around the waist with one arm. "Don't you dare faint, and don't you dare puke."

"There's . . . there's . . . " She pointed a shaking hand at the opened freezer.

On the shelf, neatly wrapped in a plastic bag, were two severed hands and a detached foot.

"I know, body parts," I said, firmly shutting the door with my other hand. "Now snap out of it." I gave her body a quick shake. "We knew what Silas was doing."

"But . . . but . . . I didn't expect to see them." Her voice quivered.

"Me, either, but finding them is proof of Tink's dreams and my vision. In both cases, the spirits were missing parts of their bodies. It shows we must be on the right track." I pulled her away from the freezer. "Come on, we need to find Silas's office."

Holding fast to Darci's hand, I led her back to the hallway and down to the last door. Behind the door was a large waiting room, and to our left a room marked pr ivat e.

"In here," I said, tugging her toward Silas's office.

A desk sat in the middle of the room, its top covered with papers. Wow, I thought, worse than mine at the library.

Bookcases and filing cabinets lined the walls. They, too, were stacked full of "stuff." A bird's nest balanced precariously on a stack of old newspapers. An old-fashioned pop bottle lay on its side at the corner of the desk. An orange hunting cap that had seen better days perched on top of a pile of magazines. Shiny shell casings littered Silas's desk.

Between the desk, bookcases, and filing cabinets, there was a path around the piles and piles of junk.

I was amazed.

Darci gave a soft sigh. "Gosh, Silas is quite a collector, isn't he?"

"Humph," I snorted, "more of a scavenger, I'd say. He must comb the woods around here and pick up whatever crap he finds." I shone my light around the room in disgust. "We're going to be lucky to find anything in this mess."

Darci motioned with her flashlight to one of the overflowing file cabinets. "You start there, and I'll look through this one," she said, pointing at another cabinet.

Holding my flashlight under my chin, I riffled through the files. Dust tickled my nose, and I sneezed, almost dropping my flashlight.

"Hey, I think I've found something," Darci said in a loud whisper. She pulled a folder out of the cabinet. "It's death certificates . . . and what looks like family consent forms."

She had my attention. "Really?" I joined her at the desk and took half of the forms from her, quickly skimming the pages. "I don't know any of these people, do you?"

"Hmm, I know this lady," she said, holding a certificate to the light. "My mother used to visit her in the nursing home. Gee, I'm surprised she wanted to be cremated." She shrugged. "She didn't have a family—I suppose that's why."

She picked up another. "I know this one, too. Myrtle Benson. She was a regular at the library until she became bedridden and her daughter had to take care of her." She paused as she read the paper. "That's funny. This has her age at time of death listed as sixty-nine—she had to be at least ninety when she died."

"Let me see that." I took the death certificate from Darci's hand.

Sure enough. Sixty-nine when she died on the second of May, 2005. I held the certificate close to the beam of my flashlight. "They whited out the age and wrote over it."

She didn't answer.

"Here's another one," Darci said. "Allen Tilton. Says here he was forty-eight. Well, that would be about right." The faint light revealed her frown. "But it has the cause of death listed as 'pneumonia.' He didn't die of pneumonia, he died of hepatitis. He'd picked it up years ago in the military. At the time, everyone was talking about his death."

I had a thought. "Hand me the death certificate of the woman your mother visited." I flipped the page over and found a family consent form granting the harvesting of the woman's tissues. "I thought you said she didn't have a family?"

"She didn't."

"This says she did," I said, waving the papers in front of Darci's face. "The consent form was signed by her 'daughter.'"

"But—"

She stopped, interrupted by the sound of metal doors rolling open from deep inside the building.

"Crap, someone's here," I said. "They're coming in through the bay doors." I shut off my flashlight as Darci did the same.

"Come on." She clutched my arm and pulled me toward the office door. "We can go out through the waiting room."

The sound of another door opening and shutting stopped us.

I heard footsteps coming down the hallway.

"This way." Not letting go of my arm, she tugged me over to the window located on the opposite side of the room.

I stumbled over a pile of old papers in my haste.

Darci released me and cranked the window open. Throwing one leg over the sill, she held out a hand to me. "Hurry up."

Grasping my hand, she shinnied out, pulling me closer to the window.

I followed suit, and had almost cleared the window when the seat of my pants caught on something protruding from the frame.

"Hurry up," she hissed from outside the building.

"My pants are snagged," I whispered back.

Darci clutched both my shoulders and yanked hard. I felt the fabric give way and tumble to the ground just as the office door opened.

"Run!" Darci exclaimed, hauling me to my feet.

We darted into the woods as a voice called out from the open window.

"Hey, get back here!"

# *Twenty-Seven*

I woke up to a silent house. Abby and Aunt Dot were still asleep in the guest room. After almost getting caught going through Silas Green's files, sleep hadn't come easy. At least now we knew Silas was illegally providing Christopher Mason's biomedical company with tissue. The question was, did Christopher know? And how did the illegal scam play into Tink's disappearance?

I needed to clear my brain. Slipping on a T-shirt, shorts, and tennis shoes, I wrote a note for Abby and quietly left the house. Too early for my neighbors to be up on a Sunday morning, I took off at a brisk pace down the silent streets of Summerset.

My shoes slapped the sidewalk while blue jays chattered at me from the trees. Squirrels scampered in the dewy grass, searching for nuts to bury. In front of me, the sun hung over the eastern horizon like a big orange ball. I wiped the perspiration from my brow. Already the day promised to be hot and sticky.

I pumped my arms, increasing my speed, and soon felt the familiar burn in my thigh muscles. I concentrated on pulling fresh air into my lungs, hoping the influx of oxygen would still my troubled mind.

What did I do now? Talk to Bill, of course. It might be a slight problem when it came to explaining how I acquired my information about Silas Green, but I'd worry about that later. Cornering Christopher Mason might be a good idea, too. Maybe another trip to Aiken to question Kevin was in order? He'd seemed very willing to talk about his former employer the night he joined us for dinner at Abby's house.

I slowed my steps. Bill wouldn't approve of these plans racing through my head, but I didn't care. Somebody had to find Tink, and soon.

A horn beeping caught my attention. I stopped, and turning my head, saw a car slowly pulling up to the curb next to me. The driver's window came down and Ethan motioned me over to his car.

"You're up early," he commented as I approached the driver's side.

"So are you. What are you doing?"

"Just driving around, trying to put the pieces of the puzzle together."

"Yeah, me, too. That's why I went for a walk," I said, leaning down.

He jerked his head to the passenger's side. "Why don't you get in and we can work on it together."

"Okay." I walked around the car and slid into the passenger's side.

"Does Bill have any leads on Tink?" I asked as Ethan eased away from the curb.

"No, I'm sorry, Ophelia, he doesn't." He shook his head. "The sheriff's office hasn't even received one single call."

I traced a line on the seat next to me. "That's not good, is it?"

"No, usually in cases like this, they at least get crank

calls." His eyes slid my way in a quick glance. "What have you turned up?"

I folded my hands primly in my lap. "Me? What do you mean?"

He made a sound in the back of his throat. "Come on, Ophelia, I've seen you in action before, remember? When you suspected me of threatening Tink, you came after me with your baseball bat. I can't imagine what you're prepared to do to whoever snatched her."

"Okay." I sighed loudly. "So maybe I have checked out a few things."

"What things?"

I unfolded my hands and turned to face him. "I'd planned on calling Bill later anyway. Silas Green is harvesting tissue from cadavers illegally and selling them to Dr. Christopher Mason's biomedical supply company."

"And you know this how?"

"We kind of went through his files—"

"'Kind of?'" He raised an eyebrow. "And who's 'we'?"

"Darci and me. Last night, at Green's Crematorium—"

He held up a hand, stopping me. "No, I don't want to know."

"You asked," I replied indignantly.

"Even though I'm on my own time, I'm still an officer of the court and bound to report a break-in."

"For the record, we didn't break anything."

"Trespassing, then."

He had me there.

"Look, I'm going to tell Bill about Silas. Once he gets a search warrant, he'll learn the truth."

"No, he won't."

My forehead puckered in a frown. "Of course he will."

"Not without probable cause."

I turned away from him. "I'm giving him probable cause."

"No, you're not. Unless you tell him the whole story, you're only relaying a 'hunch,' a 'rumor.' That's not enough for a warrant."

"What will he do, then?"

"Pull Silas in for questioning—"

"Silas will lie," I said. "Then go right back to his office and get rid of the files."

"Yup, that'd be my guess. Without a confession from you, he's got nothing on Silas."

"So you're telling me if we uncovered illegal activities because we were hypothetically trespassing and told Bill, I'd be the one in trouble."

"Right—"

"Yet Silas, who's violating the dead, would skate?"

He nodded.

"That sucks," I huffed. "Can't you guys sweat a confession out of him?"

A smirk played at the corner of his mouth. "You mean with bright lights and billy clubs?"

"Yeah." I bobbed my head righteously.

"It's called 'police brutality' and the courts frown on it."

I slapped the seat. "How do we prove what Silas is doing?"

"Slowly, carefully, building the case, one piece of evidence at a time."

"My daughter's missing!" I cried. "I don't have the luxury of moving slowly and carefully. The longer she's gone, the less chance we have of finding her. She—"

Ethan stretched out a hand, silencing me. "Ophelia, if we don't build an airtight case, the guilty walk free."

I shoved my body against the seat in frustration. "What do you suggest I do?"

"Let me ask you a question . . . Why are you so interested in Silas Green?"

"All the dreams, all the visions, seem to lead back to him. I can't help but believe he's the key." I took a deep breath. "Tink's dreams began the night before we ran into Buchanan at the airport . . . "

I quickly explained the dreams, the rumors, meeting Silas for the first time in the woods, finding the skull.

"You suspect Silas had a falling out with Buchanan, killed him, and based on town gossip, got the idea Tink knew something, so he kidnapped her?"

"Yeah."

"But based on what you saw when you tried to reach her psychically, she was safe?"

"Yeah."

"Ahh . . . " he began slowly. "I'm a cop, and unfortunately, I've seen a lot of murders." He paused, uncertain how to continue.

"Just spit it out, Ethan."

"Most killers don't leave loose ends," he finished bluntly.

I felt the blood rush from my face. "If Silas took Tink, you think he'd have killed her by now."

Gripping the door handle until my knuckles turned white, a voice in my head screamed, *No!*

"I can't accept that," I mumbled. "I'd feel it if Tink had crossed over."

I couldn't make myself say the word "died."

Ethan sympathetically patted my bare knee. "That wasn't my point. You said she was unharmed—are your visions ever wrong?"

"No one, not even Abby, is always a hundred percent correct. There's always the chance that you've interpreted a sign wrong." I shook my head. "Since all three of us sensed she was safe, I believe it's true."

"So if Tink's unharmed, and if what you suspect about Silas is true—that he did kill Buchanan—I doubt Silas was the one who took her."

"But that can't be—who else would want to take her?"

"I don't know."

I considered Ethan's argument. If he was correct, it meant I'd been following the wrong lead. No, that idea didn't feel right. The vision had shown Silas with Tink's bracelet.

Ethan broke into my thoughts. "Did all three of you see Tink in the same way?"

"No, I was with her in the woods, Aunt Dot saw her in the bedroom she described to you and Bill, and Abby saw Tink separated from me by a wide gulf."

I rubbed my forehead trying to recall exactly what Abby had said. A man standing in the shadows, a hawk and an eagle circling overhead.

Stealing a glance at Ethan, I remembered the one and only time I tried to read him. It was when I'd threatened him with my Louisville Slugger and had a bad case of the boils. The image I'd seen when I touched him was that of an eagle protecting him. It didn't make sense to me at the time, but I later learned an eagle was on his DEA badge.

"Duh," I tapped my head. "Take a left at the next corner."

"What?" Ethan asked, startled. "Why?"

I turned to him with a grin. "I'm going to find Tink, and," I said, poking him in the arm, "you're going to help me."

# Twenty-Eight

"Where are we going?"

I noticed the puzzled expression on Ethan's face. "Roseman State Park. Not only does Silas keep turning up, but so does the park. In my vision, in Tink's dreams." I snapped my fingers. "I've got it. The map Tink found in Buchanan's office."

Ethan frowned. "Huh? What was Tink doing in Buchanan's office?"

"Ah . . . well . . . umm, Tink and Aunt Dot did a little snooping around on their own."

"Like mother, like daughter," Ethan muttered under his breath.

I ignored him and continued my explanation. "According to Tink, Buchanan fished the river that runs through Roseman two or three times a week. It's also where T.P. found the skull."

"Ophelia," he said in a patient voice, "the deputies have searched those woods thoroughly and not found any remains."

"They were looking in the wrong spot," I announced as I turned toward him. "Do you have a cell phone with you?"

"Sure." He unclasped the phone and handed it to me.

I punched in Darci's number. She answered on the third ring.

"Hello?" Her voice sounded thick with sleep.

"Hi, it's me. Remember you told me about an old boy-friend who rented a place from Silas Green?"

"Yeah," she replied with a yawn.

"Would you give me the directions?"

"Go past the entrance to Roseman State Park to Two Mile Corner. Do you know where that is?"

"Yes."

"Take a left at Two Mile, and the Green place is the first lane on the right. The house is about a half mile back from the road. Got that?"

"Yeah—a right at Two Mile corner—"

"No, no, no. A *left*."

"Got it." I drummed my fingers on my knee. "Darci, is anyone living there now?"

"No, not since my old boyfriend moved out."

"Okay, good. See ya." I flipped the phone shut before she could start asking questions.

After giving the directions to Ethan, I settled back and watched the fields fly by.

Cows grazed in green pastures as black-white faced calves frolicked near their mothers. From the car, I saw ducks slowly paddling around the edges of a pond, searching for their breakfast of water bugs.

We'd almost reached Roseman when Ethan broke the silence.

"If what you've told me about Silas Green's illegal activi-ties is true—"

"It is," I insisted.

"Wouldn't dissecting a body and retrieving tissue require some skill?"

I lifted a shoulder. "I guess, but if the body's being cremated, no one would see what he does to them. He wouldn't have to worry about reconstructing them or hiding his handiwork."

"I would think there's a time frame on tissue recovery, isn't there?"

"Gosh, I don't know." I pursed my lips. "To tell you the truth, until I met Christopher Mason, I didn't even know doctors used tissue from cadavers. But to steal it from the dead and sell it for profit . . . " I shivered in spite of the warm sun coming through the car window. "It's beyond gruesome."

"I agree." Ethan's lips formed a firm line. "If Green's guilty, I want to be there when Bill slaps the cuffs on him."

I tapped on the window. "We just passed the entrance to the park. Two Mile Corner should be the next road. Take a left."

After turning the corner, Ethan slowed the car as we approached a lane coming up on our right. A corroded mailbox sat crookedly on a fence post at the end of the lane.

"Is this the place?" he asked, pointing at the mailbox.

"Yes," I answered, and he turned in.

The car bounced and jolted over bone-jarring ruts, and I watched Ethan's jaw tighten as he tried to miss as many as he could. Finally, through the trees, we spotted the old farmhouse.

The screen door hung haphazardly from one hinge, and several windows were broken or cracked. A front porch wrapped around its front, much like the one on Abby's house. Only this porch sagged badly at both ends. Thistles and foxtail flourished in the unmowed yard, with not a blade of grass to be seen. Choked out by all the weeds. An old barn, leaning dangerously to one side, sat a distance from the house. A hawk watched from his perch on the barn's cupola.

*A hawk. Yes.* I hid my smile. *We were on the right track.*

After exiting the car, Ethan walked in long, easy strides over to where I stood by the passenger door. He stopped and made a 360 degree turn as his eyes surveyed the property, taking in the old barn, the sagging porch, and the overgrown yard.

"Silas didn't spend much time keeping the place up, did he?" He opened the car door, leaned in, and removed a gun from the glove compartment.

"What's that for?" I asked, my eyes wide.

"I don't like surprises," he replied as he checked the safety. After sliding the gun smoothly into the waistband of his jeans, he opened the back door and pulled a twenty-four-inch flashlight out of the backseat. "Here, hang onto this."

Taking it from him, I was surprised by its weight. It felt like a club, and in a pinch, it could be used as one.

Both now armed, we waded through the weeds to the house. An old rusted bicycle lay by the corner of the porch. And nearby, two five-gallon buckets were overturned among the weeds. With a booted foot, Ethan pressed down on the wooden steps. Satisfied they would support our weight, he gave me his hand and we carefully eased our way over the sagging porch.

When Ethan tugged on the screen door, the single hinge holding it gave way, and I jumped as it clattered to the porch floor. With a shrug at me, he pushed the front door open and we cautiously stepped inside.

The house was small, and from the look of it, we were standing in what had once been the living room. Wallpaper peeled from the plaster walls and cobwebs hung in the corners. The air was filled with a sour, musty smell. Morning sun filtered through the cracked and broken windows, illuminating the fine layer of dust covering every surface.

"Aunt Dot saw Tink pacing a bedroom, so let's start upstairs first."

I took one step before Ethan pulled me back.

"Look," he said, pointing at the floorboards. "No footprints. It's been a long time since anyone's been inside."

"I don't care," I replied stubbornly. "I want to see the bedrooms."

He stared at me with resignation. "Okay, this is your show."

Slowly, we climbed the rickety stairs, and as we did, the air became more stagnant, the heat more oppressive, but I felt a sense of anticipation grow. I'd seen the hawk. Surely that meant we'd find something. Maybe Tink? Maybe she waited in one of the bedrooms upstairs. My steps quickened.

At the top of the stairs we found a narrow hallway with three doors.

Ethan stepped toward the first. "Shall we see what's behind door number one?" he whispered over his shoulder.

I rolled my eyes and was about to make a retort when a sound from the other side of the door stopped me.

His arm shot out and he pushed me against the wall to the left of the door. "Don't move," he said softly.

I gave a quick nod.

He pulled his gun out of his waistband.

Standing to the side of the door frame, I held my breath as Ethan slowly turned the knob. With a quick move, he threw the door open.

I winced as it hit the wall with a bang.

"Clear," he called as he secured his gun at his waist.

I peeked around the door frame. Tattered lace curtains hung limply at the windows, and dead flies and Japanese beetles littered the dirty floor. A cracked pitcher and washbowl lay discarded in the corner.

No Tink, only a very frightened mouse scurrying across the floor. Disappointment replaced anticipation.

Ethan sensed my feelings and laid a hand on my shoulder. "Come on, let's search the rest of the house."

We did. Room by room. And every room was the same—dirty, musty, and abandoned. The only occupants we found were piles of dead insects.

I stopped as we were making our way to the back of the house. "Listen, do you hear that?"

Ethan turned and faced me. "What?"

"Buzzing, and it sounds like it's coming from the walls. Is there a beehive in here?"

"It's possible. The kitchen must be this way."

When we reached the doorway, I stopped again. "Whew," I said, pinching my nose. "What's that smell? Rotten food?"

Ethan's face wrinkled in distaste. "I doubt it. Smells more like a dead mouse or rat to me."

"Rat? Did you say rat?" Horror flashed through my mind.

Ethan chuckled. "I take it you don't like them?"

"Nooo." I inched closer to him. "I can't stand them. Nasty creatures—twitching whiskers, beady eyes. Ugh." I clutched the flashlight to my chest.

He threw an arm around my shoulder. "Don't worry, I'll protect you."

Together we stepped into the kitchen and saw where the buzzing sound originated.

Hundreds of fat, black flies pinged against the windows, seeking a way out.

Ethan dropped his arm from my shoulder and withdrew his gun. "Go outside."

"No." I eyed the gun. "What is it? What's wrong?"

I don't think he heard me. He was so intent scanning the room. When his gaze landed on a door to the right of the cabinets, he swiftly moved to it and pulled it open.

I staggered as the stench rolling up from the darkness below hit me.

"Whoa, that basement must be full of dead mice," I exclaimed.

He shot me a quick glance. "Give me the flashlight and go outside," he ordered, his expression grim.

Opening the door and taking a deep breath of fresh air, I took one step outside. *Wait a second, what was he doing ordering me around? He said I was running the show.*

Holding my nose, I marched back in the kitchen. "Are you okay down there?"

No reply.

I stepped onto the top step, and the hair on the back of my neck lifted.

"Hey—"

"Don't come down here."

I saw the beam of the powerful flashlight bounce around the room below me. I took one more step and felt a warning sound in the corner of my brain. Grabbing the banister tightly, I went down another step. It creaked under my weight.

"Get back upstairs!" he yelled.

Why was he trying to stop me? What didn't he want me to see? The stink wafting up from the bowels of the house made my stomach twist. Something was dead all right, but it wasn't a mouse.

Tink!

I forgot about the smell, the warning in my head, the nausea, as my feet flew down the steps. Halfway down, my knees buckled, and I slowly sank until I rested on one of the steps, my hands still tightly gripping the banister.

Ethan crouched on the dirt floor, his gun back at his waistband. One hand held a handkerchief firmly against his mouth and nose. The other held the flashlight.

As he turned toward me, the beam played over the dirt floor, showing rotten corpses stacked deep around the room.

# *Twenty-Nine*

I sat on the passenger side of Ethan's car with the door open and watched the parade of vehicles drive up the lane. The medical examiner's van, a car holding two DCI agents, two county sheriff's patrol cars. Another car, belonging to one of the deputies, sat crosswise at the entrance to the lane, effectively blocking all curiosity seekers from joining us. I suspected one of the curious would be Ned from *The Courier*.

Once Ethan saw me trembling on the basement steps, it didn't take long for him to hustle me outside. All the time assuring me all the bodies we'd found belonged to adults, not missing teenage girls. And no, we hadn't stumbled onto a lair of a serial killer. He'd found no evidence of foul play.

When Bill arrived, he, Ethan, and one of Bill's younger deputies left me at the car and returned to the hellhole waiting for them in the abandoned farmhouse. After about five minutes the young deputy exited the house at a dead run. Seconds later I heard retching sounds coming from around the corner of the house. I couldn't blame him—the first time I'd found a body, coughing up my cookies had been my reaction, too. But the remains that I'd stumbled upon were nothing compared to the horror contained in the old basement.

And it didn't take a genius to figure out who was responsible for that horror. Silas Green. Instead of cremating the bodies as he was hired to do, he was using the old house as a storage facility.

Before Ethan rushed me up the stairs, I'd noticed several of the corpses were missing arms, legs, hands—just like in my vision, just like in Tink's dreams. Finding these bodies had to mean we were getting closer to the truth, didn't it?

I searched the trees for the hawk I'd seen earlier. Spotting him would be an affirmation we were on the right path. The branches were empty.

The front door slammed as Bill and Ethan stepped out onto the sagging porch. Even from several yards away I could see the grim expression on both their faces.

Bill barked an order to the young deputy, still pale as he leaned against the side of the old house. I couldn't make out his words, but whatever they were, they sent the young man scurrying.

Bill pulled his hat low on his head, and I felt his eyes fix on me. With purposeful strides, he walked to the car until he towered over me.

"You outdid yourself this time, Ophelia. Must be twenty bodies down there."

"Technically, I didn't find them." I got out of the car and pointed at Ethan. "He did."

Bill removed his hat and rubbed his head. "You want to explain whose idea it was to come here, and why?" He gave me a stern look. "And while you're at it, you want to explain what you were doing at Green's Crematorium last night?"

My eyes narrowed as they focused on Ethan. Someone had ratted me out.

He tapped his forehead in a salute, turned and walked away, leaving me to do my own explaining.

*Thanks, Ethan.*

"Ahh—well—it's like this . . . " I said, stumbling over my words as I tried to dig myself out of the hole into which Ethan had so thoughtfully dumped me.

He lifted a brow. "Yes?"

Tugging on Bill's arm, I pulled him over to a tree where our conversation wouldn't be overheard by all the official personnel milling around the overgrown yard.

"Are you going to arrest me if I tell the truth?"

His hand stole halfway to his head before he dropped it to his side.

"If you are," I continued in a stubborn voice, "I won't admit to a thing, and you're just going to have to prove I've been engaged in illegal activities." I kicked a dirt clod lying at my feet. "I have to find Tink, and I can't do it sitting in a jail cell."

"No, I'm not going to arrest you," he said slowly, as if he had to think about it. "I don't think you'd be a model prisoner, Ophelia, and I've enough problems without you raising a ruckus from one of my cells."

"All righty, then." I jerked my head toward a spot farther from the crowd milling around the old house. "Tink's dreams of spirits trying to contact her began the night before we met Buchanan at the airport. When she did meet him, she said later he gave her an 'icky' feeling." A thought came to me. "The day we introduced you to Aunt Dot at Stumpy's, had you just come from Buchanan's murder scene?"

"Yeah, why?"

"You gave her the same feeling."

"Are you telling me she sensed Buchanan was dead?"

"No, not exactly. I don't know how to explain how Tink's sixth sense works, or how it feels, since I'm not a medium."

"How did she take Buchanan's death?"

"She felt guilty. She thought the spirits were trying to give her a message, and if she'd been open to listening, she might have been able to warn him."

Bill scratched his head. "Buchanan would've thought she was nuts."

I nodded. "That's what I told her, too, but the guilt she felt caused her to react the way she did at the campgrounds when T.P. brought her the skull."

Bill's eyes traveled around the property. "I've got a pretty good idea where the dog found the skull."

I squinted my eyes, staring at the old farmhouse and thinking of all the unburied. "If Silas hasn't been cremating the bodies, what's in the urns he's giving to the families of the dead?"

Bill's jaw worked as he clenched and unclenched his teeth. "The medical examiner will have to determine that." He rubbed his head and exhaled a long breath. "It will be necessary to go through all his records, contact the families, and test all the ashes."

"When you do look at his files, you're going to find he falsified death certificates and family consent forms for tissue donation," I said, still watching the farmhouse.

He turned to me in surprise. "How do you—" Breaking off abruptly, he held up a hand. "No, don't tell me. I'm going to pretend you figured it out from a vision."

I dropped another piece of information. "Silas was selling the tissue to Dr. Christopher Mason's biomedical supply company."

"Should I assume that was from another 'vision,' or am I going to get a complaint from Dr. Mason? Did you sneak around his property, too?"

I gave Bill a small grin. "I think for your peace of mind . . . let's go with 'vision.'"

Bill pulled a pad and pen from his front pocket. Flipping it open, he wrote Christopher's name. "Is this the doctor in Des Moines?"

"Yeah, Darci could give you the address of his biomedical supply office."

"Darci, huh?" he said with a scowl.

My grin widened to a smile in response. The smile fled as another thought occurred to me. "I've got a question for you. Ethan mentioned that harvesting would require some skill. The bodies? Were they, um, um—"

"Hacked?" he asked, finishing my sentence.

I paled. "Yeah."

"Hard to tell." His mouth formed a grim line. "Some were . . . well, in pretty bad shape."

"That's okay," I said, wincing. "I get the picture."

"We'll know more after the autopsies." He tapped the pen on the notebook. "You're thinking maybe someone with a medical background helped with the tissue retrieval? Maybe Dr. Mason was more than just the buyer?"

"The thought crossed my mind."

Bill focused on the old house. "I don't know how much skill it would take. That's another question the M.E. will be able to answer. I do remember Silas worked for a meat packing plant up north before he went into the business with his dad."

"So he would know—"

"How to use a saw." He faced me. "You're still convinced Silas is tied to Tink's disappearance?"

"Yes."

"Well, I've got a warrant issued for him. Once we find him, we'll haul him in for questioning—"

"Once you find him? You mean he's gone?"

Bill patted my arm reassuringly. "Silas wasn't at his house

when Alan stopped, but he's checking out Silas's known hangouts. Don't worry. We'll find him, and—"

One of Bill's deputies stepped out of the barn and, cupping his hands to his mouth, yelled, "Hey, Bill, you'd better get over here. We've found more bodies."

As one of the deputies drove me home a short time later, we had to pass the group of gawkers gathered at the end of the lane. Slouching down in the seat, I shielded my face with the palm of my hand. Sooner or later the grisly discovery at the vacant Green farm would have the rumor mill churning. And sooner or later my role would be known.

I preferred later. I had enough to think about at the moment.

The house was empty when I walked in. After wandering through the kitchen, I went out the back door.

Aunt Dot sat at the patio table, tossing a ball to T.P. with her good hand. Lady lay at her feet, and Queenie watched from her perch on the table.

"Where's Abby?" I asked, flopping down in the chair next to her.

"Abby's at the greenhouse." She gazed at me with concern. "You were gone a long time. We were beginning to worry."

"Sorry. Ran into some problems." Giving a long sigh, I related my morning to Aunt Dot.

Her eyes flashed with anger as she smacked her cane on the patio. "That awful, awful, man!" she exclaimed in disgust. "Ack, such disrespect. Bad enough carving up the dead, but then to treat them like garbage."

Her words brought back vivid images of what I'd seen in that basement. I held up a hand, stopping her. "Okay, okay. Could we please not talk about it?"

She turned to me, her face full of sympathy. "Would you like some hot tea?"

"No, thanks anyway."

"A sandwich?"

I rolled my eyes and stuck out my tongue. "Absolutely not."

"No, I don't suppose you do," she said with a sad shake of her head.

T.P. gave up on Aunt Dot continuing their game of fetch and abandoned the ball to chase a butterfly flitting around the backyard.

I watched Aunt Dot and could almost see the wheels spinning underneath the cap of blue frizz. "What are you thinking?" I asked.

"Kevin—I want to grill Kevin," she replied with a determined nod.

A laugh escaped me. "Why Kevin? He's not involved with Silas."

"Are you sure?"

"I suppose in a way he is—he worked for Mr. Buchanan, so he would have had dealings with Silas." I gave her a puzzled look. "I thought you liked Kevin. You invited him to Abby's for dinner."

"There's something fishy about him."

"Aunt Dot, yesterday you were convinced Mrs. Buchanan and Dr. Mason were involved in Buchanan's death. Today you suspect Kevin. What changed your mind?"

"Humph, he gossiped about his employer's wife."

"Well, yes he did, but—"

"The fairies don't like him."

Ahh, jeez. Not the fairies again. I noticed that whenever Aunt Dot needed a reason to justify her opinion, she used the fairies. Must be nice to have such a handy excuse. Oh well, at ninety-one, I guess she was entitled. I decided I might as well play along with her.

"Did the fairies give you any more information about Tink?" I asked, trying to keep the doubt out of my voice.

Her head bobbed once with certainty. "Yes, Tink's sending you a message."

My hand shot out and touched her arm. "What? What kind of a message? Do you mean she's trying to reach me with her mind?"

"I don't know. The fairies didn't say." She lowered her head. "They don't like to meddle in human affairs, you know."

Peachy. Why couldn't they just be like the rest of us?

# *Thirty*

The need to wash away the scent of death I felt clinging to me had become overpowering, so I left Aunt Dot on the patio and went to take a shower. Grabbing the sea salt, I sprinkled tiny grains in my hair as I stood and let the hot water cascade over me. Immediately, a sense of cleansing came to me. I hadn't realized it, but the scene I'd witnessed in the basement had infiltrated me to the core with its ugliness.

I scrubbed my flesh until it felt almost raw, trying to drive the images from my mind and soul. I'd never forget what I'd seen, but I had to detach myself in order to continue my quest to find Tink.

When I finished my shower, I sprayed the rosewater that Abby had made for me all over my body. Now, instead of decay assaulting my nose, the warm summer smell of roses surrounded me.

Dressed in my long terry-cloth robe, I padded down the stairs and into my office. A quick check out the window revealed Aunt Dot still on the patio with the pets.

Good. I could count on being undisturbed for at least a little while.

Crossing to my desk, I removed my bag of runes. Just like

I had several nights ago, I made a circle of salt in the middle of the room. Lighting sage and a pure white candle, I picked up an amethyst from my desk and seated myself cross-legged in the circle's center. I unfolded a square of linen and laid the runes in my lap.

Tink was trying to send me a message, huh? Let's see if the runes would deliver it.

Placing the amethyst next to the candle, I tried to calm my fears for her safety and let each deep breath I took carry them away. I picked up the bag and focused on my senses one at a time.

Outside, I heard T.P. yapping playfully, and Aunt Dot's low chuckle.

I felt the cool stones contained in the worn leather pouch slip through my fingers.

With each breath, I inhaled the sweet aroma of sage mingled with the scent of rosewater.

I let my eyelids drift closed and saw stars dancing in the darkness as I concentrated on seeing with my mind instead of my eyes.

Carefully, I framed my question. *How to find Tink?*

My hand tingled as the runes called to me. Removing one of the stones from the bag, I placed it to my left on the linen cloth. I drew another and laid it in the center. The next rune went to my right. Two more runes followed. I placed the fourth rune above the center and the fifth one below.

I studied the pattern of runes laid out before me: a Celtic cross. I began with the center rune—the second one I'd drawn. It would show me the present problem.

Hagalaz: *haw-gaw-laws.*

*Hail, limitations, delays, circumstances beyond one's control, not an opportune time for new beginnings.*

I tapped my chin as I studied the rune.

Tink's kidnapping had been beyond my control. I'd tried to protect her and failed. Not the time for new beginnings? The only new beginning that sprang to mind was the adoption. Was that what it meant? If so, what did the adoption have to do with Tink's disappearance?

I moved to the first rune, the one to my left. It indicated what factors from the past were affecting the current problem.

Ansuz: *awn-sooze.*

*Wisdom, advice from an older person, the spoken word.*

Crud. It was inverted. Not a good sign. Inverted, the rune had the opposite meaning. Lies, trickery. Someone from the past was causing the situation I now faced through deception.

How far in the past? One week? Six months? A year? I ran over a list in my mind of people who had cause to wish ill upon my family. Hmm, the ones with the most compelling reasons either were in prison or confined to a state mental hospital like Juliet. And Bill hadn't informed me of anyone's release.

I flipped over the top rune: What help I could expect to receive with my dilemma?

Tiwaz: *tea-waz.*

I sighed in relief.

*Success, victory, enough determination to overcome all odds.*

Determination? The runes had that one right—nothing would stop me from finding Tink.

Tiwaz also indicated a strong male figure. A man who would help me.

I didn't need to be a genius to figure who that rune meant: Ethan. Its appearance also confirmed what Abby had seen. An eagle circling above a man in the shadows, and that man would help me recover Tink.

My gaze fell on the rune below center. Its position stood for that which cannot be changed. Fate. Destiny. If the rune was inverted, or perhaps one like Isa, it could indicate that I'd be powerless to change what was to be.

With trembling fingers, I turned the stone.

Thank goodness. Raido: *rye-through.*

*Movement, change, a journey, possibly an emotional one.*

Best of all, the stone wasn't inverted, so it told of a positive change, not a negative one.

I knew in my heart what the rune was trying to tell me. Never again would my life be the same. I'd welcomed Tink into my home and into my heart. For now and forever we'd be bound together with love. My friendship with Darci, for instance. Our argument had hurt more than I thought possible, and never again would I be able to shut people out of my life and return to hiding behind my wall.

Staring at the last rune, the one on the right, the one that would show either the success or failure of my quest, I took a deep breath and slowly turned it over.

Berkano: *bear-kawn-oh.*

*Birth, family, children—what we hold dear.*

It was the same rune that had showed up in my first reading several days ago. Only this time it wasn't inverted.

The runes blurred as my eyes filled with tears. Tink would be restored to us. All would be well. Unfortunately, other than showing me that I could expect Ethan's help, the runes were kind of iffy as to how I would achieve this feat.

I wiped my eyes and stared thoughtfully at the past and present runes. They were negative, but the rest were positive.

I picked up Ansuz and studied it. Lies and deceit. Silas Green lied. He'd deceived the families of the departed, falsified documents, and maybe even killed Raymond Buchanan.

Maybe he'd lied to Christopher, too.

Pulling my fingers through my hair, I tried to think of a plan. Buchanan was dead, Silas had disappeared, and they were out of my reach.

One person was left.

I intended to have a little talk with Dr. Christopher Mason.

Mid-afternoon. Would Christopher be home, or on the golf course? I hoped home. I had questions.

I checked in with Abby, but ignored the call from Darci. If I talked to her now, it would take me at least twenty minutes of arguing to convince her she couldn't accompany me. And knowing Darci, the arguments would be futile, she'd follow me.

I'd put effort into my appearance—a red silk blouse, tan linen slacks, and three-inch heels. I even wore makeup.

Grabbing my purse and shoving my sunglasses on my face, I flung the door open just as Ethan raised his hand to knock.

"Oh, you startled me," I said, pressing a hand to my chest.

Ethan didn't speak as his eyes traveled from my feet to the top of my head. He gave a low whistle and took a step back. "I didn't expect to find you like this. I expected distraught and disheveled, not attractive with attitude. Got a date?"

I leaned against the doorjamb and pulled my glasses down my nose. "Not exactly," I said, and peered over the rims.

"Where are you headed?"

"Before I answer . . . you warned me earlier that you're an officer of the court. Are you a cop now or not?"

He lifted an eyebrow. "Not."

Shoving my sunglasses back on my nose, I jingled my keys in front of his face. "You want to take a ride?"

"Where to?"

"Des Moines."

"Are you going to get me in trouble?" he asked as he shoved his hands in his pockets and grinned.

I gave Ethan the same look he'd given me, starting at the top of his boots, past his narrow waist, to the top of his streaked blond head. His jeans hugged his lean frame, and the corduroy jacket he wore made his shoulders look even broader. His gray eyes were full of humor as he watched me scope him out.

With a smile, I marched past him and down the steps.

"Buster," I called over my shoulder. "I think your middle name is 'trouble.'"

The closer we got to Des Moines, the more agitated I felt. I fiddled with the air-conditioning control. I turned the radio up. I turned the radio down. I'd just reached for the dial a fourth time when Ethan's hand reached out and took mine. He gave my fingers a quick squeeze.

"How are you going to play this?" he asked.

My eyes darted to him before focusing on the highway again. "Play what?"

"Dr. Mason. Do you want to play 'good cop, bad cop'?" He winked. "I'll let you be the bad cop."

I appreciated his attempt to lighten the building tension inside me by teasing. But his efforts failed. All I wanted was to find Tink.

"No thanks." My hands clenched the steering wheel. "I want to know where Silas Green is."

"You're still convinced he took Tink?"

"Yeah." I purposely loosened my grip. "I didn't mention this before, but in my vision, Silas carried a pile of bones—"

He frowned. "Doesn't surprise me, considering what we found in that basement."

"I saw Tink's bracelet dangling from one of the bones."

Ethan jerked his head toward the window and said nothing. An uncomfortable silence followed.

"What are you thinking, Ethan?"

"Ophelia," he said gently, "the bracelet was hanging from a bone?" He paused. "I'm not a psychic—"

My head whipped from side to side. "No, no! I told you, I'd know if something had happened to her. The runes said we'd find her."

"What you saw today didn't change your mind?"

"No. I have to believe in what I feel, what I know. It's the only thing giving me hope." My voice sounded strained.

"You need to calm down before we reach Mason's. You can't go in with guns blazing," he insisted. "With a guy like Mason, you have to use finesse. Can you do that?"

"Yes." My lips tightened. "I can do whatever it takes to find Tink."

"Okay." He nodded. "We'll get your answers. You'll do fine."

I inhaled then exhaled slowly. "Thanks, Ethan," I said, grateful for his confidence in me.

Twisting in his seat, he peeked over his shoulder at the back. "You don't have your Louisville Slugger back there, do you?"

"No," I said, giving him a wicked grin. "But if Mason doesn't give me the answers I want, I can always go home and get it."

# Thirty-One

When we pulled into the driveway twenty minutes later, Ethan faced me. "Do you have the slightest idea what you'll ask him?"

I shrugged. "I thought I'd wing it."

"Winging it is never good," he said with apprehension.

"It's all I've got," I said while getting out of the car.

Ethan hung back in the driveway as I rang Christopher's doorbell.

No answer.

I waited a couple of minutes and rang again.

Cupping my hands to the side of my face, I peered in the frosted glass door and thought I saw a shadow cross the room toward the back of the house.

I put my finger on the button and held it down.

From inside the house I heard the padding of bare feet across his tiled entry. In a moment the door opened.

"Ophelia," Christopher said with surprise. "How nice to see you."

As he stood in the doorway, one hand rested on the door, holding it open only a few inches. He didn't invite me in.

"May I talk to you?" I peeked over his shoulder. "Inside," I said pointedly.

With a sigh, he swung the door wider. "Of course, come in." His eyes traveled from me to Ethan.

"I'm sorry," I said, stretching an arm toward Ethan. "This is my friend, Ethan, ah . . . " I clamped my mouth shut.

Dang. Ethan had never told me his last name.

Ethan quickly stepped up behind me. "Clement," he said, reaching out and shaking Christopher's hand. "Ethan Clement."

Christopher motioned us into the house.

"May I get you anything?" he asked graciously when we were inside. "Wine? No, you prefer beer, don't you, Ophelia?"

"No, thank you," I replied, following him to the living room.

"You, Ethan?" he asked over his shoulder.

Ethan responded with a slight shake of his head.

Christopher strolled over to an upholstered club chair and sat. With a wave of his hand, he pointed to the couch. "Please."

Ethan took a seat on the couch while I remained standing, my eyes surveying the room as I gathered my thoughts.

The room looked different in daylight, no longer a stage set for seduction. Or was it? Two empty wineglasses were placed side by side on the coffee table. One of them was marked with bright red lipstick.

Ethan caught my eye and gave an imperceptible nod.

Christopher eased back in his chair and crossed his legs at his ankles. He watched me expectantly. "What can I do for you, Ophelia? Is this visit about your aunt? If so, my office hours—"

"When was the last time you saw Silas Green?" I blurted out.

"Silas Green?" He cast a perplexed glance at Ethan.

"The owner of Green's Crematorium."

A shadow crossed his face. "I barely know him."

"You know him well enough to buy tissue and body parts from him for your biomedical supply business," I said.

"We don't 'buy' tissue." A self-satisfied smile chased the shadow away.

His attitude annoyed me.

"No, you pay fees for harvesting, don't you?"

"A nominal amount."

Annoyance shifted to irritation.

"And you do business with Silas . . . Where is he?"

"I don't know why you would presume that I know anything about Silas. We deal with several crematoriums and funeral homes," he replied smugly. "And I don't personally handle shipments from any of them. I employ people to handle the details for me."

I crossed my arms over my chest as I felt my irritation turn to anger. "What about yesterday? Silas dropped off two coolers while you were at the biomedical office."

"I don't know what you're talking about." Christopher studied his well-manicured hands.

*Jeez, what a liar. And he's blowing me off.*

"Really?" I lifted an eyebrow. "Aunt Dot, Darci, and I saw you."

He made a sound in the back of his throat. "Ophelia, I know things didn't work out between us, but you're mistaken." Facing Ethan, he spread his hands wide and gave Ethan a helpless shrug.

I thought of Tink, alone somewhere, being held against her will. His silent appeal to Ethan caused my anger to flare even hotter.

I marched over until I stood right over him. "My daughter is missing. Silas Green is involved, and you're involved with Silas."

Christopher looked again to Ethan for help with the crazy woman standing over him—me. The strain of the past few days tipped me over the edge.

"Don't know anything, huh? Well, maybe you'll start remembering. Any minute now your lucrative, little black market body part business is going to blow up in your face."

Ethan's groan penetrated my anger.

*So much for finesse.*

Christopher surged to his feet. "How dare you attack my professional reputation? Who do you think you are?" He stood toe-to-toe with me. "I took pity on you that night at the Marriott. You were so out of your league." He rolled his eyes. "If I wouldn't have run into you at Buchanan's funeral, I never would've asked you for a date."

"Pity?" I spluttered. "Was that before or after you tried to sleep with me?"

In the background, Ethan choked.

"You can't stand rejection can you? Now you're trying to get even by slandering me." He leaned forward, right in my face.

I never saw Ethan move, but the next thing I knew, Christopher stumbled backward and landed in the chair. With a practiced move, Ethan nonchalantly brushed aside the front of his jacket. It gave Christopher a brief look at the holster and gun Ethan wore underneath it.

Christopher's face lost its color. "Who the hell are you?"

"I told you, Ethan Clement, but I did forget to mention I'm a DEA agent." Ethan's lips formed a cold smile. "Maybe you'd like to answer some questions now?"

"DEA? Drugs? I don't know anything about any drugs."

"I didn't say you did." Ethan turned to me. "Why don't you sit on the couch, Ophelia? I think Dr. Mason is willing to talk to us, aren't you, Dr. Mason?"

Christopher nodded.

Ethan joined me on the couch and withdrew a pad and a pen from the inside pocket of his jacket.

It gave Christopher another peek at his gun.

Ethan leaned forward and let his hands dangle loosely on his knees. "I'm here in an unofficial capacity, but I've volunteered to help Ms. Jensen find her daughter. As she told you, we believe Silas is implicated."

Christopher regained some of his composure during Ethan's explanation. "Of course, I'll cooperate, but my name must be kept out of the media. I have my reputation to protect."

Ethan tugged on his lower lip. "I can't make any promises, but I'll pass your request on to Sheriff Wilson." He flipped open his notebook. "About your business dealings with Silas? He's required to provide you with copies of the death certificates for all those who donate tissue?"

"Yes."

"Copies of the family consent forms?"

"Yes."

"Do you ever follow up with the families?"

Christopher looked perplexed. "What do you mean?"

"Do you ever contact the families listed on those forms?"

"No, it's not required."

"It is required to provide blood samples from the tissue donors, isn't it?"

Christopher's gaze slid away from Ethan. "Yes."

"Can you account for your time the night Raymond Buchanan died?"

"I was occupied." Christopher squirmed uneasily in his chair.

Ethan scowled. "Can you be more specific?"

"Are you prepared to charge me with something?" Christopher sat forward. "Maybe I need my attorney present?"

"If you'd prefer, Dr. Mason. Right now this is just a friendly conversation, but we *could* finish it at the courthouse," Ethan countered as he tapped his pen on his knee. He pursed his lips. "But after the discovery we made this morning, the media is probably camped out on the steps by now."

"Discovery?"

"Humph, maybe you haven't heard the news reports." He tapped his pen faster. "Silas got lazy and stopped cremating bodies. We found . . . " He raised his eyes to the ceiling. "I think last count was forty at one place and—"

"Oh, God." Christopher covered his face with his hands. "That idiot," he muttered.

Ethan fixed his gaze on Christopher. "Did you know about the bodies?"

"No, I swear." Christopher lowered his hands. "I never went to the crematorium. Silas would deliver the tissue and the forms. I had no reason to suspect he was doing anything illegal."

"Gee, Christopher," I said, hooking an arm over the back of the couch. "I'd have thought the Wite-Out on the forms would have been a clue."

Ethan touched my arm lightly to silence me. His sleet gray eyes drilled Christopher. "We have a young girl missing, a man's dead, and I can assure you there'll be a full investigation into both the crematorium and your biomedical supply business."

Christopher passed a hand over his eyes. "I'm ruined."

I watched him with disgust. Tink had been kidnapped,

Buchanan murdered, Silas had defiled bodies, and all he cared about was himself. I couldn't believe I'd ever thought him attractive.

Before I could express my thoughts, someone called from the other side of the room: "I'm innocent."

I turned to see Mrs. Buchanan in the doorway. She stared at us with wild-eyed fear, her hand resting on the wall.

She crossed the room and pointed at Christopher. "I didn't know what he was doing."

A gold heart on a thin chain dangled from her wrist. Tink's bracelet.

Ethan made a grab for me as I flew at her, but he missed. Clutching her shoulders, I shook her until her head bobbled like a rag doll's.

"Where did you get that bracelet?" I snarled.

She slapped at me, but I didn't feel the blows landing.

"Let go!" she screamed.

My fingers dug into her flesh and my hair flopped in my face as I jerked her back and forth.

"Ophelia!" Ethan's voiced sounded through the haze of my rage.

An arm shot around my waist and hauled me off my feet. Spinning me, Ethan set me behind him and away from Mrs. Buchanan.

I shoved at his solid body as I stretched my arm past him to claw at the widow.

Christopher now stood next to her, and he threw a comforting arm over her shoulders, drawing her away. "Barbara—"

She moved away from him with a flounce. "This is all your fault."

I tried to dodge Ethan, but he blocked me, then whirled on me and firmly gripped my upper arm. "Knock it off unless you want to face assault charges."

With a shaking hand, I lifted the hair out of my face.

"She has Tink's bracelet," I said, my voice trembling.

"This?" she mocked, and held up her wrist. Ripping the bracelet off, she threw it on the coffee table. "Kevin gave it to me."

Christopher looked stunned. "Barbara? Why would Kevin give—" The light of realization dawned in his eyes and he sank to the couch.

Ethan unclipped his cell phone and quickly pressed the buttons. "Bill, send a car to Dr. Christopher Mason's house."

He gave Bill the address.

"Mrs. Buchanan is here, too. I think you'll want to talk to them." He held the phone away from his ear as Bill shouted on the other end, then added, "And Bill? Pick up Kevin Roth."

# *Thirty-Two*

We waited until the patrol car arrived at Christopher's.

Back in Ethan's car, I buckled up and glanced at him.

"What was the deal with flashing your gun?"

"Achieved the desired effect, didn't it?" He kept his focus on the patrol car ahead.

"Yes, but I thought you said you weren't a cop today?"

"Honey, I'm always a cop. And you came this close . . ." He held up two fingers, an inch apart. " . . . to me arresting you."

His eyes slid in my direction as he prepared to deliver his lecture concerning my behavior, but one look at my face stopped him.

He clamped his mouth shut with effort, and we followed the deputy to the courthouse in Aiken without speaking.

TV vans filled the street in front of the old limestone courthouse. In order to avoid them, we pulled into the parking lot behind the building and entered that way.

As we came in the back door, we saw Bill standing at the end of the long hallway. He noticed us, his feet set apart in a pugnacious stance, and bowed his head, giving it a long shake.

My steps faltered as I felt a little shudder go through me. Bill might have yelled at me in the past, but I had a feeling those exchanges would pale in comparison to what he'd say to me today.

I was wrong. His anger wasn't focused on me, but on Ethan.

"I'd ask what in hell you thought you were doing taking her to Mason's," he said, "but I don't have time now." He raked Ethan up and down. "The media's gathering like vultures, and I have to get control of the situation."

"She would have gone with or without me," Ethan replied in his defense.

Bill rubbed his head. "You think I don't know that?" He shoved a finger in my direction. "With her, I expect trouble. But you're a cop. You're supposed to know how to handle people like her."

Ethan snorted. "Yeah, right."

I would have pointed out that I was standing right there and they didn't need to talk about me as if I were invisible. But in this case, maybe invisible wasn't such a bad thing.

"Did you pick up Kevin Roth?" Ethan asked, changing the subject.

"Yeah."

"According to Mrs. Buchanan, he had Tink's bracelet. Can you use that to get a search warrant for the funeral home, for his apartment?"

Bill held up a hand. "He claims Silas gave him the bracelet to pawn." .

"See," I said, tugging on Ethan's sleeve. "I told you Silas was involved in Tink's disappearance." I turned to Bill. "Have you found Silas yet?"

"No," he said shortly.

"Can I come in for Kevin's questioning?"

"No," Bill and Ethan said at the same time.

"I've called Darci," Bill said. "She's on her way to pick you up. You're going home, and you're going to stay there."

"But Bill—" I pleaded.

He cut me off. "You heard me."

I jammed my hands on my hips. "I'm not leaving. This is a public place. I can be here if I want—"

Bill took a step toward me. "Ophelia," he growled.

"Ethan? Please?"

"Ah, let her stay, Bill. Her daughter's missing, and those three"—he motioned to the door behind him—"might be able to shed some light on the case."

Bill eyed me with uncertainty.

"You won't cause any trouble, will you, Ophelia?" Ethan asked, pressing the advantage.

"I swear." I motioned to the bench opposite the door. "I'll sit there, quiet as can be."

"Humph." Bill's face softened. "If you so much as move—"

A deputy running down the hall interrupted him. "Bill, we've found a body at the crematorium."

"Dumped?"

"No, this one's in the oven Silas uses."

Bill's forehead wrinkled in a frown. "Maybe Silas was trying to catch up on his work."

The deputy shrugged. "The M.E.'s on his way to Green's to check it out."

Bill gave him a curt nod and pointed to the door. "I'll be in there. I want the reports as they come in." He looked at me. "You plant your butt on that bench and don't you dare move."

"Yes, sir," I replied, and crossed to the bench.

* * *

Ethan and Bill disappeared into the room holding Kevin Roth.

The minutes ticked by as I stared at the closed door. How long did it take to sweat the information out of him? I had to fight the urge to bust into the room and demand what he knew about Tink, but I figured if I did, my next stop would be a cell.

The familiar click of heels on the linoleum floor had me turning my head.

Darci hurrying toward me. When she reached the bench, she slid down next to me. "Have they found Tink?"

"No." I shook my head forlornly and proceeded to tell her the events of the day.

When I was finished, she sighed deeply. "What a mess . . . Mrs. Buchanan and both Dr. Mason and Kevin?" She rolled her eyes. "She was busy."

"It would appear so. I guess Aunt Dot's suspicions were correct. Christopher looked very surprised when he figured it out."

"Do you think Kevin kidnapped Tink?"

"I don't know. He was the one who gave the bracelet to Mrs. Buchanan, but he claims Silas was the one who gave it to him." I drummed my fingers on my thighs. "They need to find Silas."

Another deputy hurrying down the hall caught our attention. He rapped sharply on the door and stepped back when Bill opened it. Leaning close, he talked to Bill in a low voice.

I strained to hear what he said.

Bill shot a look in my direction and then nodded at the deputy. Taking a step back, he firmly shut the door.

"What was that about?" Darci wondered.

"I don't know," I said, jiggling my leg with nervousness. "Maybe they found Silas."

Darci took my hand in hers. "Don't worry. Bill will find her."

"*What* is taking them so long?" I exclaimed.

Before Darci could reply, the door opened again and Ethan stepped into the hallway, a grim expression on his face. Crossing to us, he sat next to me and stared straight ahead, as if trying to marshal his thoughts.

"Ophelia—" he began.

"It's not good, is it?" My stomach sank to my toes.

"They think they've found Silas—"

"'Think?'"

"The ashes and bone fragments at the crematorium—"

I clutched Ethan's leg. "Not Tink?" I asked, my voice laced with fear.

He shook his head. "The M.E. found a piece of melted plastic in with the fragments. He thinks it came from a knee replacement."

I bowed my head in relief. Not Tink.

"They've also found traces of blood in Silas's office."

My eyes narrowed in suspicion. "Whose?"

"Silas. It's his remains in the oven."

My mind raced, trying to put what Ethan was saying together. "But how do you know? And if Silas is dead, then where's Tink? Do you have any idea where he's hid her?"

"Ophelia, Silas didn't kidnap Tink," he said softly.

"He had her bracelet—"

"According to Kevin, Silas found it at Roseman."

My shoulders sagged as I remembered our campout. Tink had put the bracelet in her pocket after she caught it on the tent pole. It must've fallen out later that night. "So the bracelet wasn't a clue," I stated in a stunned voice.

"No."

"But—"

Ethan laid a hand on my knee. "There's more."

"M-m-more?" I stuttered.

"Kevin Roth just confessed to killing both Raymond Buchanan and Silas Green," he said simply.

I slapped the seat. "Then Kevin took Tink." I made a move to stand, but Ethan put pressure on my knee, stopping me.

"Kevin was running the body snatching scheme with Silas's help. He used his medical school background to harvest the tissue. Silas was the deliveryman." Ethan leaned forward and propped his elbows on his knees. "Buchanan didn't die Saturday night, as we thought. He went out to Roseman late that night to do some cat-fishing. While there, he stumbled over one of Silas's stashed corpses. He recognized the corpse as someone Silas was hired to cremate."

"But Kevin killed him before he could report what he'd found?" I asked.

"Yes, Buchanan went to the funeral home to make the call. He trusted Kevin, so he told him about the body. Kevin knew an investigation at Green's would uncover what they were doing to the bodies."

I sat in stunned silence.

Darci cleared her throat. "Did Christopher know?"

"I think he knew the whole thing was shady, but he didn't ask questions," Ethan answered.

"When did Kevin kill Silas?" Darci asked.

"Last night, after you were almost caught—"

She picked at the seat. "Ah, well—"

"Never mind, you don't have to explain. I already know." Ethan slowly moved his head from side to side. "You girls were lucky Kevin and Silas didn't catch you."

I shook myself out of my stupor. "But what about Tink?"

"I don't know, Ophelia. Kevin swears they didn't take her—"

"He's lying." I shot to my feet. "Every dream, every vision, has led us to this point!"

I spun on my heel and rushed the door. Before Ethan could stop me, I flung it open and ran to a surprised Kevin. Yanking him to his feet, I grabbed his shirt and yelled in his face, *"Where's my daughter!"*

It took two deputies to pull me off of him.

# Thirty-Three

The tears wouldn't stop.

But they were the only reason I wasn't sitting in a cell instead of driving home with Darci. I'd never seen Bill as angry as when I'd burst through the door.

At the moment, I didn't care. My talent had betrayed me and led me down the wrong path. Precious time had been wasted while I was off chasing handless spirits and body snatchers. I despaired of ever finding Tink.

"I don't understand," I said, slamming my fist against the seat of Darci's car. "The signs all pointed to Silas."

A deep hiccup stopped my tirade.

Wiping my face, I stared bleakly down the road. "I can't think."

Darci's face tightened with worry. "You need to calm down. This isn't good for you."

"I don't care." I sighed as hopelessness swamped me.

"Do you think having a case of hysterics will help find Tink?"

"Hysterics? They're the only reason Bill didn't arrest me. The last thing he wanted was a wailing woman in his peaceful jail."

"You'll feel better after you see Abby and Aunt Dot." Darci's voice was soothing. "They're waiting for you at home."

I gave her a bitter look. "Yeah, Aunt Dot and her fairies. A lot of bloody good help they've been."

"She said the fairies didn't think Silas was smart enough to be behind the body snatching," she reasoned. "You mentioned that they didn't like Kevin."

I blew my nose and took a deep breath. "I'm not one hundred percent sure her fairies aren't a result of delusions. Or tippling." I wiped my face with the heel of my hand. "Maybe they're just a figment of her imagination, which she uses to explain her psychic gifts."

"Doesn't matter, she's been right at least twice now." Her eyes slid briefly in my direction. "And I don't like pointing this out, but when it comes to what's happening with Tink, that's better than you or Abby have done."

I puffed out my cheeks and blew out slowly. "You're right. Maybe I should pay more attention to what she's saying."

When we arrived at the house, I spotted Abby waiting for us on the front porch, wringing her hands. I flew out of the car and into her arms. The tears flowed again.

"Why? Why?" I cried, my sobs muffled against her shoulder.

Abby made soft tsking sounds as she led me through the house and into the kitchen, where Aunt Dot was sitting at the table. Pulling out a chair, she helped me ease my trembling body down and slid a cup of tea over to me.

"Drink it," she commanded.

I took a cautious sip, and the hot liquid felt good flowing down my aching throat. Warmth, starting in the center of my body, spread outward, and my shaking stopped.

"Better?" she asked, placing a hand on my shoulder.

I bobbed my head.

With a small smile, she took a place at the table next to Aunt Dot.

Darci sat, too. Scooting her chair forward, she propped her arms on the table. "Tell me about your fairies, Aunt Dot."

Aunt Dot cast a nervous look my way. "Ophelia doesn't believe in them."

"She just doesn't understand," Darci said gently.

"Ack, I've seen them ever since I was a little girl." Her eyes widened. "Not the bad ones, though, just the good ones." A dreamy expression softened her face. "They're beautiful and playful. And their voices sound like the tinkling of bells. They don't like to interfere with the doings of humans, though. Mind their own business, they do." She gave an emphatic nod.

"Is that why they won't say where Tink is?" Darci asked.

"Yes, it's one of the reasons." Aunt Dot's body rocked back and forth. "But she is still safe. They told me this morning."

I cleared my throat. "What's another reason, Aunt Dot?"

"The things that have happened are part of the pattern."

"What pattern?"

"The pattern of your life, child. You had lessons that needed learning."

I pulled my hair back from my face. "Pretty hard lessons, I'd say."

"They have been, but the end is in sight. You've learned, and your life will never be the same. There'll be more down the road for you, but for now the lesson is almost finished."

"Can you be a little more specific?"

She smiled, her wrinkles deepening. "That's for you to figure out."

I rose and carried my now empty cup to the sink. "Answers like *that* is what I *hate* about all this psychic stuff," I grumbled. "Why can't you just know what you need to know, without all the mumbo jumbo 'Here's a sign' crap."

Aunt Dot exchanged a look with Abby. "I'd bet her next lesson will be one in patience," she said in a wise voice.

"Listen, messages from the fairies aside," I said, leaning against the counter, "the way I see it, we're no closer to finding Tink than we were—"

Aunt Dot turned to me in surprise. "Didn't Tink contact you?"

"No," I replied in a clipped voice.

"Hmm, the fairies said the message is there. It's going to show you the way."

I clutched the edge of the counter. "I did a Celtic cross reading with the runes."

Aunt Dot nodded in approval. "Good, good."

"They were all positive except the one representing the present." I snorted. "Go figure. Oh . . . wait a second . . . the rune in the 'past' position was inverted."

"And it said what, dear?" Abby asked.

"The current situation is being affected by lies and trickery."

"Someone is lying to you?"

"Abby, all we've run into so far is liars. Kevin Roth, Silas Green, Christopher Mason." I crossed the room and joined them again at the table. "And none of them know anything about Tink."

"Maybe you need to look a little deeper?" she suggested, patting my hand. "You'll figure it out. You can't let what's happened shake your belief in your gifts."

"That's kind of hard at the moment. I—"

The sound of a car pulling into my driveway interrupted me.

"Dang, I don't want company now," I exclaimed.

"Don't worry." Darci rose with a determined expression on her face. "I'll take care of them."

Moments later Darci's strident voice filtered into the kitchen. "This isn't a good time."

"Nonsense."

Crap. Gert.

She bustled into the room, holding a plate in her hand. Placing it on the table, she threw her arms around me. "You poor, poor thing. It just goes from bad to worse for you, doesn't it?"

Releasing my shoulders, she stepped back. "I heard what happened. Have they found Tink's body yet?"

"What?" I exclaimed.

"That's an awful question to ask, Gert." Darci stood in the doorway with her hands fisted at her sides.

Gert looked at each of us in turn with complete innocence. "I'm sorry. The story I heard said that terrible man, Silas Green, kidnapped Tink. It—it only made sense to assume he'd hide her body with the rest of the unburied."

*The fairies said she's safe.* I repeated it over and over in my head while I fought the sickness gripping my stomach.

Abby took charge of the situation. "I know you didn't mean to be unkind, Gert—"

She waved her hands. "No, no, I didn't." She pointed at the plate. "Mama made cookies as a way to offer our condolences."

Darci moved to the table. "They don't need condolences."

"Darci, dear, why don't you have a seat?" Abby got to her feet. "Gert, here, take mine. Would you like a cup of tea?"

Gert seated herself. "No. Thank you for asking. Mama and I just feel so sorry for y'all. I can't imagine. It all must seem so hopeless to you."

"Humph." Aunt Dot quickly stood and hobbled over to the sink.

"One can never give up hope," Abby replied in a firm voice.

Gert pivoted in her chair. "You haven't given up even though the sheriff doesn't have any clues? You must have a plan to find her."

"I'll find her if I have to go house to house myself."

Gert looked at me with pity written all over her face. "Ophelia, sometimes it's best just to accept the inevitable."

Darci's open palms hit the table. "What are you trying to do, Gert, shove the knife in and twist it?"

Gert's hand flew to the pendant around her neck. "Whatever do you mean? I'm only trying to help."

"Ha!"

"I am," she huffed.

"Well, so far there hasn't been a single 'helpful' remark come out of your mouth." Darci waved a hand toward the door. "You come waltzing in here, saying you heard Tink's dead, telling this family their situation is hopeless." Her eyes narrowed as she scowled at Gert. "How 'helpful' is that, huh?"

"What an insulting thing to say. You never have liked me," Gert sniffed. "And I've tried so hard to do a good job at the library."

"You have, Gert," I said in an effort to placate her and ease the tension building in the room.

"She doesn't think so," she replied, her tone injured.

"Sure she does." I nudged Darci with my foot from under the table. "Don't you, Darci?"

Darci leaned back in her chair, crossing her arms over her chest, and frowned at Gert with hostility. She refused to answer.

"Come on, everyone's upset right now. I'm sure Darci didn't mean to insult you, Gert."

A smirk played at Darci's mouth. "Yes, I did. I don't like her sowing her negativity."

"Darci—"

Gert surged to her feet. "I've heard stories about the two of you, but I didn't believe them. I'd heard you're so grateful for her friendship that you let her run all over you. Now I see it's true."

"Gert," I said in a cold voice, "she does *not* run all over me. Darci is a valued employee and a friend. I'm sorry if you have a problem with that."

"A friend? You should hear what she tells the other employees about you."

I grabbed Darci's arm to prevent her from rising. "You must be mistaken. I trust Darci."

"Humph, but you don't trust me. I had such hopes for this job. There's so much to be done." She lifted her chin. "But it's impossible for me to continue working in such a hostile environment. I'll be calling Claire with my resignation."

She turned on her heel and stalked out of the kitchen.

For a moment no one spoke.

"Hey, she forgot her cookies," Darci said, picking up one and taking a bite. "Bleah. That's the worst cookie I've ever tasted."

She grabbed the plate and dumped it, cookies and all, into the garbage.

# *Thirty-Four*

I wandered the dark, silent house. I'd tried to sleep, but it eluded me. I found myself alone in my office. From the window, near the ring of trees circling my backyard, I saw lightning bugs flitting amid the flower beds. Huge lightning bugs. Their lights blinked on and off in a mesmerizing, almost comforting pattern.

I paused at the window, watching them.

When would this nightmare brought on by Tink's disappearance end? Abby had said I couldn't lose faith in my talents, but they hadn't helped me find her. I still felt she was safe. But did I know it or was it because I needed so desperately to believe it was true?

The thought scared me.

Aunt Dot had said I'd learned a lesson. What lesson? I thought back to the rune reading. Raido had shown an emotional journey—one that would change my life. My life had changed. It was unrecognizable from how it had been six years ago. Trust and friendship mattered more to me now than ever before.

Sitting at my desk, I picked up the old leather pouch holding my runes and leaned back in the chair. The weight of it felt good in my hand. I shifted the bag from one hand to the next.

With Gert quitting, I had no choice but to go to the library tomorrow. I groaned. Working the counter would be impossible. The town gossips would be on me like a pack of dogs, all wanting to know about Silas Green, the bodies, Tink's disappearance. My nerves were strong enough at this time to handle their stares and their questions.

I'd go in early and hide out in my office.

I opened the pouch, and sticking my hand inside, let my fingers play among the cool stones. Suddenly, I felt a tingle on the side of my palm as if I'd touched a hot electrical wire. Running my fingers through the stones, I felt it again. Strange.

Sitting forward, I withdrew my hand and placed the bag on the desk. I unfolded the linen square, emptied the pouch, and closed my eyes as I ran a finger over the runes.

The shock hit me again. Opening my eyes, I looked to see which stone had called to me. By their position, it was impossible to tell.

Leaving my eyes open, I ran my finger across them. *Ouch.* The shock tingled all the way up my arm. Taking a pen, I flipped the rune over.

Ansuz inverted. Lies, trickery, deceit. The same rune that had appeared earlier in the Celtic cross reading in the "past" position. The runes were making a point—someone from my past was deceiving me, and somehow it was related to Tink's kidnapping.

Was this the message the fairies had described?

Early the next morning I stood on the library steps unlocking the front door for the first time in days. My car had been returned the prior evening by one of Bill's deputies and now sat in its usual parking spot in front of the building. Ha, I thought, it would be like a beacon drawing the curious to the library.

I stepped inside, and all the familiar smells greeted me. Lemon oil, old leather, the funny, kind of musty smell that old buildings have. Taking a deep breath, I paused and drew comfort from the fact that some things never change.

Darci was already here. Spotting me, she smiled, and I felt a tinge of sadness. Her presence here every day would be a change. In all that had gone on over the past couple of weeks, I'd not thought about how soon she'd be starting college.

"Hey, how are you? Did you get any sleep?" she asked.

After strolling to the counter, I shoved my backpack in its regular spot underneath. "Yes."

"No dreams?"

"No." I straightened the pens on the counter. "I did think about the rune reading." I paused, staring off into space. "A funny thing happened. I picked out Ansuz again. In fact, it was almost as if the rune was shouting at me."

"What do you mean?"

"I felt a shock when I touched it. The rune was inverted, too, just like in the reading."

"And that means what?"

"Someone's lying." I pursed my lips, thinking. "You don't suppose it could be Ethan, do you?"

Darci snorted. "Are you kidding? That guy's as straight up as they come." She thought for a moment. "Do you think the rune is Tink's message to you?"

"If it is, it's not clear." I shook my head. "Do you believe the stuff Aunt Dot said last night about the fairies?"

She lifted one shoulder in a careless shrug. "I don't know—a couple of years ago I wouldn't have." She nudged me in the ribs. "But after hanging out with you, I've seen a lot of things I'd never thought possible." She tugged on her lip and frowned. "That night at the old cabin in Minnesota when Juliet tried summoning the demon—the black fog that rolled in?" She shuddered. "I never would have believed in something like that. So why not fairies?"

She picked up a book from the stack sitting in front of her. "Would you look at this?" she said with disgust. "Someone's bent the corners on a bunch of the pages. Honestly." She carefully smoothed the pages.

Bent corners?

"Let me see that." I slid the book over and looked at the title. *Down the Rabbit Hole*—one of our most popular young adult selections.

"Here's another one. I tell you, people just don't have any respect anymore."

I grabbed the stack of books and began flipping them open. Every single one had curled corners, and every single one was a young adult selection.

Grabbing Darci's arm, I gave it a shake. "Who brought these books in?"

"I don't know. Gert worked Saturday."

"They didn't come from the book drop?"

"No. They were on the counter when I walked in this morning."

"Are these in our bar coding system yet?"

"No."

"Who checked them out?"

Darci ran through the card file. "The cards are here, but there's no date or number on them." A confused look crossed her face. "I don't get it. Did someone snitch these, then bring them back?"

"I need to call Gert."

Darci's eyebrow shot up. "After last night and the way she huffed out, you're the last person she'll talk to."

I clutched one of the books. "Darci, I have to know who had these books."

Cocking a hip against the counter, she looked at me in disbelief. "What are you going to do? Fine them for damaging library property?"

"No," I said, my eyes wide and holding a book up. "This is a message from Tink."

She snatched one of the books and rapidly turned the pages. "She wrote in them?"

I laid a hand on top of the open book. "No. It's the curled pages. It's a bad habit Tink has. Instead of using a bookmark, she turns down the corner. I can't tell you the number of times I've talked to her about it."

"So whoever's holding Tink took these books?"

I felt my excitement rising. "Sure. Why not? It would be a good way to keep her occupied." I moved swiftly around the corner of the counter. "I'm going to my office. I'm calling Aunt Dot to ask her if this is the message."

Grabbing my backpack, I ran down the stairs and into my private office. I picked up the phone and quickly dialed my house. Abby answered on the second ring.

"Abby, may I speak to Aunt Dot?"

"Of course." She sounded perplexed.

A moment of silence followed as Abby handed Aunt Dot the receiver.

"Hello?" Aunt Dot's voice shouted in my ear.

"Aunt Dot, did the fairies mention any books?" I asked, and held the receiver away from my ear while I waited for her reply.

"No, no, I don't think so," she yelled.

"When you saw Tink in your vision, did you see any books lying about?"

"Ack, I don't remember. I don't think so. I just noticed the fairies."

"Okay, thanks," I said, feeling a little deflated.

"Do you want me to ask them about books?" she offered.

"Yeah. Put Abby on the—" I stopped, realizing I was speaking to dead air.

Aunt Dot had hung up on me.

Fisting my hands on my hips, I scanned my office. Where had I placed Gert's file? I rummaged through the piles of paper on my desk. Pages slid to the floor, but I didn't take the time to retrieve them. *Nope, not there.* Opening the file cabinet, I riffled my fingers over the folders. I pulled one out and quickly turned the pages. Another sheet fell to the floor. Nothing.

Frustrated, I smacked the folder on top of the file cabinet and moved on to the next drawer. Soon, stacks of papers covered every surface and the floor was littered with random pages.

*Okay, this wasn't working. What next?*

I snapped my fingers. Claire. As library board president, she'd have Gert's number.

My fingers flew over the keypad as I entered Claire's number. When she answered, I got right to the point.

"I need Gert Duncan's phone number," I said quickly.

"I don't think she'll want to talk to you," Claire replied. "She called me about nine, very unhappy, and gave me a real earful about you, Darci, the library. What happened?"

"Claire, I'm sorry she was upset, but I don't have time to explain now—"

She cut me off. "You have news about Tink?"

"Ah, no, but I do need to speak with Gert."

Snagging a pen, I rapidly wrote down the number she gave me.

"Thanks." I hung up before she could ask any more questions.

Before I could dial Gert's number, the phone rang.

*Do I answer and waste more time, or let Darci take care of the caller?*

I answered. "Summerset Library."

"Ophelia?" Aunt Dot hollered in my ear.

"Hi, Aunt Dot. Look, I'm really busy—"

"I thought you wanted to know about the fairies?"

"Well, yes I do. Did they say anything about the books?"

"No, but they said to tell you you're a very clever girl." She sounded pleased.

"Umm, well . . ." I faltered, trying to think of a response. "Tell them thanks."

I disconnected and stared at the receiver in my hand. *Duh, Jensen, what did you expect? You really don't believe in fairies in the first place.*

After punching in Gert's number, I shifted nervously back and forth on the balls of my feet while I waited for her to answer.

"Duncan's," said an unfamiliar voice in my ear.

Must be Mama.

"Hello, Mrs. Duncan, this is Ophelia Jensen."

"Ophelia Jensen? What do you want?" Her voice dripped ice.

"May I speak with Gert?" I asked, trying to sound chipper.

"After the way you treated her last night?"

"It's really important, Mrs. Duncan. It's about the library."

"Going to beg her to come back, are you?" I heard smugness in her words. "Well, she'll never work for you again."

Her receiver slammed in my ear.

Gert hadn't been kidding when she said Mama was grumpy. Her voice could have frozen the telephone lines. Her voice—funny thing—she didn't have an accent. One would think after living in Louisiana all those years that she would've sounded more southern. If anything, her speech was clipped, as if she came from a state even farther north than Iowa . . . like Minnesota.

The pieces of the puzzle that had been tormenting me slammed together into one whole picture.

They'd been bold and taken a huge risk that I wouldn't figure out their game.

They were wrong. I knew who kidnapped Tink, I knew why, and most important, I knew where she was.

# Thirty-Five

I tore through the library, passing a startled Darci and almost knocking Edna Walters, walker and all, down.

"Wait!" Darci called after me. "Where are you going?"

I yelled over my shoulder, "Can't explain now."

After half running, half sliding down the front steps, I hit the button on my key ring to unlock the car doors. As my hand gripped the handle, an arm snagged me at the waist and whirled me around.

"Ethan, you scared me to death," I exclaimed.

"Where are you headed in such a hurry, and what trouble are you into now?"

"I'm not in trouble, and I don't have time to explain. If you want information, you'll need to come with me." I opened the car door and flung my backpack behind the driver's seat.

Without a word, Ethan got in on the passenger's side.

He gave me a wry look as I pulled away from the curb. "Last time I went with you, I got the butt-chewing to end all butt-chewings."

"Don't worry—I think I've found Tink." I paused at the stop sign and turned left. "You were right. Her kidnapping had nothing to do with Buchanan's murder. It has to do with the adoption."

"What adoption? Aren't you her legal guardian now?" He sounded perplexed.

"No, her uncle, Jason Finch, is, but not long ago his attorney notified us that he was willing to relinquish his rights."

"Is this the husband of the criminally crazy aunt in Minnesota?"

"Yes. I don't know how much you know about that story—"

"A little—Bill kind of filled me in on your background."

"I bet that was a fun conversation," I said with sarcasm.

He winked. "Maybe not fun, but very interesting."

"Did he mention the Finches had a small cult?"

"No, no, I think he left that part out."

"One of the cult members was absolutely devoted to Juliet—Winnie Clark—and she hated Abby and me, especially me. Tried hexing me, locked me in a box, etcetera, etcetera." I finished with a wave of my hand.

"Pretty cavalier about it, aren't you?" he asked with a grin.

"I wasn't at the time, but these things seem to be happening to me a lot lately. I guess a person could get familiar with it."

Rolling his eyes, he shook his head. "So what about this Winnie?"

"She escaped into the woods during one of Juliet's spells . . . " My voice trailed away.

*Do I tell him she was trying to summon a demon? Nah.*

"Anyway, I'm pretty sure the new employee I hired, Gert Duncan, is somehow mixed up with Winnie."

"Pretty sure? How did you come to that conclusion?"

"I recognized Winnie's voice when I called Gert this morning. She's pretending to be Gert's mother."

"When was the last time you saw Winnie?"

"Over a year ago."

"You haven't talked to her for over twelve months, and you still remember her voice?"

I flashed him a look. "Yeah. The woman threatened me with a gun and locked me in a box. She's not someone I'm likely to forget."

"Why would she take Tink?"

"Juliet tried to use Tink's gifts for her own selfish reasons, and I suspect Winnie thinks she'll do the same." I drew my lips back in a sneer. "Ha—she wasn't even a very good witch. I don't know how she thinks she can use someone as talented as Tink."

"We're hurtling down the road because you suspect a bad witch is holding your daughter?"

"Yeah."

His attitude surprised me. Witches, folk magick, restless spirits, all in a day's work for me.

"You have to trust me, Ethan," I said as I focused on the road ahead. We were almost to the gravel road leading to the old Blunt place.

"Do you have a plan, or are you going to wing it like yesterday?"

I drummed the steering wheel. "Winging didn't work so well."

"Depends on how you look at it. We didn't find Tink, which was your goal, but we caught a killer and busted a body snatching ring. Not bad, Jensen."

Out of the corner of my eye, I saw his smile.

His face sobered. "But we are walking into a hostage situation. Tink might get hurt if we're not careful."

"You're the cop—you got a plan?"

He turned in his seat to face me. "First, since Gert

worked for you, she'd recognize your car. We'll park down the road . . . "

"What else?" I asked when he didn't continue.

"This isn't what you want to hear, but I think we should call Bill. He'll send a car out—"

"Oh no he won't," I said, cutting him off. "You saw how mad he was at me. If he thinks I'm sticking my nose in again, he'll lock me up and ditch the key."

"How about an anonymous tip?" he suggested.

"About what?"

"You said Winnie escaped. I presume that means she's a fugitive?"

"Yes."

"We call in a tip about her location—"

"If Bill shows up, she's not going to answer the door," I scoffed. "She'll hide out until he leaves."

"Scratch that idea." He thought for a moment. "Best scenario . . . we watch the house until we spot her, then call Bill. She's got to come outside sometime."

"I don't know . . . " My uncertainty echoed in my voice.

"Remember what I told you yesterday—the way to build a case is slowly and carefully? If you're correct, you don't want Winnie to escape again, do you?"

The thought made me shudder.

We left the car on the side of the road and cut across the pasture to reach the old Blunt place, coming up from behind the house. Using the windbreak located on the north side of the property as cover, we snuck around to the front.

A small white car sat in front of the house. The trunk lid was up.

Grabbing the sleeve of Ethan's jacket, I stared at him with fear in my eyes. "They're leaving."

"Maybe not. Maybe Gert's been grocery shopping."

As he said it, Gert came out of the front door carrying a big box. She stowed it in the trunk and returned to the house. A few seconds later she was back. This time lugging two suitcases.

"They are leaving," I whispered. "What do we do now?"

"I guess what you're good at—winging it." He reached for his cell phone and made a quick call.

"Bill, Ethan. I'm out at the old—" He covered the phone with his hand and looked at me. "Where did you say we were?"

"The old Blunt place," I said quietly.

Ethan repeated it into the phone. "Yeah," he said as he cast a glance my way. "No, we won't. Don't worry about it, Bill, I'll take care of everything."

He flipped the phone shut. "Bill's on his way."

"We don't have time to wait," I hissed. "They might leave with Tink any minute. It takes at least twenty minutes to get here from Aiken."

The front door slamming caught our attention. Gert again. She moved down the steps toward the car. She got in and we heard the motor turn over.

"We have to move now."

Before he could stop me, I was on my feet and headed through the grove of trees to the back of the house.

With three long strides, Ethan caught me. "Sneak in the back while I keep them busy at the front of the house," he whispered. "They could be armed, so no heroics."

"Not to worry," I said with a weak smile. "I hate getting shot."

As he turned away from me, I heard him muttering under his breath, "Bill is going to kill me."

I skirted around the edge of the property until I'd reached

the backyard. I closed my eyes, took a deep breath, then ran across the yard. Peeking around the corner of the house, I saw Ethan walking up the short drive. Satisfied he'd provide a distraction, I crept up to the enclosed porch and quietly slipped in through the screen door. Another door leading into the kitchen stood open. Plastering my body to the wall next to the door, I heard voices in the front of the house. They were suddenly silenced by a loud knock.

Footsteps went in two different directions. One set to the other side of the house, and the second set to the front door. The front door opened and I heard Ethan's voice.

*Move, now, Jensen.*

But to where? In Aunt Dot's vision, Tink was being held in a bedroom. In most farm homes, the bedrooms were on the second story, with the stairs leading up from the kitchen.

I peeked around the doorway and saw another door on the wall to my right. It either concealed a pantry or stairs leading up.

*Please let it be the stairs!*

Slipping into the kitchen, I clung close to the wall as I made my way to the next door. Carefully, I turned the knob and gently opened the door.

Yes. Stairs.

Shutting the door behind me, I hurried over the worn treads. At the top, I found myself standing in a large bedroom containing two twin beds. Two other doors led to the rest of the bedrooms. I tried the first—it swung open easily, revealing an empty room. Crossing swiftly to the next door, I grabbed the knob. Locked.

Lightly, I tapped on the wooden panel.

"Go away, Winnie," exclaimed an angry teenage voice.

My body slumped with relief. I'd found her.

"Tink," I called in a loud whisper. "It's me."

The sound of footfalls on a wooden floor came from the other side of the door.

"Ophelia?"

"Shh, Winnie and Gert are downstairs."

"The door's locked."

"I know. What about the window?"

"No, I already tried using my bed sheets, but they weren't long enough."

"I'll find something to pry the lock."

I looked madly around the room for something, anything, to pop the door open.

A hanger? No, the wire would bend too easily.

I ran my hand through my hair and chewed on my lip. A nail?

Stepping back to the center of the room, my eyes roamed the walls, looking for a nail protruding from the plaster.

I spotted one above the door. Standing on my tiptoes, I reached for the nail. A piece of string or ribbon seemed to be hanging on the metal shaft. I looped my finger around it and pulled it down.

Staring at the string dangling from my finger, I couldn't believe my luck.

Swinging back and forth at its end was a key.

I fitted it into the brass lock and turned. I heard a soft click, and then the door swung open.

The next thing I knew, thin arms flew around my neck in a tight hug. I gave myself a moment to just feel the joy of finding Tink again.

I stepped back and cupped her face with my hands. "You okay?"

She nodded. "Winnie and Gert grabbed—"

"Not now, sweetie, we have to get you out of here." I threaded my fingers around hers. "Follow me down the steps to the kitchen. We're going to sneak out the back door. Once we're in the yard, run for the grove of trees. Okay?"

"Okay," she replied in a soft voice.

"And Tink, don't let anything stop you. You keep going no matter what happens."

Her mouth took on a stubborn line. "I'm not leaving you."

I squeezed her fingers. "Yes. You *will.* A DEA agent is somewhere outside. You'll find him and send him back if I don't follow. Got it?"

"Got it," she grudgingly said.

Together we crept down the stairs. At the bottom, I put a finger to my lips and slowly opened the door. Peering out, I checked the kitchen. All clear. I tugged on Tink's hand. As we stood in the kitchen, I moved her in front of me and guided her toward the back porch.

A sudden yank on the back of my head almost pulled me off my feet.

"Run!" I screamed and turned to face my assailant.

Gert stood holding strands of my hair in her hand. She dropped them and came at me.

I shoved her away, and as I did, my hand caught her pendant, ripping it away from her neck. It flew across the room and clattered to the floor.

With a screech, her open palm flew to her throat. "My Eye of Horus! You took my Eye of Horus!" she cried, staring at the broken necklace. "I've lost my protection."

"Shut up and grab her, you fool!" Winnie yelled from the kitchen doorway.

Gert lunged at me, but I dodged her. Spinning on my heel, I headed toward the door.

A hand clutched the hem of my T-shirt and tugged me backward. I jerked and struggled to keep moving. My shoes slid on the slick linoleum floor as my body was pulled away from the open door and freedom.

"Freeze! DEA! On the floor now!"

The hand released me, and I staggered to regain my balance.

I whirled around to see Ethan standing in the doorway with his gun drawn.

Winnie and Gert dropped to the floor like a couple of stones.

# *Thirty-Six*

I couldn't let go of Tink's hand as Bill took her statement. I knew it embarrassed her, but I didn't care. She'd get over it.

"They grabbed you at Abby's mailbox?" Bill asked.

Tink nodded. "Gert stopped and called me over to her car. When I got there, Winnie jumped out and threw me in the backseat. Then they took off and brought me here."

"Did they mistreat you?"

"No." Tink rolled her eyes. "They pretended to be really nice." She gave a small snort. "They didn't fool me. They're almost as crazy as Aunt Juliet."

With that one sentence, Tink summed up the whole situation.

I found Ethan leaning up against the side of one of the patrol cars, his long legs stretched out before him.

"Bill said you're leaving?" I asked, shoving my hands into my pockets.

"Yeah, just got the call," he said, straightening.

"A new assignment?"

He gave me a cheeky grin. "Sorry, can't say."

I lowered my eyes. "Right . . . " Scuffing the ground with

the toe of my shoe, I tried to think of the proper words to express my gratitude.

It was impossible. There weren't enough words written or said to do that.

"Ethan," I began, raising my eyes to his face. "I can't tell you how much I appreciate—"

"Hey, it's okay, Jensen. I told you I always pay my debts."

"Well, this is a debt I can never repay you."

He laid a hand on my shoulder. "Don't worry about it. I'll be around again. Maybe by then you'll think of a way." Dropping his hand, he opened the door to the patrol car and got in.

I cocked my head. "You'll be back?"

"Sure," he said, shutting the door and resting his arm on it. "Whenever my life gets boring, I'll look you up."

"Ha—you're an undercover agent. Your life is a lot more exciting than mine."

"I'm not too sure about that," he said with a laugh. He glanced at the deputy behind the wheel and gave him a quick nod.

As the deputy turned the key in the ignition, I stepped away from the car.

Ethan raised his finger in a salute as they slowly backed away.

They were almost out of the driveway when Ethan leaned out the window. Cupping his hand to his mouth, he yelled, "Jensen, remember—don't fall off your broom!"

I shot a look over my shoulder to see if anyone else had heard him. When I looked back, he was gone.

At the end of the week we were all gathered on the patio, enjoying the warm summer night. It would be our last get together before Aunt Dot left the next morning for home.

Watching Aunt Dot and Tink stroll around the backyard, I faced Abby. "Aunt Dot got her adventure, didn't she?" I asked, sipping my ice tea.

Abby's brows shot up. "She certainly did. Her stories will have the mountain talking for the next six months. I just hope Aunt Mary doesn't decide to come to Iowa for an adventure now, too."

I choked. "Aunt Mary?"

"Um-hm, she never did like Aunt Dot to get one up on her."

"But—but—" I stuttered.

The idea of another aunt from the mountains of Appalachia visiting made me shudder.

Abby laughed. "Don't worry, dear. Aunt Mary's one hundredth birthday is fast approaching. We'll be expected to visit her for that."

"To Appalachia?"

"Yes, I've promised Tink a trip there."

Aunt Dot had been a handful in Iowa. What would she be like on her own turf? "Gee, Abby, I don't know."

Abby said nothing—just gave my hand a quick pat as Aunt Dot made her way back to the patio.

Guess we'd be headed to Appalachia one day.

Aunt Dot took a seat next to Abby and smiled over at me. "It's been an exciting visit, Ophelia." Her eyes traveled to Tink playing with T.P. "Could have done without that awful Winnie. I hope they lock her away forever."

"They will. It will be a long time before she gets out."

"Did you ever learn the why of it, my dear?" Abby asked.

"She had a crazy idea she'd take Tink back to Juliet, and enlisted her cousin Gert to help."

"But Juliet's still confined."

"I know. Doesn't make sense, does it? Oh, and here's a good one—the pendant Gert wore?"

"Yes, I remember. She said she'd bought it on the Internet."

"Um-hm. When I ripped it off of her, she kept yelling 'my Eye of Horus,' so I looked it up. The Eye of Horus is an ancient Egyptian symbol of protection . . ." I paused. " . . . against witchcraft. I guess she was afraid of us."

"Humph, she should've feared Winnie. Thanks to Winnie, Gert will be serving time right along with her," Abby said, her voice full of disgust.

Tink's laughter drew my attention. "Isn't that a great sound?" I said in wonder.

"Yes, it is," Abby replied, reaching out and clasping my hand. "And soon she'll be a permanent member of the family."

I nodded as I watched Tink run across the yard in the pale light of the moon.

As she ran, lightning bugs seem to follow her. They hovered above her, their bright glow shining in the night.

I pointed at Tink. "Would you look at those lightning bugs? I saw them out my office window the night before we found Tink. Have you ever seen any that big?"

From her chair, Aunt Dot cackled and turned to me with a wise expression on her face. "I told you the fairies liked her."

# The *Agatha Christie* Collection

# THE HERCULE POIROT MYSTERIES
## Match your wits with the famous Belgian detective.

The Mysterious Affair at Styles

The Murder on the Links

Poirot Investigates

The Murder of Roger Ackroyd

The Big Four

The Mystery of the Blue Train

Peril at End House

Lord Edgware Dies

Murder on the Orient Express

Three Act Tragedy

Death in the Clouds

The A.B.C. Murders

Murder in Mesopotamia

Cards on the Table

Murder in the Mews and
Other Stories

Dumb Witness

Death on the Nile

Appointment with Death

Hercule Poirot's Christmas

Sad Cypress

One, Two, Buckle My Shoe

Evil Under the Sun

Five Little Pigs

The Hollow

The Labors of Hercules

Taken at the Flood

The Underdog and
Other Stories

Mrs. McGinty's Dead

After the Funeral

Hickory Dickory Dock

Dead Man's Folly

Cat Among the Pigeons

The Clocks

Third Girl

Hallowe'en Party

Elephants Can Remember

Curtain: Poirot's Last Case

AC1 0411

# RETURN TO THE HOLLOWS WITH
## *NEW YORK TIMES* BESTSELLING AUTHOR

# KIM HARRISON

## WHITE WITCH, BLACK CURSE
### 978-0-06-113802-7

Kick-ass bounty hunter and witch Rachel Morgan has crossed
forbidden lines, taken demonic hits, and still stands. But a new
predator is moving to the apex of the *Inderlander* food chain—
and now Rachel's past is coming back to haunt her . . . literally.

## BLACK MAGIC SANCTION
### 978-0-06-113804-1

Denounced and shunned by her own kind for dealing with
demons and black magic, Rachel Morgan's best hope is life
imprisonment—her worst, a forced lobotomy and genetic
slavery. And only her enemies are strong enough to help her
win her freedom.

And coming soon in hardcover
## PALE DEMON
### 978-0-06-113806-5